THE BIG SILENCE

*Also by Stuart M. Kaminsky
in Large Print:*

Poor Butterfly
The Devil Met a Lady
Rostnikov's Vacation
Hard Currency
The Dog Who Bit a Policeman
The Rockford Files: The Green Bottle

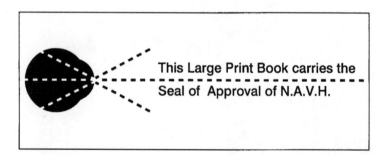

This Large Print Book carries the
Seal of Approval of N.A.V.H.

THE
BIG
SILENCE

AN
ABE LIEBERMAN MYSTERY

STUART M.
KAMINSKY

Thorndike Press • Thorndike, Maine

Published in 2001 by arrangement with St. Martin's Press, LLC

Thorndike Press Large Print Basic Series.

The tree indicium is a trademark of Thorndike Press.

The text of this Large Print edition is unabridged.
Other aspects of the book may vary from the original edition.

Set in 16 pt. Plantin by Rick Gundberg.

Printed in the United States on permanent paper.

Library of Congress Cataloging-in-Publication Data

Kaminsky, Stuart M.
   The big silence : an Abe Lieberman mystery / Stuart M.
Kaminsky.
      p. cm.
   ISBN 0-7862-3148-3 (lg. print : hc : alk. paper)
   1. Lieberman, Abe (Fictitious character) — Fiction.
2. Police — Illinois — Chicago — Fiction. 3. Chicago (Ill.)
— Fiction. 4. Jewish men — Fiction. 5. Large type books.
I. Title.
PS3561.A43 B47 2001
   813'.54—dc21   00-066618

This one is for Renata
and Vern Sawyer.

Vengeance has made its unappeased way with every dart of death and visited your family one by one. And now with eager hand Fate is pursuing you. Your turn has come.

— EURIPEDES, *Iphigenia in Tauris*

CHAPTER 1

Bill Hanrahan had been in Cleveland only once before. That was about ten years ago, when he and Maureen were still married. A Cleveland cop, a detective named Morello, had remembered when Bill was a young football hero with bad knees that had kept him out of the pros.

Three decades ago Hardrock Hanrahan had been the fastest lineman on the Chicago Vocational High School football team. Dick Butkus, who had graduated from CVS a few years later, told Bill at a reunion that Hardrock had been an inspiration to him. And then the knee went in a practice game and so did the speed and any chance at Notre Dame or Illinois or even Wisconsin. He lasted two years at Southern Illinois University and managed a *Parade* magazine second team All-American spot. But the knees wouldn't hold. He gave up to join his father as a Chicago cop, as his father had joined his grandfather before him.

Morello, who followed college football down to the Division III teams, found out that Hanrahan was passing through to Chicago and had a few hours between planes. Morello, a guy in his late fifties maybe, with lots of dyed too-black hair and the face of a Coke can run over by an eighteen-wheeler, had driven through Cleveland showing Hanrahan the sights, apologizing here, showing pride there. Hanrahan, who had been drinking hard then and hated flying, would have preferred being in the airport bar, but he couldn't hurt the man's feelings.

So he had seen Cleveland and had a few drinks on the plane.

Morello was dead now, his name on a plaque. Line of duty. Shot by a sixteen-year-old drug dealer in a stolen car. According to Morello's partner, the detective's last word was "son" before the kid in the car shot him in the face. Morello's partner had shot the kid four times. The kid died. Morello's partner had faced charges and been put on unpaid leave for sixty days.

Now Detective Bill Hanrahan was back in Cleveland, but he wasn't going to have time for any sightseeing. His knees were no better but he was sober and meant to stay that way. He had gone to AA after he had let an informant die while he was drunk in a restaurant across from her apartment building. Hanrahan's partner, Abe Lieberman, had covered for him, but Hanrahan had been a Catholic, a lapsed one to be sure, and guilt was his lot.

A few years later he had seriously considered sliding back to the bottle when he killed a young lunatic named Frankie Kraylaw whose wife and child he had been protecting in his house. Hanrahan had set up the lunatic and lured him to the house, knowing that if he had not killed the man, the man would surely have killed the young woman and the boy.

With the help of a young Catholic priest, AA, Iris Chen, and his partner, Abe Lieberman, Bill had slowly, shakily come through it still carrying guilt.

Now the divorce from Maureen was complete and Bill Hanrahan hoped and expected to marry Iris Chen in a few months. He was also slowly and with some caution returning to the church. The assignment he was on was Captain Kearney's way of giving Hanrahan a few days away from the city, away from the reminders of the past.

It was early October. A bit cold for fall in Ohio. Hanrahan had watched the Weather Channel and was prepared with the zippered lined jacket Iris had given him. The job was simple, even boring.

He sat in the car he had rented, heater on

9

low, radio on an oldies station he had found by pushing the right button. The Beatles were singing "Help."

Hanrahan was a burly man who looked like a cop and didn't find it easy to hide, but that wasn't a problem on this one. Back in Chicago a mob witness, an accountant named Mickey Gornitz, had agreed to talk about his boss's highly illegal operation, but only to Hanrahan's partner, Abe Lieberman, with whom Gornitz had gone to Marshall High School. No surprise. Abe was easy to talk to, and Abe and his brother had been basketball stars in a basketball school. Articles had been written about the brothers, who were both starting guards on the same team, a team that won the city championship the three years they played. Besides talking to Lieberman, Gornitz had several conditions. One was that his ex-wife and his seventeen-year-old son should be protected until Mickey finished testifying and went into witness protection. The assistant Cook County state attorney didn't think it was necessary. Gornitz hadn't seen his wife or son in fifteen years, when she had walked out on him, changed her name and the boy's, and moved to Boston. Mickey hadn't spoken to either his son or his ex-wife since they went out the door, but he had sent her money, plenty of it. The assistant state attorney gave in. This was a big case and watching a couple of people, humoring his witness, was a small price to pay.

A Boston cop named Persky, weary and yawning, had come on the flight to Cleveland from Boston with Gornitz's ex and the kid. They didn't know he was there. Persky knew a Chicago cop was going to take over, and he had found Hanrahan waiting for him when the crowd came off the plane.

Hanrahan had shown the man his ID, but Persky had waved it away, saying "They're yours. I'm headin' for the bar. Got a plane back home in about an hour."

So they were Hanrahan's. He had a recent photograph of the woman and the boy. They were easy to spot. She was about Hanrahan's age, in good shape, not bad looking if a little hard around the edges and a little loud. The kid was little, thin, and wore a gray sports jacket, tie, and slacks. His hair was dark and combed straight back. He was wearing glasses and looked like a classic case of what Lieberman's grandson called "the nerds."

Hanrahan had done his footwork before they arrived. The Boston and Cleveland police had helped. The mother and son had a rental car waiting. They were on their way for a trip to four colleges in Ohio that were all interested in the boy, who was a straight A student with an interest in computers and theoretical mathematics. Hanrahan had their itinerary from the Boston police and had made reservations at the same motels as the mother, Louise Firth, and her son, Matthew.

No trouble. They would make their rounds in three days, wind up at a motel in Dayton near the airport, and catch a plane back to Boston where Persky or someone would be there to meet them. It was almost a minivacation on the State of Illinois. Football on television at night with his shoes off, dinner watching the mother and son — at a table discreetly far away — back to bed and early to rise, providing Mom and son didn't decide to take in a movie.

Hanrahan followed the pair in front of him to baggage claim. He had only a carry-on. A skycap helped the woman and boy to the Hertz minibus, and Hanrahan got back in his rented car parked illegally at the curb and followed them.

Now he sat outside the Hertz gate listening to "When My Dream Boat Comes Home" by Louis Prima and Keely Smith.

First day went easy. About forty miles to Oberlin, tour around the campus with Hanrahan a safe hundred yards behind, back to administration for talk, and on to the motel where he had a room next to mother and son.

Because of his size, Hanrahan had learned a great deal about being inconspicuous. Most of it depended on staying as far back as possible and never doing anything to call attention to himself. It was especially easy when the people he was following had no reason to think they were being followed. Like today. In any case, knowing that they were going to colleges, Hanrahan had brought his briefcase, which he found dust-covered in the back of the bedroom closet. He filled it with papers, wore his suit, and tried to look like a college professor.

Food the first day was ribs. Drink was diet root beer. It was a Monday. The Bears were playing the Bucs silently over at the bar, and a juke box played Sinatra. The mother and son ate, looked like they had a disagreement about something small, and went right to the motel with Hanrahan behind them.

He was up well before them the next morning and had already eaten when they came down. He read the paper in the lobby to find out what, if anything, the Cleveland *Plain Dealer* said about the game. Hanrahan had watched. The Bears had lost, again. And to the Bucs. The glory days of Payton, Butkus (Hanrahan's idol), MacMahon, and the rest were long gone.

The next two days were about the same.

Kenyon, Wooster, and finally Wittenberg. The campuses didn't look very different from each other. Small, right out of a movie about small colleges. Hanrahan liked Wooster best, but his experience had been at Southern back in Illinois, a state school already grown to the size of a small metropolis. These schools were no bigger than CVS, his old high school.

After each tour and interviews, the son had come back to the car burdened by catalogs, flyers, and copies of who-knows-what. The Wittenberg visit was last. Mother and son had gone to that motel near the Dayton airport, and Hanrahan had bedded down in the room next door. His plane was about two hours after theirs in the morning.

The walls were thin in the motel, but not thin enough to hear what they were saying. They didn't seem to be arguing. Hanrahan would have been happier if the rooms had been on the second or third floor with no entry possible from the outside, but they were on the first. No big problem. The windows were thick and didn't open, and bushes, dense and deep, stood before each window. He was just a professional wanting everything to be right, which it was till just before three in the morning. Hanrahan leaped up at the sound, unsure of what he had heard. He looked at the television screen. A man was

14

talking silently. No doubt about the second sound, a shot, followed by another. In shorts and a Southern Illinois T-shirt, Hanrahan fumbled for his .38, found it, went into the hall where a few brave souls were opening their doors. Hanrahan went for the door of the room next to his. When the curious in the hall saw the gun in the big man's hand, they retreated, closed and chained their doors.

Hanrahan crashed his fist into the door once and shouted, "Open up. Police."

He didn't expect an answer and didn't get one. Weapon held high, he threw his shoulder against the door. He tried three times, failed to budge it, and finally shot the lock open. It took two bullets.

The lights were out and the light from the hallway sent a path of yellow to the nearest bed. Nothing moved. No one spoke. Crouched, Hanrahan went for the switch, which he assumed would be in the same place as the one in his room. It was.

White light from the lamps on the table snapped on and Hanrahan pointed his weapon at the figure on the closest bed. It was clearly the mother though there wasn't much left of the top of her head and there was a hell of a lot of blood. She was wearing pink pajamas and a surprised look; her remaining eye was open. They didn't usually die with their

15

eyes closed. Not like in the movies and on television.

The second bed was empty.

"Matthew?" Hanrahan said, looking around.

No answer. The bathroom door was open. The room was empty.

Hanrahan felt the night breeze from the broken window and stepped on a shard of glass. He knew what had happened before he could put it into words. He ran to the light switch, clicked the room back into darkness, and went for the window, ignoring the glass that cut into his bare calloused soles. The mother's rented Hertz car, which had been parked in a space a few cars down, was still there. He listened and thought he heard a car pulling out of the hotel parking lot.

Hanrahan went through the window, plowed through the bushes, and ran, leaving a bloody trail of footprints. He was in reasonably good shape and didn't get winded easily, but the knees, the knees would make him pay later, the joints scraping against each other, the cartilage long gone. He didn't even think about or really feel the cuts or even anticipate the slings and arrows he would have to face from Kearney.

When he reached the front of the motel, a large white car, maybe a Buick, pulled out of the lot onto the six-lane street that would be

16

packed if it weren't the middle of the night. It was hopeless. By the time he threw on his pants and got to his car, whoever it was would be long gone in who knows what direction with the kid.

On the way back to his room to call the airport and the state police, Hanrahan wanted a drink, wanted a drink so badly that he prayed silently for Jesus to show mercy and have a large double bourbon on his nightstand when he got back to his room.

There was no bourbon, but there was a telephone and he followed procedure, feeling in his gut that some of Jimmy Stashall's coke-filled piss-heads had the boy and were heading with him toward someplace he felt was safe. Hanrahan had the feeling that place would be in or near Chicago. All feelings. Little thought. He had lost another witness. His job was supposed to have been easy. The stakes had been high, but the police had put the mother and son on low priority in spite of star witness Mickey Gornitz. And now . . .

While he sat on the bed removing glass from his feet, two uniformed policemen suddenly appeared at his open motel room door. Their guns were drawn, their faces serious and scared. One of them looked at the bloody trail of bare footprints that led to the man seated on the bed who was pulling glass from the bottoms of his feet. Hanrahan figured they had visited the room next door. He figured they saw the .38 next to the big man sitting on the bed. He figured they took him for the killer. Well, so did Hanrahan.

He put up his hands and said, "Hanrahan. Chicago police. Wallet's in my jacket. I just called in to the state police. Woman was with her kid. Someone took the kid."

The uniformed cops had heard many stories, none this big. Their guns stayed out and focused. One of them checked Hanrahan's wallet and I.D. and said, "William Hanrahan? Aren't you the football player who —"

Hanrahan stopped listening and supplied his own ending to the sentence. His ending wasn't filled with the admiration the cop was probably giving. It was supposed to have been easy.

"Aren't you the cop who keeps fouling up," Hanrahan thought, and reached for the phone to call Chicago while the two cops who were way over their heads wished for someone to come fast and take over.

Hanrahan hobbled to the bathroom, ignoring the pain. He would wash off his feet till the bleeding stopped and then bandage them as well as he could. Then he would put on two pairs of white sweat socks to cushion the pain.

He didn't want to think about anything else. Not now.

"You're lucky," said the big man in the overalls to the ancient little woman in a white wig tilted slightly to the left.

The big man was filling out papers at a dining room table across from the woman who kept offering him things — coffee, tea, cake, candy. The big man accepted some cake and coffee and finished making out the document. He examined it and handed it to the little woman, who kept putting her glasses on and taking them off to find the best way of reading what was in front of her. It really didn't matter. She had no way of understanding the complicated words written on page after page. But the big man with the smiling face had been very patient in explaining everything to her.

"It's a good thing my assistant spotted your driveway, Mrs. Lawton," said the big man. "You were lucky. Another week, maybe even a day or two and it would have collapsed."

"You don't think I should call my grandson in Houston?" she asked, looking at the confusing document before her.

"Frankly, I think we should get started on that driveway tomorrow. I'll have to pull a few men off of other jobs, but this is an emergency. Don't worry. There won't be any extra charge."

"Thank you," the woman said. "You said

three thousand dollars?"

"Total cost," the big man said. "You can pay it all up front. You've got my guarantee and I'll give you a receipt. I'm sure your check is good. If you want to put up two thousand till we finish . . ."

"No," said the old woman, adjusting the front of her dark dress. "My husband knew how to do things like this. That's him."

She pointed at a large photograph on the wall, a couple in their thirties. Both of the people in the picture stood erect, smiling. The man shorter than the woman. He was thin, wore a light-colored suit, and had a head of curly black hair.

"A fine-looking man," the big man said, admiring the photograph.

"A saint," the woman whispered reverently. "Didn't fool around. Worked hard his whole life. Never hit one of the kids. Never. Not once even when Tony took the car without permission."

"Kids," said the big man. "Got two of my own."

"That's nice," she said. "Don't hit them."

"I won't."

"More cake?"

"Yes," he said. "About the check . . ."

"Checks confuse me," Mrs. Lawton said. "I go to the bank. Make money orders from the Social Security or savings. My neighbor drives me once a week. I get enough cash for the week. Would it be all right if I gave you cash?"

"That would be acceptable," said the big man, taking a plate of neatly cut coffee cake from the thin fingers of the old woman.

"I wouldn't want to get you into tax trouble," she said. "I know Tony worries about that. He's a good boy. Busy. Wants me to live with him in Houston, but . . . my husband and I lived here all our lives. I'll live here till they carry me out."

"Let's hope that's a long, long time from now."

"Thank you," she said, holding up her coffee cup to drink. It took both her hands to hold the cup steady.

"You were saying you have cash? The entire three thousand?" the big man asked with a warm smile.

"I don't like it."
"What?"
"This Salt and Pepper shit."
The young man on the sofa shrugged, started unwrapping his second sandwich, and kept his eyes on the television where Michael J. Fox stood with a perplexed look on his face while the sound track gave off laughter.

"This show ain't funny," the young man on the couch said.

The man on the couch was named Irwin Saviello — Jewish mother, Italian father. Irwin was big and burly — heredity, but he also worked out. The papers and the television had been calling them Salt and Pepper for the last two months. Irwin, who was thirty-one and had a baby face, sort of liked it. His partner, Antoine Dodson, Pepper, was black, his head shaven. He shared Michael Jordan's birthday and wanted to look like the superstar. The truth was he looked more like a bald, nervous version of Richard Pryor on crack, which Antoine used as well as whatever he could get.

Saviello, on the other hand, was clean, always had been.

The two men had met in prison. Dodson had been doing time for breaking and entering. Saviello had been sitting in his cell for manslaughter, a fight in a supermarket in which he had thrown a man into the frozen fish display. The man had died. At the time, Irwin had not quite remembered what the fight had been about. His appointed attorney had told him and then had plea-bargained down to manslaughter.

There was no doubt about who was the brains of the duo. It was Dodson, who had not only graduated from high school but had gone to the University of Illinois at Chicago Circle for a semester. Saviello had not quite made it through Austin High. Neither man had ever had an I.Q. test, but there was a note on each man's record saying that Dodson probably had a high I.Q. and was definitely a sociopath. The note on Saviello was that he was at least slightly below the low end of normal in intelligence.

Something had brought the two together. Saviello normally didn't like niggers, but he had met some decent ones in jail. None of them had messed with Irwin. Irwin was big. Irwin was strong. Irwin didn't mind fighting and didn't seem to mind getting hurt. He had once taken a makeshift knife in the back and kept fighting the two Mexicans who had attacked him on a clean-up detail. When the fight was over, Antoine had removed the knife, wiped it clean, and stuffed it in his shoe. Irwin had stoically gone to Doc Mirron, an inmate and a veterinarian on the outside, who took care of the wound.

Irwin's rep had gone up. He hadn't gone to the infirmary. He hadn't complained, and though he should have been in pain, he was working and looking normal the next day.

The fact that Antoine and Irwin got out on the same day made it easy for the two of them

23

to just drift into a partnership. It was Antoine who hit on the idea of knocking off convenience stores. The clerks there were told to turn over their money, not fight back, and pray that they didn't get killed.

The two would enter a 7-Eleven or something late when no other customers were there. Irwin would go in first, walk over to the counter, reach over, grab the clerk and hit him, hard, not hard enough to kill him, but hard enough to break a nose or a jaw. Antoine would follow, show his junk gun, a Raven MP-25 he had picked up on the street for forty-five dollars, and tell the reeling clerk to put all the money in a bag and give it to him fast or die. Since the weapon was so small, Antoine sometimes had to fire a shot into the ceiling or through a glass refrigerator window to convince the clerk to cooperate.

While the clerk was moving, Irwin would climb up to the video camera and rip it out. Then he would go in the back room where the tape was recording and remove the tape and stuff it in the bag in his pocket. Later, he would throw the tape away.

It had worked eight times. The money wasn't bad. The furnished room in Uptown wasn't bad, though the neighborhood stunk with druggies and drunks looking for small action or trouble. The television worked fine.

The two men visited their parole officers regularly, each not saying that he was rooming with a former convict, and went out on job interviews when they were told to do so. Each man had a job, but they both knew they would be fired. It was what they wanted.

"The system is so up to its ass in paper, bodies, and bullshit," Antoine said, "that they're letting assholes who rape kids out in two years for good behavior. Shit, sure they behave. There ain't any kids behind the bars. They're not gonna send us back 'cause we can't hold down a job."

That was all right with Irwin. Let Antoine do the thinking. Irwin sat in front of the television whenever he could. Now he was on his second sandwich. He had taken five from the store they had robbed that night. Irwin liked the tuna best. He always took Twinkies, Little Debbie cakes, and anything sweet and wrapped he had time to grab. He liked unwrapping the cellophane. It was like getting a present.

"Will you turn that shit off?" Antoine said, pacing the floor behind the sofa.

While chewing on his sandwich in one hand, Irwin reached over and pushed a button on the remote. He didn't much care what he watched. Something that looked like it might be *The X-Files* came on.

"Salt and Pepper," Antoine said, sitting in the chair near the sofa and draping one leg over it. "Shit, can't they come up with somethin' halfway original? Racist bastards."

Irwin shrugged and watched the screen where a woman was turning into something that looked like a big white worm.

"I'm goin' out," Antoine said.

"Okay," Irwin said as the white thing slithered behind an unsuspecting security guard in a blue uniform. The guard was sitting at a desk with a night-light reading a book. Irwin had never been able to finish a book. He didn't think the guard was going to finish this one.

The door closed. Antoine was gone. Irwin finished his sandwich and reached for the fourth one on the sofa next to him.

He was a mongrel with no name, born in an alley, the only one of the litter of four to survive. He had no memory of how he survived. He never thought about it. For him, life was simply staying alive. There were no dreams, no goals. He did have a small territory in two alleys that he protected. One was behind a run-down transient hotel off of Lawrence Avenue. It had once been a respectable place to stay, even a nearly prestigious place. But that was decades ago, long before the dog was

26

born. Now there was the remnants of discarded meals in the alley at night, put out by an indifferent staff. The dog protected his right to the garbage from homeless cats, large rats, and, occasionally, another dog. Sometimes, though, when the humans were more careful with their garbage, he would have to roam for dark miles with cautious eyes.

The dog's other main territory was behind an abandoned and boarded-up bread factory on Damen Avenue. It had been closed for years, and the neighborhood was so rundown that no one had any interest in bothering to spend the money to tear it down. There was a loose board in the building's basement. The dog knew how to push it away so he could get inside and out of the worst of the winter cold. There were corners inside, small rooms, that were almost warm.

The dog without a name slept during the day and roamed for food at night. He did not seek fights, but he did not hold back when he felt there was food or a female worth fighting for. He lived alone and had no instinct to find a permanent mate.

He was a gray and black creature, a bit scrawny, and about average for dog height. One ear was almost gone, the result of a battle with a larger dog over a piece of hamburger. Were he ever brought in to the Humane Society, they would find it impossible to guess the many breeds that had gone into his creation, and there would be no chance that anyone would want the ugly creature.

He saw humans abuse and steal from each other. He had seen them kill each other. They were the breed that ruled all space and time and were definitely to be avoided. On the two occasions when he couldn't avoid them, when they had trapped him for sport or possibly to eat him, the dog without a name had attacked. He had badly injured a man with foul-smelling clothes, had bitten his face and neck. The man had run bleeding and screaming. The dog had never gone back to that place again. His other encounter with a human had been more dangerous. This creature trapped him in a dead-end alley and held something in his hand and that had made a cracking sound and had spit something small, hard, and fast at the dog. The dog did not know how to cower. He had attacked the surprised man, leaped on him, knocked him down, and bitten at the hand and the spitting thing it held.

The man screamed. Others were coming. The dog stopped his attack on the bloody mass that had been the man's hand. The man punched and tried to crawl away. The dog ran.

People, the animals that ruled without

sense or understanding, were to be avoided and hidden from during the day. That was the dog's rule, and it had helped keep him alive.

And now, in darkness, a chill October wind ruffling his fur, he wandered.

It was nearly midnight when Rita Bliss, whose real name was Rita Blitzstein, cruised up and down Lunt in East Rogers Park just off Sheridan Road. She was tired. She was irritable, and someone had parked in the space for which she paid forty dollars a month. Parking in the neighborhood of six- and ten-story apartment buildings and older courtyard buildings three or four stories high was never good. At night it was nearly impossible. Rita had once spent an hour cruising for a space and finally parked in the gas station two blocks away and left a note on her windshield saying she'd be back early in the morning and pay for having parked there. The gas station proprietor, a Croatian immigrant, had charged her twenty dollars. He had a family to bring over, he explained, and he had been cheated on the price of the gas station, a price that would take him three years instead of two to pay back with the advance he had borrowed from a fellow Croatian loan shark.

Rita was forty-one, a dark, thin, well-groomed woman with very short hair and a reputation among others she worked with and for as a television producer at Channel 5 as a no-nonsense, unflappable career woman. It was agreed that it was only a matter of time before she was grabbed by the NBC network or another network to produce a national talk or investigation show.

Meanwhile, she lived alone in a comfortable apartment in what had once been class and was now on the fringe of respectability. She had a reasonable grip on herself when she left the station after calmly doing take after endless take with Cliff Swenson, the director of *Investigative Eye*, the show she produced and which had taken off well and had been picked up by twenty-seven stations. The problem was the star, Betina Young, who was neither young nor named Betina. Her real name was Alice Birdsell. She was older than Rita, but still a beauty with or without the makeup. However, time to be discovered nationally had run out on Betina Young. The clamor for beautiful black anchors and talk show hosts had passed. This made Betina less than a bundle of fun to work with. Betina kept demanding retakes, different dialogue. One of Rita's primary jobs was to keep Betina calm and happy. Happy wasn't possible. Calm wasn't either, but the semblance of calm was.

Tonight had been one of the worst. And after driving around for more than half an hour looking for a space, Rita decided she had enough of staying in this apartment and waiting for her call from the network. She would get an appreciably more expensive, if smaller, apartment in Lincoln Park nearer the studio. Life would be easier.

The space wasn't a miracle. It wasn't legal, too small and too close to a fire hydrant a block from her apartment. A small car pulled out of the illegal space. Rita took it. It took her five or six moves forward and back to make it in, and she wasn't sure the red car behind her could get out, but she was in. Maybe she'd be out in the morning before she got a ticket. Even if she got a ticket, it would, at this point, be worth it.

She got out, locked the car, put her keys away, picked up her leather briefcase, and headed across the street trying to decide which of the "investigative" reports to feature for next week's show, probably the one about the landlord on Diversey who was extracting sexual favors from his welfare mother tenants in addition to rent.

There was almost no traffic on the street. Every two or three minutes another late lost soul like Rita would roll slowly down the street praying some driver would pull out and let him park and get home to bed.

She was walking almost in the middle of the street when she heard the sound. Metal against . . . ? Metal? Concrete? It was ahead of her in the shadows between two cars. There were streetlights, but there was more than enough darkness for the neighborhood muggers. Rita hurried and was about to cross between two parked cars half a block from her apartment building when the monster appeared.

He was suddenly there, hovering over her, arms extended over his head, something big and catching spots of light in his hands. Rita froze. She should have run. She could have done other things. She was a woman with a strong head on her shoulders, a woman who remained calm in a crisis and was the rock of her crew. But not now.

She recognized him, had seen him in the neighborhood. He had approached others. Once she had even glimpsed such an encounter, but this was the first time he had approached her and it was night and the street was empty.

Rita wanted to say, with the authority she had learned, "What do you want?" But she didn't speak. The man holding a metal garbage can over his head took another step toward her. He was close enough now that he could, by reaching out, have brought it down on her head.

"Son of a bitch," the huge black man said. "Whore. Dirty piece of ass. Shit. Fuck. Cock."

He was growing more angry. Rita looked around for help, anything. She would have flung herself on the hood of any passing car, but there were none and most of the windows in the nearby apartments were dark. She should have screamed, but she couldn't.

The huge man suddenly spun around, garbage can over his head. He looked down the street. He looked at parked cars. He looked at darkened windows and he looked at Rita Blitzstein. And then he turned and threw the garbage can down the street toward Sheridan Road, which it would never reach though it was rolling quickly and noisily, clattering and scraping. He had thrown the can at least three car lengths.

"Shit," he shouted, turning back to her.

Rita tried not to but she backed up. She was determined not to shake or cry but she couldn't stop doing both. In the light of a nearby streetlamp she could see the man's black shining face, his eyes madly open, his knit sweater with a ragged hole about the size of a cassette in the chest.

"You know whose street this is?" he

shouted, looking around at the windows.

She wasn't even sure he was talking to her, that he wanted an answer.

"Nobody's," he said, looking down the street at the garbage can that was just coming to a halt against a Toyota's fender. "I do what I want. See what I want. I live on the cats, dogs, and rats and the water from the fountain in the park. These are dangerous streets. You'd best be careful."

His face was inches from hers now and she tried to do something . . . answer, run, scream, hit him, though she feared hitting him would do little good. Finally, as he stood over her, his head suddenly cocked to one side like a curious bird looking at an unfamiliar object, she ran. Rita ran expecting two huge hands to grab her, lift her in the air, and throw her down the street.

She wasn't sure if she heard footsteps behind her. Her low wooden heels clacked against the cracked sidewalk. She made it to her lobby door. She had fumbled for her keys as she ran and found them. She went into the lobby and glanced back. Was that a bush? Was it him? She pushed all the bells and panted to the inner door. No one opened. She forced herself to insert the key quickly, turn it, and go inside, closing the door behind her. But what was such a door to a monster like that? It was glass and thin wood from another era. He could burst through it with a lunge.

Rita went up the stairs two at a time till she was so exhausted she had to pull herself up by the wooden railing. She heard nothing behind her, but she would not feel safe till she was behind her apartment door. She was on the third floor. She got inside, closed the door behind her and locked it, throwing the bolt. There was a light on her desk, one of those cheap table lamps with the green glass that you see in all the movies. She left it on all the time, day and night.

Rita took her briefcase and moved to her bedroom, where she switched on the light and sat panting and then she did something she hadn't done in almost ten years. She called her parents because she needed them. She needed them badly.

CHAPTER 2

Lieberman didn't hear about his partner's troubles until Abe reported in to the Clark Street station about five hours after the event.

Detective Abraham Lieberman was tired. No one could tell, of course, because Abe always looked tired though once in a while he could simply manage to look weary. Lieberman was a little over sixty and looked more than seventy. On a good day, he weighed about 145 pounds. He told everyone that he was five seven as it said in his personnel record, but every day he felt as if he were growing imperceptibly shorter. Today the face in the mirror looked like that of a basset hound with curly white hair and a little white mustache. Abe had learned to live with that face and marvel at the clear evidence that his wife, Bess, who was nearly his age, looked about two decades younger. She thought her husband looked distinguished and wise.

This morning Abe felt neither distinguished nor wise. The night before had been a series of family confrontations, though it had started peacefully enough.

Lieberman's grandchildren were now pretty much at home in the house on Jarvis in West Rogers Park. Barry was twelve, into baseball and the Cubs almost to the degree of his grandfather, who still snuck away to home games during the season and remembered fondly the long slow swing of Hank Sauer, the peppy blasts and lightning moves of Ernie Banks, and even the lanky lunges at shortstop of Roy Smalley who would have been right up there with the best of them if he only had been able to hit. Barry's Cubs memory went only as far back as Rick Sutcliffe and Andre Dawson.

There was a tape of a last-season Cubs-Atlanta game on the night before. Neither Abe nor Barry remembered who had won though they had their suspicions that it wasn't their team. Even Abe's eight-year-old grand-daughter Melisa had curled up in his lap in her pajamas clutching her stuffed bear and trying to understand the game.

Peace should have prevailed. Around the fifth inning, the moment should have arrived when Bess came in and said it was time for the children to go to bed. The dialogue was al-ways the same and strangely comforting to

Lieberman, who savored a reliable routine when it managed to exert itself on the chaos of his life. Bess would say there was school the next day. Barry would plead for one more inning, claiming he was older than his sister. Lieberman, if necessary, would agree with his wife and kiss the kids as they slouched off toward the stairs to the room where their mother had once slept.

That was the way it should have gone with Lieberman in his socks and favorite chair in the dark until Bess turned a light on repeating for the thousandth time that you should watch television with lights on.

"Not the Cubs," Lieberman would say. "You watch the Cubs in Wrigley during the day or at night on TV in the dark. It's the rules."

Bess turned the lights on.

The batter was Mark Grace. He hit a single to right.

"Grace always hits a single to right," said Barry, sitting with feet crossed on the floor.

"It could be worse," Lieberman said.

"It could be better," said Barry, who looked exactly like his father and nothing like Bess or Abe.

"Next season we win the division," Lieberman had said decisively. "Your grandfather proclaims it. Sammy will hit sixty-five home runs."

"You shouldn't ask God for things like that," Melisa said dreamily.

"Why not?" asked Lieberman, kissing the top of her head. "If he doesn't want to do it, who's there to make him? Maybe he needs a little easy work, a rest from Russia, Bosnia, Africa. It's not that much to ask."

"It's blasphemy," said Barry. "Rabbi Wass said."

"You asked him about the Cubs?" Lieberman asked, as someone he had never heard of popped up to end the inning and Bess returned to end the conversation.

"Bed," she said.

No argument. Melisa climbed out of Abe's lap, leaving it warm and slightly damp. Barry got up from the floor.

"Baseball's not about important things," Barry said. "You learn that when you prepare for your Bar Mitzvah."

"To me the Cubs are important. Not as important as you and your sister and your grandmother and your Bar Mitzvah, but important. I've spent half a century waiting for the Cubs to get to the World Series. I'm not even asking for that, just the division title. Good night."

"They're losing twelve to one," Melisa said with a yawn.

"It's just an experimental game," Lieberman said. "Playing some new kids, resting the veterans."

"Aren't the Braves doing the same thing?" Barry asked.

"We're better at losing than they are," Lieberman said. "Enough philosophy. Go to bed."

They went. Lieberman heard Bess putting them to bed. Abe considered changing the station, watching an old movie if he could find one. Maybe Bess would join him. They'd eat popcorn and she would observe inaccuracies of human nature from time to time. Bess was a realist. Like it or not, in spite of the horrors he had seen, Abe had remained a romantic. If his unshaken love of the Cubs was not evidence of this, what was?

And then the knock at the door came.

Lieberman checked his watch. It was nine, still reasonably early. He hit the mute button, got up slowly, pausing to scratch the bottom of his right foot through his wool sock, and headed across the living room to the door, wondering why the visitor hadn't rung the bell.

He opened the door and stood facing his daughter.

"You look very much like my daughter," he said. "But you can't be. She's in California."

"Abe," she said. "I'm standing in the cold."

"It's not cold. It's fall. The night is clear and cool. I'm watching the Cubs. I don't want to fight with my daughter who's not supposed to be here."

"We won't fight," said Lisa.

"A new world arrives," Abe said, standing back to let Lisa in, knowing as she did that this was the beginning of the first round, the first gambit, and that he would never keep her out of the house, that a bed waited always for her upstairs.

Lisa came in and closed the door while Abe turned on more lights and considered turning off the game. He couldn't bring himself to do it. It would concede the loss of the evening to chaos.

"You look good," he said, turning to face her.

"You always say that, Abe," she said.

"You always look good," he said. "You almost never look happy, but you always look good. From the second you were born you looked good."

"You've told me that," she said.

"I suffer from an as-yet-undetected variation on Alzheimer's," he said. "I repeat myself endlessly and count on the kindness of my friends and family to hide my terrible secret."

"It's not funny, Abe," she said.

"Which is why I am a policeman and Don

41

Rickles is a comedian."

"The kids are in bed?" she asked, walking into the dining room and looking up the stairway.

"Which is why you knocked instead of ringing the bell," Abe said. "Coffee?"

She sat at the dining room table and brushed her hair back with her hand. Lisa looked like Bess only darker. She was a pretty woman, still young at thirty-five. A bit on the thin side, but good features. Thank God none of the Lieberman looks had been passed down to her and she, in turn, had passed none of them to her two children.

Lieberman went into the kitchen and poured two cups of coffee from the pot that was on hot. Coffee, no coffee. It didn't matter. Abe was an insomniac. He had ceased fighting the situation decades earlier. He had learned to live with it, spending thousands of hours in hot tubs reading magazines and books, thousands more hours watching television till dawn with a sleepy-eyed Robert Mitchum or a wide-eyed Joan Crawford for company.

When Lieberman made his way through the kitchen door, careful not to spill, Bess was back downstairs and sitting across from Lisa.

"You want tea?" Abe asked his wife, placing one cup of coffee in front of his daughter and the other at his place at the head of the table.

Bess shook her head and looked at her daughter.

Abe decided to say nothing. It was the safest thing to do. He sipped and tried not to glance back into the living room at the television screen in the hope that the Cubs had miraculously overcome the Braves' overwhelming lead.

"Marvin wants a divorce," Lisa said, hands folded in front of her on the table, voice striving to remain calm and even, to remain the Lisa her parents had always known.

"Why?" asked Bess, looking at Abe who sipped more coffee and knew that all chances of a movie were gone.

"I cheated on him," Lisa replied.

Abe put down his cup and stared at his daughter, who met his eyes for an instant and then looked down into the dark liquid she hadn't tasted.

It was Lisa's second marriage. Her first husband, Todd, the father of Melisa and Barry, had remarried an older colleague at Northwestern University, where Todd Creswell taught classics and had the annoying habit of quoting morbid passages from Greek tragedies.

Now Marvin Alexander. The man was nearly perfect. An M.D., internationally respected pathologist, forty-nine. He had taught at Hebrew University in Jerusalem and spoke nearly perfect Hebrew. Lisa was a biochemist who had left her husband with her children and later left her children with Abe and Bess and moved to California to "put her life together." Imagination had never been Lisa's strength. She had always been an outstanding scholar, a serious child and woman.

Todd had not been Jewish. Abe and Bess could live with that. He was, as far as they could tell, a good husband, a good father.

Marvin Alexander was an African American, which bothered Bess and Abe only insofar as knowing that if Lisa had another child he or she might be black and have to face the trials of growing up black in America. Both Abe and Bess liked Marvin and, frankly, in bed in the dark, on more than one occasion, they wondered what Dr. Marvin Alexander had seen in their daughter that made him decide she would be a good wife. Her history so far had indicated otherwise, and Marvin Alexander had seemed to them smart enough to see that.

"Cheated?" Bess repeated, looking at Abe for help that he was not yet ready to give. He was a cop. He believed in letting witnesses or suspects talk themselves out before he started asking questions.

"An intern at the hospital where Marvin

works," she said. "Where I work. I didn't know . . . Morris is so young. I just . . ."

"How young is this Morris?" asked Bess.

"Twenty-five."

"He's Jewish?"

"Yes."

"Married?"

"No."

"How many times did you . . . ?" Bess asked.

"Never," said Lisa. "Close, but never. Marvin found out. Does it matter how many times?"

Bess looked at Abe. It clearly didn't matter to him.

"Marvin's a good man," said Lisa. "I can be difficult. You know that. He knew that."

"There's difficult and there's . . . never mind," Bess said. "Go on."

"I don't want to live with Morris. He doesn't want to live with me. I don't want to marry him. I want Marvin to forgive me, to take me back."

"Did he hit you when he found out?" Bess asked, trying to keep her voice from cracking.

"Marvin? He'd never hurt me. I hurt him. This is the kind of person you've helped turn me into."

The last was directed at Abe. He hoped he was not about to hear the list of charges against him once again. Lisa had the memory of an advanced computer and every error, every missed conference, every intended comic remark to a date, every absence because of a homicide, every . . . well, Lisa's failures were primarily the fault of Abraham Lieberman. He had come, in fact, to believe that she was probably right though there had to have been some point many years ago when Lisa should have taken responsibility for her own life.

"As I recall from reading the Bible in the bathtub, God even forgave Cain for killing Abel," Lieberman said.

"There is no God," Lisa said wearily. She had first said it when she was eleven. She had gone on saying it. Lieberman was not sure she was wrong though he was now, largely to please his wife but partly because it gave him some peace of mind, an active member of Temple Mir Shavot on Dempster Street who spent much of his nonworking time considering the question of God's existence or nonexistence and the meaning of whether He existed or did not exist.

"You want Marvin to take you back?" Bess asked.

"Yes," Lisa said, and a miracle happened. Lisa wept. Lisa never wept. At least not before others. Abe had felt that his daughter had cried when her cousin David had been mur-

46

dered, but she had kept it private and had done a far better job of comforting Abe's brother Maish and Maish's wife Yetta than Abe would have expected.

"He told you he wanted a divorce?" Abe asked. "He just said it like that?"

"No, he never said he wanted a divorce. I could tell from his voice, his . . . I could tell."

"Call him, Abe," Bess said.

"Me?"

"Call him, Abe," Bess repeated. It wasn't an order. It was a plea. A necessity.

Abe held back his sigh, finished his coffee, and reached for the telephone that Bess was now placing in front of him. Lisa reached out and almost touched her father's hand. This, he decided, was a Lisa who needed help. The former Lisa would never have shown her weakness, her need, and would not have accepted help from Abe Lieberman. The two had been nourished and exhausted by years of debate, argument, and resignation. Abe had, almost 100 percent of the time, been able to keep from getting angry, or at least showing it. In fact, he seldom felt anger toward Lisa. Whatever guilt he felt came from the relief he experienced when Lisa was not living at home.

Lisa was giving him the phone number when the doorbell rang.

Bess got up to answer while Abe continued dialing. He had almost finished dialing when two men pushed a third through the door Bess had just opened. The two pushers were talking Spanish so quickly that Abe could barely follow their conversation, which, he decided immediately, was not worth following.

The man they pushed in past Bess stumbled forward and almost fell. He was young, younger than Lisa. He was Korean. He had only one arm, his left, and he looked angry. The Korean wore jeans and a dark brown shirt. The two members of the Tentaculos wore black slacks and tight-fitting long-sleeved black shirts.

Lieberman stopped dialing and put down the phone. Bess closed the door.

"In English," Lieberman said.

"*Viejo*," the leaner of the two Tentaculos said. "We found him outside. He had a gun."

The lean Guatemalan was named Fernandez. He was known as Chuculo, the Knife. He had more than earned his nickname. The bigger of the two Tentaculos was an almost feebleminded enforcer known as Piedras, the Stone. Ironically, his last name was, indeed, Piedras. He simply lived up to it. Piedras held up the gun they had taken from the Korean, a black Glock.

The Tentaculos were a gang of Mexicans, Panamanians, and Guatemalans led by the nearly legendary El Perro, Emiliano Del Sol. Emiliano was generally conceded to be mad and extremely violent and dangerous. He was also known to have a symbiotic and almost friendly relationship with Lieberman. To the degree that he could, Lieberman provided protection for all but the worst of El Perro's crimes. In turn, El Perro provided information. They also shared a passion for the Cubs though El Perro's extended only as far as the team's Hispanic players.

"*¿Que quiere, Viejo?*" said Fernandez.

"*Nada ahora,*" Lieberman replied. "In English."

Lieberman knew that all he had to do was tell the two Tentaculos to get rid of the Korean, whose name was Kim, and it would be done. Only once had Lieberman condoned El Perro's killing of a criminal. It had been pure vengeance, and Lieberman could have pretended that he didn't know the murder would take place. But he did know and he accepted.

"El Perro found out that this *chinga tu madre* was coming for you tonight," Fernandez said. "One of the guys he used to have in his gang told him."

"Tell Emiliano I said thanks," said Lieberman. "You want coffee?"

49

"No, *gracias*," Fernandez said. "You want us to just leave him here?"

"*Sí,*" Lieberman replied.

El Chuculo shrugged.

"*Bueno, pero cuidado Viejo. Este hombre es muy loco.*"

"*Voy a recuerdo,*" said Lieberman, looking at the tottering Korean.

"*Hasta luego,*" said Chuculo, and then to Kim, "You a lucky gook, you know that? El Viejo should let me cut your heart out."

With that Chuculo turned to Bess and Lisa and said, "*Dispensa me, mujeres.*"

"He said 'excuse me,' " Lieberman translated. Then to the men: "*Gracias, hombres.*"

Chuculo and Piedras left. The blank look on the face of the hulking Piedras didn't change. They closed the door behind them and the one-armed Kim stood wobbly and defiant in the living room.

"Coffee?" Lieberman asked.

Kim didn't answer.

"See what I mean?" said Lisa, looking at her mother, her voice raising. "This was my life. Murderers, drug dealers, gang members. In our own living room. I don't want this for my children."

"You left them here, Lisa," Bess reminded her. "Your father and I didn't let anything happen to you. We won't let anything happen to Barry and Melisa. I think it would be a good idea if you went up and said good night to your children. You can sleep with Melisa."

"What about the call to Marvin?" Lisa said, standing and looking at Kim, whose eyes glistened with hatred.

"After Kim and I have a talk," Lieberman said.

Bess led a reluctant Lisa toward the stairs and up. The two women whispered, but there was an angry near whimper in Lisa's voice.

"Sit down," Lieberman said, pointing to the chair Lisa had left.

Kim shook his head no.

"I'm not asking," Lieberman said. "I'm telling you. Sit down or we walk outside and talk there. Believe me, it'll be far more civilized in here. I am sorely displeased that you've come to my house again. It will be the last time. You know what those two wanted to do to you?"

Kim reluctantly staggered to the chair and sank into it. It was clear that the two Tentaculos had not been tender in ushering the Korean into the house.

"They wanted to take your other arm and then your life. You want a couple of Tylenol?" Lieberman asked.

Kim shook his head again.

"Suit yourself," Lieberman said. "I've got

some things to tell you and I want you to listen. You don't listen, you've got problems. You don't come near my house. I told you that once. This is twice. The next time . . ."

"I can walk where I want," Kim said through nearly clenched teeth.

"No," Lieberman said, "you can't. You can't come within two miles of where I live. No, let's make boundaries. You can't go south of Howard Street or north of Touhy. You can't go west of California or east of McCormick. If you do, I'll know and you'll probably be lucky just to lose your other arm. Chuculo wanted to kill you. For him it's easier that way. I think he's right."

"I will kill you," Kim said. "On the honor of my father, I will kill you."

"Your father's dead," Lieberman said. "He died cursing you for being a third-rate gangster. Your mother and sister want you to go away. Your gang is gone. Everyone needs a meaning in life. I don't want to be yours. I didn't shoot your arm off. That was a Korean girl in a cleaning store you were extorting from. I brought you in. What the hell's wrong with your memory?"

"You set me up," said Kim.

"That I did," Lieberman replied. "It's what I do for a living. Kim, I'll give you my advice. You won't listen but I'll give it anyway. Move

West. Santa Fe is supposed to be nice, or California. Not L.A. Someplace north. Santa Rosa maybe."

"I will kill you," Kim said. "I have vowed. You destroyed my honor, turned me from my family, made my friends desert me, taken my self-respect."

"Wrong," Lieberman said, reaching over for Lisa's untouched cup of coffee. It was still warm. He drank. "You are a really incompetent criminal. My partner and I kept setting you up. Your own people, the ones you were preying on, turned you in. You could have made twice the money working in a factory instead of walking around in suits, ties, and dark glasses with big guns trying to get tribute from Korean businesses."

"I will kill you," Kim repeated. "You put me in disgrace. I cannot walk down Devon without people smiling at my dishonor or turning their heads. I am a one-armed parah."

"You mean 'pariah,' " Lieberman corrected. "You like the Cubs?"

"The Cubs?"

"Baseball," Abe explained.

"No." Kim, confused, was trying not to show it.

"Listen, I have family business to take care of and I'd like, if possible, which seems unlikely, to watch the last inning or two of the baseball game. So, I've got your gun, which I feel confident is not registered. I don't want to get my shoes on and take you in for carrying a concealed illegal weapon. I don't like paperwork and I don't think it would get you more than a few months in jail if anything. That missing arm is good for at least five percent sympathy. So I'm going to let you walk out of that door. If you want a job out West, I'll make some calls, but I have a feeling you won't take help from me. So, think about it and take a warning instead. You come near here again, you're dead. I think it's better to be alive than dead, but you make up your own mind."

"I can go?" Kim asked warily.

"I wish you would. I've got an important phone call to make."

Kim rose, confused. "You won't even arrest me?"

"No."

Lieberman's foot was driving him crazy. He had to scratch it, and he did.

"So, more dishonor from the Jew devil," Kim said.

"You get your dialogue from very bad Hong Kong movies," Lieberman said. "You need a slightly higher grade of culture. You ever see *Mildred Pierce*?"

"Mildred . . . ?" Kim said.

"Forget it."

"You're ridiculing me again," Kim said angrily.

"Maybe," Lieberman said. "I'm tired and I think I have a long night ahead with my family problems. You know how that is. Go now, and don't say 'I'll be back.' "

Kim stood in confusion trying to think of something to say while Lieberman finished Lisa's coffee. Lieberman wondered what, if anything, was sweet in the kitchen. He knew there was a Ben & Jerry's Cherry Garcia frozen yogurt, but he had a taste for something baked and comforting. All he could remember in the pantry were Fig Newtons, which was the last resort.

Kim blinked once and looked around the room, not to remember it but to make sure he was really here, that this was really happening. And then he moved slowly, nearly shuffling, to the door.

"Don't turn around," Lieberman said, still seated at the dining room table. "Just leave and close the door."

Kim paused at the door, defeated, and then opened it quickly and left, closing the door behind him. Lieberman had to give the young man some credit. He hadn't slammed the door. Maybe there was a small sign of hope. Frankly, and only to himself, Lieberman didn't believe that Kim would give up. It would all probably end with Kim dead, which Lieberman regretted since he had developed some sense of what the Korean had gone through. From dreams of being a successful American-style gangster, he had fallen to one-armed outcast seeking revenge against the man he blamed for his fall.

Seconds after the front door closed Bess and Lisa came down the stairs.

"Kids hear any of this?" he asked.

"They're asleep," Bess said.

"We have any cake, coffee cake with that white swirly frosting?" Lieberman asked.

"In the freezer," Bess said. "I'll thaw it in the microwave. Abe, a small piece."

"Cholesterol," Lieberman said. "I know."

"Abe," Lisa asked, "who were those people?"

"Business acquaintances," Lieberman said.

"Business? They were criminals. In this house. With my children."

"I had it under control," Lieberman said.

"Lisa," Bess said, "I have learned over the course of the past forty years to accept the possibility that anyone might phone or knock at our door. Your father is a policeman. Madness from time to time comes with the badge."

"Not when my children are in danger," Lisa said.

"They weren't in danger," Lieberman said. "The only one in danger was Kim, the young man with one arm."

"Why was a one-armed Chinese man at your door?" Lisa demanded.

"He's Korean," Lieberman corrected. "I remind you, you lived through many a colorful visitor to our home."

"And that contributed to the confused and bitter person I became," said Lisa.

"We've had this conversation before," said Bess. "Let's get back to your father calling your husband."

Bess went into the kitchen through the door and Lisa sat, not in the same seat she had been in before, but at the opposite end of the table.

"Coffee?" Lieberman asked.

"Killers bring in killers," Lisa said. "In your house, my mother's house, the house where my children are sleeping, the house where I grew up."

"My house is safe," said Lieberman. "I keep it that way."

"With a gun," she said.

"Like Fig Newtons," he said. "The gun is a last resort, and I've never had to take it out of the drawer in my bedroom where I lock it every night."

"And you wear the key around your neck," she said. "I know."

"You want me to call Marvin now?" Lieberman asked. "Or do you want to complain further about my lifestyle?"

"Call," she said, glaring at her father.

"Give me the number again."

She did and he dialed.

The phone rang five times before Marvin Alexander picked it up and said, "Hello."

"*Shalom*," said Lieberman.

"*Shalom*, Avrum," said Lieberman's son-in-law.

"Do I have to tell you why I'm calling?" asked Lieberman.

"Lisa wants to come back," said Marvin. "She says I threw her out."

"Yes."

"I didn't throw her out, Avrum. I found out about her and the intern and talked to her on the phone, told her we had to discuss the situation. When I got home, she was gone. She left a note. That was yesterday."

"And?"

"I talked to the intern," said Marvin. "He was frightened. He was apologetic. He promised to stay away from Lisa. He swore that they had never — to use a biblical phrase — consummated their relationship. In fact, that's not the issue. Part of the blame is mine. I've been caught up in some forensic cases and I haven't spent much time with Lisa. Her

58

work is basically nine to five. Mine is whenever someone dies. Much like yours, I imagine."

"I understand," said Abe, looking at his daughter, who was trying to figure out from her father's minimal dialogue what was happening.

"I love Lisa," said Marvin. "She is not easy, but I love her. Tell her to come home. We'll talk. I know a good marriage counselor."

"You want to talk to her?"

"No, just tell her to come home. And, Abe, I'd still be happy to have Barry and Melisa live with us, but, just between us, for now at least I still think they'd be better off with you."

"I think you're carrying understanding a bit further than a saint," said Abe.

"Someday I'll tell you my life story. I think it might help you understand. Meanwhile, you might still qualify for special treatment from your God. Remember Abram became Abraham when God told him he would be a prophet and renamed him."

"I don't think that's going to happen to me," said Abe, "and I'm afraid of what God might rename me and what he might tell me to do."

"Tell Lisa I love her. Good-bye, Abe. To tell the truth, I don't have the heart for a discussion with Lisa right now, but I've got a homicide victim who needs attention back at the hospital."

"Good-bye, Doc," Abe said, and hung up.

Father and daughter simply looked at each other as Bess came out of the kitchen with a microwaved Sara Lee coffee cake and three plates, three forks, and a knife.

"Well?" asked Lisa.

"He wants you to come home," Abe said as Bess cut and served and sat to listen. "He says he didn't throw you out. You ran. He said he loves you and thinks you should both see a marriage counselor. He talked to the intern. The intern confirmed that nothing much had happened between you."

Abe took a bite of the warm cake. It was just what he needed. He knew he would try for a second piece and that Bess would stop him.

"I can't face him," Lisa said, looking at Bess who touched her daughter's hand.

"Wear a mask," said Abe. "He's a good man. Get a plane ticket and go back to California tomorrow."

"I've got a round trip," Lisa said softly. "Open ended. It was cheaper than one way."

"Then go back to your husband in the morning. Your mother will drive you to the airport."

"I'll drive you," Bess confirmed.

Lisa hesitated and said, "You think he really wants me back?"

"He really wants you back," said Abe.

Abe ate. He tried to eat slowly. It didn't work.

"I'll call TWA," Lisa said.

"Settled," Lieberman said, glancing at the television set. The score was flashed. The game was over. The Cubs had been trounced.

"You're tired," Bess said to her daughter. "I'll take you upstairs. We'll worry about your travel arrangements in the morning."

Bess was the president of the Temple Mir Shavot, and there was a big meeting in two days. Her pile of paperwork and the number of calls she had to make to appease, persuade, and cajole was monumental. She wouldn't get much more finished tonight. Bess wasn't an insomniac.

When Bess finally came down, she went to the sofa and sat across from Abe who had turned off the television set and was simply sitting with his feet up on his almost ancient hassock.

"You know how much our daughter's spent on airfare over the last three months?" Lieberman said. "We could spend a month in Florida, not that I want to spend a month in Florida."

"You ate Lisa's piece of cake," Bess said.

"You're the one who should be a detective."

61

"You left the evidence."

"I *ate* the evidence," he said.

Bess smiled and said, "Do us all a favor, Abraham. Try harder to keep company like we had tonight away from the house."

"You mean Lisa?"

"You know what I mean. Remember, I said 'try.' "

"You are a realist," he said.

"I've been married to you for a little more than forty years," she said. "I just know the way things are. I'm going to sleep. Tomorrow promises to be busy."

She had given him a kiss on the cheek and gone to their bedroom. Lieberman sat up watching *Out of the Past* for the sixth or seventh time and then sat through about half of *Oklahoma* coveting another piece of coffee cake and resisting the urge. Then he took a bath, running the water as quietly as he could, though it let out a nearly maddening hiss when it was on anything but full power.

He read an article on George Bernard Shaw's Irish heritage and how it appeared in his work. The article made sense. By three-thirty in the morning, Abe had turned off the lights and was in bed. He slept till seven.

And now, tired and with three cups of coffee in him, he entered the squad room, looked across the morning victims, suspects, and weary policemen and women and saw Captain Kearney in the door of his office motioning for Abe to come to him. Kearney did not look happy, but, then again, he seldom did.

Kearney was only in his early forties. He had been a rising star, headed for the top, possibly chief of police, and then, about a year ago, it had all gone bad. His ex-partner had lost control, held the city hostage for two days from a high-rise rooftop, and accused Kearney of seducing his wife. The ex-partner, Sheppard, had hit every newscast and front page. Kearney had denied the accusations, but the department needed a scapegoat and Kearney was it. When Sheppard was killed, so was Kearney's career. He would never be more than captain of detectives at the Clark Street station.

Lieberman made his way around the desks and through the smells, past his own desk, and into the captain's office with Kearney behind him. Kearney closed the door and faced Lieberman.

"Your partner's in deep shit again," Kearney said. "The woman's dead. The kid's gone. The state attorney's office thinks you better talk to our witness before whoever took his son gets to him. What are you working on?"

"Convenience store robberies," said Lieberman. "Salt and Pepper. One black, one white. Armed. About every other night. The black one is skinny, nervous, has a gun, uses good grammar. The white one is big. Hits the clerk with his fist. The last clerk looks like he has some brain damage. If it keeps going, I think Pepper's going to start shooting and Salt is going to hit someone a little too hard."

"Stay with it," Kearney said. "Press coverage on it?"

"Nothing on television. A few small articles in the papers. At one I'm supposed to be at a house on the paving scam."

"Juggle," said Kearney. "If you need help . . ."

"I need Hanrahan," said Lieberman.

Kearney shrugged and said, "Gornitz is priority. Hanrahan'll be back later in the morning. Go see what you can do with your old friend Mickey."

CHAPTER 3

"Remember Hal Litt?" Mickey Gornitz asked.

Mickey was thin, liked to wear cheap baggy clothes. He sat on the sofa, hands on his legs, clutching deep. Once he had been called Red Gornitz, but that was a long time ago. Gornitz still had hair, but not much of it and none of it red. Mickey had the face of a nervous accountant, which he was, and the perpetual half smile he wore since childhood as a mask.

The hotel room they were in was a decent size with a view of Lake Michigan between a pair of high-rises along the lake. They were downtown, east of Michigan Avenue in a hotel that had been seen a lot and once been the luncheon meeting place of the Chicago Press Club. Lieberman had covered a murder here about twenty years back. A department chairman at Loyola had picked up a pair of young men. The closet gay professor had given in to his need. The pair of young men had robbed him and thrown him out the window. Catching the pair had been easy. Telling the professor's family had been hard.

Sitting here with Mickey wasn't too bad, but Abe really had other things on his mind.

"I remember him," said Lieberman, sitting across from Mickey on an old fading sofa.

"Crazy guy," Mickey said, reaching into his pocket and then pulling it out as he remembered that he no longer smoked. According to Mickey, he had quit more than seven years ago. Old habits. "Took his clothes off on graduation night and stood in the middle of Roosevelt Road directing traffic. He wasn't even drunk. What happened to him, Abe? You know?"

"He got crazier," said Lieberman. "He's dead."

"I wonder what made me think about Hal," Mickey said, looking down at his lap. "So?" he asked, looking around the room and slapping his legs.

There was a young cop in plain clothes standing next to the door. Another cop, also in civilian clothes, stood outside in the hall pretending to read the *Sun-Times*. An investigator from the state attorney's office was in the bedroom watching a monitor that showed the hotel's lobby.

Mickey had spent a life of anonymity. Old acquaintances didn't recognize him in the street, and when he ran into someone from high school or college and stopped them to say hello, it was clear to him that he was not remembered.

Now all that had changed and one of the Lieberman brothers, half of one of the best back-court duos in the history of Chicago high school basketball, was sitting across from him, talking about old times.

Mickey had been an accountant for his father's paper box factory when he got out of the University of Illinois and then, when his father died and the factory went into bankruptcy, Mickey had gone to work for Jimmy Stashall. As Jimmy Stashall's bookkeeper, Mickey had led a life of relative comfort, though a solitary one since his wife took their son and left him more than a decade ago. Still, Mickey had been resigned to his lot. Then something, who knows what, maybe the need to change things around, stay ahead of the game, had gotten to Jimmy Stashall, who decided that Mickey Gornitz was getting a little old and was maybe a little dangerous because he knew too much.

The state attorney's office had picked up Mickey and played him a tape of Stashall's number-one man, Carl "the Fish" Cataglio, telling someone unknown that Mickey Gornitz was beginning to smell funny, that he needed a bath. The guy he was telling it to simply said, "Yes."

The state attorney couldn't use the tape in court, but he used it on Mickey, who understood exactly what the conversation meant. Mickey's lawyer made a deal and Mickey never even went back to his apartment to pick up his clothes and a toothbrush. Witness protection in exchange for copies Mickey had kept on floppy disks of Stashall's illegal activities. Mickey would also have to appear on the stand to testify that the disks were authentic.

Now came the waiting. Convinced that Stashall had gotten to the first lawyer, Mickey fired his lawyer and got a new one. Living in the hotel room for three months, talking and talking and talking to lawyers and cops and prosecutors and the FBI, Mickey was beginning to go a little mad. Everyone expected it. Then one day Mickey insisted on talking to Abe Lieberman and no one else. He knew Lieberman was a cop.

Mickey got what he wanted, including, he assumed, protection for his son and ex-wife.

A television was on across the room. The sound was off. It looked like C-Span.

"Hal Litt's dead," Mickey said, shaking his head at the more than forty-year-old memory. "One of the greatest. Best all-around player I ever saw, like French silk pie to play with, wasn't he? Could have, should have been the best Jew in the NBA. What was he? Six seven? Should have gone to a major college. Would have set records up the ass."

"Hal was stupid," Abe said, reaching for a cup of coffee Mickey had leaned over to pour for him. "A basketball idiot savant. Genius on the court. Couldn't read past fifth-grade level. Couldn't add numbers over the low hundreds."

"Couldn't carry numbers," Mickey said, handing Abe the coffee cup. "I tried to help him. You know that? With you, Hal, Mel Goldman, your brother Maish, and the black kid . . ."

"Alvin Garrett," Abe supplied.

The coffee was bad, very bad.

"What happened to him?" asked Mickey.

"Went to Pepperdine," said Abe. "Got a Ph.D. Heads a department out there."

"And Hal's dead."

Abe shrugged.

"He worked in Fetterman's bagel bakery. Went to park district games at night. Looked older than any of us."

"Time," Mickey said with another shake of the head. "How's Maish?"

Abe said his brother was fine.

"Still owns the T&L on Devon?" Mickey asked, glancing at C-Span and over at the cop at the door.

69

"Still," said Abe.

"Okay," said Mickey sitting back. "Now we talk about what you're really here for. The days of the Marshall Commandos can wait for better times."

"Bad news," said Lieberman.

"How bad?" asked Mickey, the small smile still in place, hands clasped together white in frightened mockery of prayer.

"Someone killed your ex-wife," said Lieberman.

"The boy?" asked Mickey. "Did they . . . ?"

"We don't know," said Lieberman. "Happened just outside of Dayton. Motel. We were watching. You can't be one hundred percent sure of protecting people who are out . . ."

"Stashall's got him," Mickey said, standing up and running his hand through nonexistent hair. He began to pace.

"Maybe," said Lieberman.

"There's no maybe," Gornitz said, pacing around the sofa. "How did they do it?"

"She was shot during the night. Window smashed. Cop guarding them came in, just missed them. Your son was gone."

"I don't care about her," he said. "She was a bitch, took my kid, told him lies about me, tried to make him hate me, kept me almost broke."

Which Lieberman knew was a lie, at least

70

the part about his ex-wife keeping him almost broke, but he sat quietly listening.

"She was a warning," he said. "That's how much I can count on you people. They told me that my kid would be protected and . . ."

"They won't kill him," Lieberman said.

"I know that," Mickey said, pausing and glaring at Lieberman. "I shut up, Matthew lives. Happens fast, doesn't it, Abe? One minute we're talking basketball and the old days. The next . . ."

"Happens fast, Mickey," Abe said, flashes of his own nightmares held back.

"Now we —" Mickey began, but he didn't finish.

Two men came through the door to the hallway. One man was short, stocky, black, head shaved and wearing a well-pressed dark designer suit. The short black man was about forty-five and not happy. At his side carrying a briefcase was a thin, towheaded white man in a nondesigner suit. The towhead looked thirty at the most.

"What the fuck is going on here, Lieberman?" asked the stocky black man who was an assistant state attorney and whose name was Eugene Carbin, Eugene A. Carbin. The "A" was for ambition.

"Kearney sent me," Lieberman said without getting up.

"And I suppose you told . . ."

"He told me," Mickey said, standing behind the sofa.

"You should have checked with our office," Carbin said, adjusting his tie. He didn't look comfortable in the tie, possibly because he had so little neck.

"I assumed Captain Kearney had . . ."

"You assumed shit," said Carbin, motioning for the thin towhead to move to the table near the window.

"Abe stays. He's the one I talk to," said Mickey.

"Okay," said Carbin, holding out his hands. "We've had that straight for some time, but that doesn't give Detective Lieberman the right to keep my office uninformed . . ."

"What the hell difference does it make who tells me my ex-wife was murdered and my son kidnapped?" Mickey shouted.

Unspoken was the likelihood that Carbin may well have withheld the information indefinitely.

Lieberman leaned forward and drank some more of the awful coffee. He exchanged looks with Carbin and they understood each other. If Matthew Firth was kidnapped, by Stashall or by someone Stashall paid to do it, someone would be calling to talk to Mickey Gornitz, someone who would insist with the threat of killing the boy if he didn't.

"We don't know if your son was kidnapped." Carbin moved past Gornitz and sat at the table where the towhead was setting up shop with the contents of his briefcase. Carbin looked out the window. It looked as if it might rain. "It could have been a coincidence. Locals after money. Wouldn't be the first time that motel was robbed, room broken into."

"Then Matthew is dead," said Mickey.

"I didn't say that," Carbin said, rising again.

"If Stashall has my son," said Mickey, "I'm not talking. I'm not testifying. No disks."

Mickey was shouting now and pointing to his chest.

"I'm not talking. I'm goddamn mad. If Stashall hurts my boy, I'm gonna get out of here and kill Jimmy Stashall. I never killed anyone in my life, but I'm gonna kill Jimmy Stashall. You get my boy back alive."

"Talk to him, Lieberman." Carbin stared at Abe across the room.

"You can put Jimmy Stashall away for twenty, thirty years, maybe more," Lieberman said without conviction.

"With his lawyers? With this system? He'll do ten if you're lucky. He'll do ten years and my son will be dead. Ten years isn't enough."

"Gornitz," Carbin said in the deep, slightly preaching voice he usually saved for juries. "You have enough to put a lot of people away, to break open a major criminal activity, to make connections to the mob no one has ever made. You have the obligation . . ."

"Stow it," said Mickey. "Abe, you remember when Maish used to say 'stow it' when anyone on the team complained?"

Abe nodded to show he remembered.

The towhead had set up some phone equipment as the conversation had gone on. Lieberman had ignored him.

"Your son's alive," Carbin said with a sigh.

"How do you know?" asked Gornitz.

"Call to our office," said Carbin. "About two hours ago. A guy. Said he'd call back at eleven. That's a few minutes."

He looked at the towhead who nodded.

"We're patched in here," said Carbin. "He'll call my office. It'll come from there here. We'll check the call. We have automatic . . ."

"It'll be from a stolen cell phone," Mickey said, coming around the sofa and sitting again to face Lieberman. "Any calls we get from them will be from stolen cell phones. Having the number won't do you any good. Tracing won't do you any good. Well, Abe? What would you do? Your kid? Your grandchildren?"

"Stall," said Abe.

"For what?" Mickey asked, putting his head in his hands. "I can't believe it. Five minutes ago we're talking Hal Litt. I find out he's dead. Now . . . I can't believe it. But I should. What I've seen working for that bastard. I should."

The phone rang. Mickey jumped up. Carbin stepped in front of him.

"Let it ring a few times," he said.

"Don't you understand? You can't catch him by tracing the damn call. Get out of my way or so help me you lose any chance you got of my testifying. I don't testify. You don't become a judge. We understand each other?"

The phone continued to ring.

"We're putting it on a speaker phone and recording," said Carbin. His face remained calm. He stepped out of the way. Carbin nodded to the towhead who pushed a button.

Mickey stopped.

"Hello," he said, voice unsteady into the sudden silence of the room.

"We're having a nice talk with one of your relatives," the voice said. "We hope you're not having nice talks with your friends."

"I talk to Matthew or I talk to the state attorney," said Mickey.

"Get off the speaker phone," said the voice. "I hear the room echo. Now, or I hang up."

Carbin nodded. The towhead turned off the speaker phone as Mickey picked up the regular receiver.

"Put my son on the phone," said Gornitz. "That's it. Nothing else. No threats. Prove he's alive."

There was a pause. Lieberman looked at Mickey, who slumped, rubbed his forehead, listened, and hung up.

"They cut him," said Mickey.

Lieberman was out of his chair and at the side of the man who used to sit in the wooden bleachers a lifetime ago.

"He's hurt," Mickey said as Lieberman led him back to the sofa. "And they're gonna hurt him more, a lot more."

"Gornitz," Carbin said. "This isn't easy, but it's history and common sense. They aren't going to let your boy live. And you don't stand a chance of getting to Stashall even if you get out of here, which you won't because my office plans to prosecute you even if you don't testify against Stashall. You've given us more than enough for that. You can't kill anyone from prison, and if you're not in witness protection, you can get yourself killed when you're a prisoner. It's not pretty, but we don't have a hell of a lot of time. We're going to do our best to find your son, but . . ."

"I'll work something out," Mickey said to

himself but aloud. "I've got to think this through."

"You don't have any options," said Carbin. "Think about it, but not too long. Did you recognize the caller?"

"No," said Gornitz. "But I recognized my son."

Mickey's head was down and he said with self-pity, "I don't even have a good picture of my own son. That bitch wouldn't send me one."

"What did he say, Gornitz?"

"Matthew was scared. Real scared. He saw them kill his mother. They've told him things they're gonna do to him if I don't promise to shut up. They —"

"And how do they keep you quiet when they release your son?" Carbin said.

"They want me to kill myself," he said.

"Then they'll kill your son, and you know it," said Carbin.

"You're a son of a bitch, Carbin." Mickey looked up, eyes moist.

"But I'm telling you the truth and you know it."

"I've got to think."

With that, Carbin motioned for Lieberman to follow him and nodded for the towhead to stay where he was. Out in the hallway with the door closed, Carbin strode away out of earshot of the plainclothesman pretending to read the paper, then he said softly to Lieberman, "Convince him."

Carbin was definitely invading Lieberman's space. Their noses were inches apart.

"Of what?" asked Lieberman.

Carbin sighed and shook his head. "Lieberman, you going to be retiring soon?"

"Few years."

"Pension, party, citation, the whole shmear?"

"You're threatening me?"

"Every cop has done something that can be looked at in his career," said Carbin. "*Every* cop."

God and Lieberman knew that Lieberman was no exception.

"Mickey's smart," said Lieberman. "He's a crook, but he's smart. Let's give him some time to try to work something out."

"Work something out," Carbin said, turning his head. "For starts, talk him out of any thoughts he might have about jumping through a window or sticking his finger in an electrical outlet."

Lieberman shrugged. He didn't really owe Mickey much but some nostalgia and a lot of ancient basketball games that seemed to matter a hell of a lot once but had been forgotten by almost everyone in what seemed like a short time. He would talk to Mickey. He would also do some thinking on his own about how to save Mickey's son.

"We'll pick up Stashall, talk to him," said Carbin, "but it won't do us any good. I understand your partner was responsible for watching Gornitz's kid and ex-wife."

"Yeah," said Lieberman.

"Great job," Carbin said dryly, turning his back on Lieberman and heading back to the hotel room.

Bill Hanrahan sat in his car in the parking lot of O'Hare Airport. No one had come to meet him when he arrived from Dayton. That suited him just fine. There would be questions, lots of questions, and he was supposed to head directly for the station where Kearney was waiting, probably with someone from the state attorney's office.

The run through broken glass and across the parking lot at the motel hadn't done his feet or knees any good. In fact, his right knee hurt, not enough to go to the doctor but enough to need ice, which he did not have. The cuts on the bottom of his feet made it painful to walk. He knew he was punishing himself with more than a touch of pain for blowing the job.

It was raining in Chicago. He could see it falling from his space on the sixth level of the

79

parking garage. Simple. Turn the key, start the car, and get into the city where he would deservedly be torn apart.

Bill Hanrahan considered a number of stops. He could stop by the Black Moon restaurant and get some solace and a cup of coffee from Iris Chen who, as yet, didn't know what had happened. He could go see Whizzer, the priest at St. Bart's whose football career had been far longer and more illustrious than Hanrahan's and who would give it to you straight. He could stop at home and stall seeing if there were any messages, or he could fly off the wagon and get that drink he wanted, the one that would carry him through the morning and into the afternoon. He wasn't out of options there. He could call Gerald Resnewki and get Gerry or someone from AA to talk to him, see him.

They all seemed like good ideas. Hanrahan started the car, went down the winding ramp, drove into the rain, paid his toll being careful to pocket the receipt to be reimbursed sometime in the distant future.

Hanrahan thought as he drove down the expressway that it would be a needed consolation if his son Michael were still at the house. Michael was probably strong enough to talk to and Michael, too, was an alcoholic, but Michael was dry now and sober and back with his wife and kids after spending a month with his father, a month of drying out and reconciliation.

No, the house would be empty. Bill's best bet was his partner. He never knew what Lieberman would say, but it would usually make things look less bleak than they certainly seemed. Lieberman knew how to accept failure and was cautious about celebrating anything that resembled victory. "Hope for the best. Expect the worst." Lieberman's motto number one or two. He got it from a Mel Brooks movie, but it made sense. Lieberman said he had also found it in the Bible.

Hanrahan pushed the button and listened to the Chicago oldies station. Buddy Holly and the Crickets were singing "Peggy Sue." Where was he when that song was popular? Dating Maureen, being courted by Division One colleges. He pushed another button and listened to a grumpy talk show host. The words didn't matter. It was company.

When he took the off-ramp at Touhy, Hanrahan compromised by stopping at Big Eddie's for a pair of hot dogs with everything. Big Eddie's was a shack whose owner had been fighting condemnation for years. The ancient black man who had owned Big Eddie's for about half a century made the best dogs in the city, bar none. His name was Ben. No one knew who Big Eddie was or had been. The atmosphere left something to be desired for many customers, particularly first-timers, but regulars and semiregulars like Bill Hanrahan didn't mind the darkness and the three tables that required endless matchbooks underneath the legs to keep them close to level. People left you alone at Big Eddie's. Ben didn't even say hello. He was a surly son of a bitch, but the food was good and fast and hot and brought back memories of the old days and the Sanborn Drive-In not far from Chicago Vocational High where Bill had reigned before Dick Butkus. Hanrahan didn't dwell on the memory, but it was there. He could have stopped at Maish's T&L, but that would take too much time and he might have to answer questions. He would be answering enough questions soon.

It was almost noon when he pulled into the parking lot behind the Clark Street station. The rain had stopped but the sky rumbled with the threat of another torrent. Hanrahan would have welcomed it. It suited his mood. He made his way through the back door and up to the squad room. The place was busy. It was probably the rain. People got cooped up by the rain, got on each other's nerves, got into fights about what show to watch on television or whether the Yankees would beat out the White Sox or what someone actually said about some relative's cooking. Sometimes people got killed. Burglaries went down. Burglars, unless they were desperate for drug money, were like other people. When the weather was bad, they stayed home. Same for muggers. That was one of the reasons they became criminals. So they could stay out of the rain when they wanted to. At least most of them.

Hanrahan looked around for Lieberman. He wasn't there. A few faces lifted toward him. Detectives at their desks hovered over suspects or witnesses. He saw sympathy, but no one spoke. It could have happened to any of them and they knew it, but Hanrahan would take the drop for losing someone whose life he was supposed to protect.

He knocked at Captain Kearney's door.

At a desk behind him, he heard a young man's voice with a heavy Hispanic accent saying "I don' know, man. If the guys says it was me, he's crazy nuts. I din't stab him. I don't know him. Swear on the holy mother, on my own mother. He's mistakin' me for some other guy. You know?"

"Come in," Kearney called, and Hanrahan entered.

Kearney was behind his desk. The office was large, large enough for both a desk with two chairs in front of it, a small couch and a small conference table. Behind the conference table was a blackboard with a list in blue chalk of the cases that Kearney felt were top priority.

There were three narrow windows in the office. One was behind Kearney. The other two faced Clark Street. Kearney was just hanging up the phone. The lights were not turned on in the office in spite of the rain-threatening darkness. Not a good sign.

Kearney's handsome, worn face turned to Hanrahan.

Bill opened his mouth to speak but was interrupted by the captain, who said, "Put it in writing. I want it in an hour. Cover your ass. Make it long. Here's an address. Be there by two whether you finish the report or not. It looks like we can take the guy who's been running the paving scam."

Hanrahan stood at the door and Kearney looked at the window. His job was a reasonably high-ranking one and it kept him busy, but those who knew him also saw the occasional distant look at what might have been. The spark of ambition wouldn't die completely.

Kearney brought Hanrahan up to date on the Gornitz business, including the phone call and the pressure from Carbin and the state attorney's office. Kearney didn't ask what had happened, didn't complain about how Hanrahan's failure would reflect on both of them. Kearney was remembering the accusations that had sat him permanently at the Clark Street station.

Hanrahan's mother would have said "He needs a nice Irish girl."

Maybe she would have been right, but for now, it looked as if Kearney's history would dampen his criticism of his detective.

"I'll go write the report," Hanrahan said.

"Remember, make it long and boring. If it's long and boring enough, Carbin will probably stop reading it by the middle of the first page."

Hanrahan nodded and went back into the squad room, where three detectives were holding down the young Hispanic who had claimed to be innocent of stabbing someone. The young man was shouting in Spanish. Some of the detectives at other desks ignored the battle and went on working. A few paused and waited for the battle to end and the young man to be dragged off screaming for a public defender.

Hanrahan had escaped. Kearney was going to protect him. It wasn't because they were both Irish. The Chicago police department still had more Irish than any other ethnic group. Kearney and Hanrahan shared failure.

Hanrahan went to his desk and worked on his report wondering where Lieberman was. He could sure use a dose of Abe Lieberman.

"I don't know," said the old man holding an umbrella over his head though there had been a pause in the rain. He wore an oversized gray sweater and a look of uncertainty as he looked down at the driveway.

"Look at the cracks," the big man at his side said.

The big man had introduced himself as Mike. He looked a lot like the guy on television and in the movies John Goodman, but Mike was deadly serious and he wore serious gray overalls and a matching gray baseball hat and tucked under his arm was a clipboard with a black plastic cover. Behind him in the driveway stood Mike's white van.

"I don't know," said the old man.

"I'm tellin' you," said Mike. "Not just the cracks. See the gravel leaking from under the drive into the street there?"

"Yeah," said the old man, rubbing his chin.

The street was wet with puddles and streamlets gliding toward the sewer.

"Two thousand'll save this driveway, Gerald," Mike said.

Mike had started calling the old man Gerald from the start and had urged the old man to call him Mike.

"If you wait," Mike said with a shrug, "the whole thing collapses, could run you five thousand and someone might get hurt. You know. It might fall in when a car pulled up. Heck, Gerald, it could maybe even fall in if a big guy like me jumped on it in the right place."

"It's gotta be?" the old man asked, shaking his head.

"Gotta be," said Gerald. "I can get the whole thing taken care of any day next week. Done in a few hours and then we need a few more hours to let it dry. You want I can come out with my crew on the first clear day."

"The money," said the old man.

"Half up front," said Mike. "Check'll do. Other half when we finish the job to your satisfaction."

"A thousand dollars," said the old man with a sigh.

"Actually, fifteen hundred to cover materials, an extra man. The other five hundred can wait till you approve. Fair?"

"Sounds fair," said the old man as a car drove by. A woman was driving. A boy about six made a face at Gerald and Mike from the backseat as the car kicked up a stream of rainwater.

"Written guarantee," Mike said, holding up his clipboard. "Just write out the check. Make it to cash or Mike's Driveways."

"I think I'd like to think about this overnight," said the old man. "Talk to my son. He's a lawyer."

"But he doesn't know driveways," said Mike, squatting to poke his pen into a narrow crack in the drive that looked like an anemic bolt of lightning. "Gerald, you need this work. You need it now. I wouldn't have stopped at your house and left my flyer and card last week if I didn't see immediate danger here, and you wouldn't have called me to come if you didn't know deep in your heart that I'm right."

"Next week?" asked the old man.

"First clear day," said Mike, opening the cover of his clipboard and handing his pen to the old man.

The document Mike was holding was in tiny type. It ran for three pages, which Mike flipped open to the page with a signature line.

"My work is guaranteed," said Mike. "One hundred percent for the life of your drive."

The old man held the umbrella high in one hand and signed with the other.

"I'll go get my checkbook," said the old man. "I wouldn't want anyone hurt or, God forbid, killed on my driveway."

"Right is right, Gerald."

"Wait here. I'll be right back."

"I'll wait in my van," said Gerald. "Startin' to rain again."

Mike went back to his van and climbed into the driver's seat, where he sat listening to the news while he waited. The old man was out in a few minutes walking slowly to the driver's window, which Mike rolled down.

"Could you get out of the van?" the old man said. "I don't see so good without my glasses and I don't see so good with them when they're covered with rain."

"Sure," Mike said obligingly as he opened the door and stepped out.

As soon as Mike closed the door, a dark car came quickly down the street and pulled into the driveway behind Mike's van.

"You've got visitors," said Mike. "I'll just take the check and go. I've got four more stops today."

"Only one more," said the old man.

Something about the way he said it made Mike pause. He was looking down at the old man and heard the door of the car in the driveway open behind him. He didn't look back.

"I don't get it, Gerald, but if you'll just give me the check, I'll sign the contract and give you your copy."

89

"You are under arrest," said the old man, holding out his wallet and showing his badge.

"Arrest," Mike said with a laugh.

"Fraud," said the old man. "Bunch of other charges too. Plenty of witnesses, including me."

Mike took a step toward the old man and said, "Get out of my way."

The old man took a step toward Mike. The two were inches apart, and Mike suddenly felt something poke hard into his belly. He looked down at the gun in the old man's hand. He didn't know what kind of gun it was, but it was a big one.

"Push me and you're resisting arrest," said the old man. "Then I can only assume you plan to run me over with your van. I would take umbrage at that and have to shoot you."

Mike considered. The old man was looking him in the eyes.

"You're making a mistake," Mike said with a laugh.

"No, he's not" came a voice behind him, the voice of the person who had gotten out of the car that blocked Mike's van.

Mike turned toward the voice and saw a man as big as he was with a pink Irish face. Definitely a cop.

"I think you'd better let me get back into my van and call my lawyer," Mike said indignantly.

"Detective Lieberman just told you you're under arrest," said Hanrahan. "He'll tell you your rights and we go to the station. You make it easy or you make it hard. I think I'd prefer hard. I've had a bad few days."

"Put it that way, so have I," said Lieberman. "So, try to get away, Mike. I'll just put my gun away and watch Detective Hanrahan subdue you. He doesn't subdue gently."

Mike's angry indignation slipped and his shoulders sagged, then he made one more try.

"You're making a mistake," he said. "I'm an honest businessman. This is false arrest."

"You've been scaring old people into giving you money for months," said Lieberman. "Turn around and put your hands together."

"You're gonna cuff me?" asked Mike.

"Unless you can think of something else effective I could do with your hands behind your back," said Lieberman.

Mike turned around. He was facing Hanrahan now.

"Last chance," Hanrahan said softly. "Just get by me, get in your van, and run us over. We'll shoot, but you might get lucky and live."

Mike looked up at the sky. There was a loud clap of thunder. Lieberman clasped on the cuffs.

"I didn't do anything wrong," Mike insisted as the two detectives ushered him toward Hanrahan's car. Lieberman's was parked in the garage. The owner of the house, a man named Jankitis who would be celebrating his eighty-fifth birthday in a few days, was inside watching a *Wheel of Fortune* rerun.

"There's nothing wrong with this driveway," said Lieberman. "We had a contractor check it."

"My professional opinion against his," Mike said as they moved to the passenger side of Hanrahan's car.

"You are not a professional," said Lieberman. "At least not a professional contractor. You are a professional con man who takes deposits from people who need their money. Then you disappear. Now, do me the courtesy of being quiet while I tell you your rights. If you listen, really listen, you may find them useful and interesting."

"Can't we work something out here?" Mike pleaded, looking from one policeman to the other. "I've got a wife, two little kids. I'm just a guy trying to make a living."

"You think our friend Mike is suggesting a bribe?" asked Lieberman.

"It's a distinct possibility," said Hanrahan.

"My roof needs fixing," said Lieberman.

"My son Michael could use money to send my grandson to a Catholic school," said

Hanrahan. "I'd say five million dollars would do it."

"Five mil—" Mike began.

"You're safe," said Lieberman, guiding the big man in overalls toward Hanrahan's car. "Maybe you didn't offer a bribe. Maybe you've got no conscience. It happens a lot. Maybe my partner and I like to look in the mirror in the morning and see a face we can live with. I got a feeling you don't understand what I mean. I suggest you not say another word till you talk to a lawyer."

Mike shut up as he was shoved into the backseat of Hanrahan's car.

"My van," Mike cried.

"We'll have it towed in," said Hanrahan.

"You okay, Father Murphy?" Lieberman asked as he closed the door on Mike.

"Could be better, Rabbi. Could be a lot better."

"We'll talk," said Lieberman.

Hanrahan moved around to the driver's side of his car and opened the door. Before he got in, he said, "That is one hell of an ugly sweater."

"Guy who owns the house was going to give it to Goodwill," said Lieberman. "I bought it from him. Comfortable. A little large, but comfortable."

CHAPTER 4

"Bess called," Maish said, standing by the booth at the T&L where Abe sat.

The T&L on Devon wasn't exactly packed but it was busy. The short-order cook, known to all as Terrell, an ex-con whom Abe had gotten his brother to hire a dozen years ago, was a genius with Jewish food, a black culinary genius. Jerome Terrell had learned to cook in prison and had quickly developed a passion for Jewish cooking after Maish hired him. He loved the smells, the taste, the lack of concern about what the ingredients might do to the human body. He cooked by taste and smell, never used measuring spoons or cups.

"She wants me to call?" Lieberman asked in answer to his brother's statement.

"She wants me to be sure you eat right when you come here," said Maish.

Maish wore his ever-present white apron, his ever-present sour look on his sagging face, and a few more pounds than he should have been carrying for the sake of his own health, but owning a deli wasn't the way to stay slim and whatever little care Maish had taken of himself had vanished with the murder of his son David by muggers less than two years earlier.

"Then give me something that's right," said Abe. "A magical something that tastes great and doesn't send cartoon cells scurrying to block my arteries with cholesterol like the slaves scurried with blocks of stone to build the pyramids."

"The Jews who were slaves in Egypt didn't know from cholesterol," called Herschel Rosen from the reserved table of the *Alter Cockers*, the old men who gathered every day at the T&L. The members of the group who might appear at any time of the day. The time changed depending on their schedules, but you could always count on at least a few of them when you came in for a meal or a nosh at the T&L. The *Alter Cockers* were all old Jews except for Howie Chen, a full-fledged member who had owned a Chinese restaurant one block away before his retirement. Howie had lived and worked in the neighborhood for fifty years. He spoke better Yiddish than most of the *Alter Cockers*, some of whom couldn't speak Yiddish at all. A few of the members could actually speak Hebrew, not well, but they had picked up enough in pilgrimages to Israel over the years.

"It's a bad analogy," Rosen continued emphatically. "Pyramids, cholesterol."

Howie was at the table. So was Sy Weintraub. Sy, at eighty, was the group's athlete. He walked at least five miles a day, rain or shine. When the weather was really bad, Sy could be found at the Jewish Community Center on Touhy not far from Abe's house. Sy walked resolutely around the basketball court softly humming till he did his five miles. Sy could hold his own in the table banter, but it was the company he savored, not the conversation. He would have been content to sit at the table near the window with the other old men and simply listen. This information on Sy Weintraub had been given to Abe by Maish, Nothing-Bothers Maish, except lots of things bothered Maish, more since David died. Maish just didn't show it.

"I'll live with the bad analogy," Abe called back. "It should only be my biggest faux pas of the day."

"Faux pas, again," said Herschel. "You and Bess planning a trip to gay Paree or something or are you just showing off?"

"I've decided to emulate the eloquent repartee of the great French lovers of history," said Abe, straight-faced. "I've launched a personal campaign to woo my wife with poetry in

French and Romanian. So I'm practicing French words at every opportunity."

"Romanian?" asked Herschel. "Romanian poetry?"

"Great Romanian poetry," said Abe.

"Joking again," said Herschel looking at the others at his table. "Another Myron Cohen we've got here."

"Where's Al Bloombach?" asked Abe.

"Bloombach and his wife are on a cruise," said Herschel with some disdain. "My wife, *alevai shalom,* may she rest in peace, went on a cruise about ten years ago. Too much food. Too many kids. Too many islands with too many stores trying to sell you stuff. He can have it. Al will be back tomorrow."

Two clerks from the Rosenthal Men's Shop down the street were hunched over the table in their booth trying to carry on a conversation over the banter between Abe and the *Alter Cockers* but the two salesmen were trapped in the booth between the cop and the Cockers.

The T&L was the last of a dying breed. Once Devon was Jewish with a sprinkling of Chinese restaurants and a Greek fruit store or two. Now the street was Korean with a minority of Vietnamese who probably outnumbered the Jews from Ridge Avenue to McCormick Boulevard. Actually, business at the T&L was better than it had ever been. A lot of Koreans liked corned beef and matzoh ball soup or a good brisket.

Three women on stools at the counter downed bowls of cabbage borscht. Two of the women talked to each other, usually at the same time. Abe recognized them. One was the daughter of Myrna Kransky, whom Abe had dated in high school. The daughter was in her thirties, pretty, with thick glasses. The other woman he recognized, Irene Richman, was a member of Temple Mir Shavot where Bess was president and Abe was constantly being shoved into committees, some of them with Irene, a plump, always suited, even-tempered assistant vice president at a bank on Irving Park Road. Irene had an MBA from the University of Chicago, a fact her mother often brought up when Irene put forth an argument during a committee meeting. Irene's mother, Rose, was a widow who had a modest income from her husband's insurance. Rose's goal in life was to be on every committee her daughter was on at the temple.

The third woman, the one sitting alone, looked familiar, but he couldn't place her. She was good-looking, dark, short business-like haircut, pearl earrings, wearing no-nonsense makeup and a look that could have been anything from determination to blank daydreaming. He would place her, remember her name. It used to be easier.

The T&L door opened. The two salesmen went out. Bill Hanrahan came in. For a late-weekday afternoon, business was booming.

"Look who walked in," said Herschel Rosen. "The Irish Republican Army delegate."

"Here to make another attempt at contacting the Israeli government through those of us with connections," said Morris Hurvitz, the short, smiling, bespectacled, and still-working seventy-eight-year-old psychologist.

"Irish and Jews against the British," Hanrahan said with a sad smile as he headed toward Abe's table. "Unbeatable. We'd have the British out in a week."

Hanrahan sat across from his partner and Maish brought a cup of coffee without being asked.

"You want a bowl of soup, a sandwich?" asked Maish.

"You decide," Hanrahan said, touching his brow and closing his eyes.

"Corned beef and chopped liver on rye?"

"Sounds fine," said Hanrahan.

Maish joggled slowly back behind the counter to place the order and to ring up a customer on the cash register.

"Booked and out on bond?" asked Lieberman.

"Booked on five counts of fraud," said Hanrahan. "Judge was Mason Harvey. Old Mason must be seventy-five minimum. Doesn't take kindly to people who pull scams on our senior citizens. Set the bond so high our pal Mike almost couldn't post. By the way, his name isn't Mike. It's Mikhail Piniescu. Not a citizen. Things go right, Mikhail could be on his way back to the old country."

"If things go right," Abe said, drinking some coffee.

"Which they almost never do," said Hanrahan.

Abe nodded. The *Alter Cockers* chattered behind them. Two of the three women at the counter paid their bill and left together. The third woman, whom Lieberman was still trying to place, checked her watch and picked at her food. A couple of guys in hard hats and overalls came in and sat at the counter.

"I blew it, Rabbi," Hanrahan finally said, opening his eyes and lifting the cup of steaming coffee.

"You blew it," Lieberman agreed. "Anyone would have blown it. One man on a job like that would have to be damn lucky to keep a determined, connected *shtick dreck* like Stashall from pulling this off. Face it, Father Murphy, you were there because Mickey

100

Gornitz wanted someone there. Part of the deal. No one thought Stashall would go after the ex-wife and kid. Cunning, yes. Clever, yes. Smart, no. Jimmy Stashall is not one of the great minds of the century. One man on the road to protect an unlikely target . . . Anyone would have blown it."

Hanrahan nodded, unconvinced.

"So, you either go into another depression, blame yourself, try to get AA or your priest to keep you together — neither of which is a bad idea — or we get the kid back, nail Stashall, and keep Gornitz convinced that he should talk. What's your pleasure?"

Hanrahan sighed, finished his coffee, and said, "We get the kid back and nail Stashall."

"Am I right or am I right that anyone would have blown it?" Abe asked as Maish ambled slowly to the booth with their food.

"Anyone would have blown it," Hanrahan agreed. "But it was me. And it wasn't the first time."

"Probably won't be the last either," Abe said, looking at the food placed in front of him and his partner. "I've still got my share to screw up. You want to keep score? Most screw-ups in the next year commits suicide."

"Let's make it the most screw-ups pays for dinner for four at Houlihan's," said Hanrahan.

"Let's," Lieberman said, looking at his plate and then up at his brother who hovered over him. "What's this?"

"Cottage cheese, pineapple, on top of a little lettuce," said Maish.

"Don't I get a little maraschino cherry?"

"I'll get you one." Maish turned and moved back to business.

Lieberman looked at his plate and at Hanrahan's. Hanrahan was about to take a bite of his corned beef and chopped liver on rye.

"Despondency doesn't seem to have affected your appetite?"

"Life goes on," Hanrahan said, taking a big bite.

"You going to eat both halves of that sandwich?" asked Lieberman.

"Both and maybe a big bowl of matzoh ball soup," said Hanrahan, his mouth full.

"You wouldn't consider taking half my . . ."

A deep-red cherry complete with stem dropped atop the hill of cottage cheese in front of Lieberman.

"You eat that sandwich, I tell Bess," said Maish. "You wanted a maraschino cherry. You got a maraschino cherry. Eat. Enjoy. Indulge."

Maish left. It was Lieberman's turn to sigh as he picked up his fork and dug into the lumpy white mound.

"A little sour cream mixed in wouldn't kill me," he mumbled.

"Abe," Herschel Rosen called across the room. "Opinion. You got an opinion on all this new stuff about Genesis?"

"If you Cockers are so interested in the Torah," Lieberman said, gulping down the cherry, which he had planned to save till the end, "you should go to the study group at Mir Shavot."

"With Rabbi Wass?" asked Louis Roth, a former jeweler with astonishingly thick glasses. "I'll take my chances at this table, thank you very much."

"Amen," said Herschel Rosen. "You got an opinion? You don't have an opinion? Which is it, Abraham?"

Abe glanced toward the counter behind which his brother had stopped cleaning and straightening and pouring and was giving his full attention to the conversation.

"There was a beginning," said Lieberman.

"And?" Herschel prompted.

"That was enough to screw things up," said the detective.

The two men in hard hats were half turned listening to the conversation. One of the two men was as black as Lieberman's son-in-law. The other hard hat was a stocky young man in his thirties with a round cheerful face. They definitely did not fit the description of the salt-and-pepper holdup men.

"And they'll stay screwed up," Hanrahan said so low that the old men at the table couldn't make out his words. "Just trying to stay sane in a mad world. We can do without God being crazy too."

"What'd he say?" Louis Roth asked, squinting around the table.

"God's crazy," said Herschel Rosen.

"Amen. So tell me something new?"

Lieberman had finished his cottage cheese and pineapple and even eaten the thin sheet of lettuce. He was still hungry. Hanrahan's sandwich was gone. Maish was back to filling the coffee cups.

"How was the cottage cheese special?" asked Maish.

"Healthy," said Abe. "I feel healthy now. I feel like I could conquer giants."

"A simple 'good' would be enough," Maish said, picking up the empty plates.

"Actually," said Abe, "it wasn't bad."

"Frankly," said Maish, "I can't stand the stuff. Herschel's right. God is crazy."

And then he was gone.

"What now, Rabbi?" asked Hanrahan.

"We could go back to all the places the Salt and Peppers have hit," said Lieberman.

"Maybe get a lead, some piece of identification we can follow up."

"We could," said Hanrahan.

"Or," said Lieberman, "we could go visit Jimmy Stashall for a friendly conversation."

"Eugene A. Carbin wouldn't like it," said Hanrahan.

Lieberman stood, used his fingers to take a last tiny lump of cottage cheese he had overlooked, and said, "I am firmly convinced he wouldn't like it at all, Father Murph."

"Then let's do it," said Hanrahan.

And they were about to do it when the T&L door opened again and a man came in, a man about Lieberman's age, a thin man with dark receding hair and a gaunt look. He was wearing a dark sweater under his open flannel-lined jacket. His hands were thrust in his pockets. The man spotted Lieberman and headed for him. It was then that Lieberman placed the lone woman at the counter: Rita Blitzstein, daughter of the man who was advancing on him, Robert Blitzstein.

"Blitzstein," Lieberman said to the man who was a member of the congregation at Temple Mir Shavot.

Blitzstein who had lost his wife five years earlier offered his hand and looked at Hanrahan.

"Detective William Hanrahan, my partner," Lieberman said.

"Good," said Blitzstein. "Can we sit?"

Lieberman shrugged and sat back in the booth. Hanrahan moved over to make room for Blitzstein, who folded his hands and looked at his daughter at the counter. She saw the look, got off of the stool at the counter and joined them, sitting next to Lieberman across from her father.

"Is that Blitzstein?" Hy Rosen asked from the *Alter Cocker's* table.

"It is," said Howie Chen. The Blitzsteins used to be regulars at Howie's restaurant. Every Sunday. Howie had watched Rita grow up. Had served them the same meal week after week and received the same tip even when inflation was on them.

"Blitzstein," called Rosen. "Come over when you're done. We'll insult you for a few minutes, buy you a coffee or two."

Blitzstein didn't answer. He was in no mood. Blitzstein had moved out of the neighborhood long before the Koreans and Vietnamese started to come in. He had moved north, beyond Skokie into Winnetka. Blitzstein had a successful children's furniture and clothing store. Actually, he had three of them and was one of the more affluent members of Temple Mir Shavot though in actual dollars his annual contributions were well below that of Lieberman and Bess. Blitzstein had, however, been on the building committee with Lieberman, the committee that had been responsible for raising the money for the new temple in the renovated bank building on Dempster in Skokie. The two men were not friends, but neither were they enemies. "Acquaintances" would be the word Lieberman would have used.

Lieberman knew, though Blitzstein hadn't talked about it, that Blitzstein had received four combat medals during the Korean War. He knew that Blitzstein had never gotten over the loss of his wife to cancer nearly five years earlier. Blitzstein was a man who held tightly the memory of his suffering and that of his family. He was not an easy man to know or like, but he was, Lieberman knew, a man who prided himself on his honesty. The word of Robert Blitzstein was good, though his company might not be.

"They told me I might find you here," said Blitzstein. "You weren't at home. You weren't at the police station."

Lieberman and Hanrahan sat back. Whatever it was, was important to Robert Blitzstein.

"Rita, tell Detective Lieberman."

Slowly, clearly, precisely, and in detail Rita

Blitzstein told the two detectives about her encounter with the huge man in the street the night before, about the garbage can, the obscenities.

"Clarence Millthorpe," Lieberman said with a sigh.

Hanrahan nodded his agreement.

"You know him?" Blitzstein asked.

"We know him," said Lieberman. "Known him for almost three years, when he first appeared. We don't know where he lives. His fingerprints don't show up on any local, regional, or national files, which means he was never in prison and never in the armed services under any name. He has no identification. On the street, he's crazy, but when we get him in for questioning, he could give Gerry Spence a run for his money."

"So, what are you telling us?" asked Blitzstein.

"Miss Blitzstein," Hanrahan said, "did he threaten you?"

"He held the garbage can over his head in front of me, for God's sake," she said.

"Did he say he was going to hit you with it, show signs that he was?"

"I —"

"What did you say he did with the garbage can?" Hanrahan pressed on.

"Threw it down the street," she said.

108

"Say anything threatening to you?" asked Lieberman.

"Obscenities," she said. "Loud, angry."

"No direct threats," Lieberman went on. "No witnesses."

"He's done this to other people," she said, her eyes moist but holding back tears. "I've seen it. I —"

"My daughter's afraid to go home," said Blitzstein. "I'm going to move her in with me till she feels up to finding a new place, subletting her apartment."

"No," Rita said firmly. "He's not driving me from my home. I'm not a child. He's terrorizing a whole neighborhood. I'm sure you can find witnesses."

"We've had maybe thirty complaints over the last three years," said Hanrahan. "Never enough evidence of anything but trying to frighten people. We put him in with a shrink. He doesn't cooperate. We can't even charge him with disturbing the peace. Not enough evidence."

"Something's got to be done about a madman like this before he hurts someone," said Blitzstein. "Look what he's done to my daughter."

Rita looked at her father and let her tongue touch her upper lip to keep back the tears.

"We'll find him," said Lieberman. "Pull

him in. See what we can do."

"When?" asked Blitzstein.

Lieberman looked at Rita and then at his partner.

"Now," said Hanrahan.

Blitzstein nodded with cautious satisfaction and reached over to touch his daughter's hand. From what Lieberman could recall from bits and pieces over the years, Rita Blitzstein had left her parents' home after college and had had little to do with them after growing up under the morose domination of her father. She worked for a newspaper or a television station. She had been on her own, professional, and then this happened and she was back seeking the power and determination of her father. Lieberman read defeat in the woman's eyes, but he may, he decided, be imagining the scenario. She had said that she wouldn't move in with her father. Maybe the threat of Clarence Millthorpe wasn't quite as bad as becoming a little girl again. He knew he didn't particularly care for Blitzstein, but he had never witnessed anything really bad from the man but the flashes of temper at committee meetings.

"Stashall will wait," Hanrahan said.

Lieberman nodded and the four people got out of the booth and headed for the door.

"You'll probably have to identify him face

to face if we can come up with a charge," Lieberman said.

"I'll identify him," Rita Blitzstein said with determination.

"Blitzstein," Rosen said as they passed the *Alter Cockers'* table near the window. "You want to sit, *kibbitz* a minute or two, or you got people to talk to in Highland Park?"

Rosen knew Blitzstein didn't live in Highland Park. Blitzstein took his daughter's arm and left the T&L. Hanrahan and Lieberman were right behind.

Abe turned to wave good-bye to his brother, the little Jimmy Cagney flip of the hand for Pat O'Brien they had been using since they were kids. Maish wasn't looking at his brother. He was staring glassy-eyed at the sparkling coffee cup in his hand as if it were a crystal ball that might hold an answer to any of his questions.

Lisa hadn't gone back to Los Angeles yet.

Lieberman would be in for a surprise when he saw her sitting there waiting for him whenever he came home. Bess knew her husband was good at handling such surprises from his daughter. They didn't make him happy. He just handled them well. Providing Abe got home from work at a reasonable time — and probably even if he didn't — there would be a

111

long session of reason, persuasion, exasperation, and frustration. Bess did not look forward to it any more than she looked forward to the first in a series of afternoon Torah studies sessions that she was about to open.

The reason was not the small turnout, only a dozen people, but the fact that her brother-in-law Maish had shuffled into the session before anyone arrived and sat in the first row of seats in the small sanctuary nodding at Bess, the stoic look on his bulldog face emotionless. He was dressed in his one gray suit and even wore a tie and in his lap was a yellow legal-size pad. Bess, from the lectern of the small *bema* on which she stood, could see that Maish's pad was filled with notes.

Maish had essentially dropped out of the congregation when his son was murdered by a mugger and David's pregnant wife was shot during the attack, killing her unborn baby. At least that was the story. As Bess knew, there was much more to it than that, more than she would ever be able to tell Maish and his wife, Yetta. Bess had chatted with young Rabbi Wass, who kept adjusting his glasses while people straggled in. Rabbi Wass nodded at Maish, who didn't respond, and said to Bess with a pleased smile, "You see who's here?"

"My husband's brother," Bess answered, trying to get some sense of why Maish might be here with his yellow pad. She sensed that he had not simply returned to the fold.

At ten after the hour, Bess suggested that they begin with the dozen people seated before them. Rabbi Wass agreed.

"I think I know all of you," she began. "I'm Bess Lieberman, president of Temple Mir Shavot, and this is our rabbi, who has made the study of the meaning of the Torah, the first five books of the Holy Bible, his life's work. This is the first in a series of conversations with the rabbi on questions you may have and wish to discuss. All of you have been asked to read the Torah in preparation for this series. We hope and expect that others in the congregation will join us in the future. Rabbi Wass."

Bess descended from the *bema* and moved to one of the many empty wooden seats toward the rear. There were plenty of empty seats. The sanctuary could hold 107.

"The Torah," Rabbi Wass began in his most rabbinical voice, "is a living work of mystery, contradiction, wisdom, and great literature. It is God's solace and warning to us. It teaches us that we can never know God but that we must love and obey. It teaches us that we are the chosen people and that we will survive if we revere God and behave cleanly and with respect for each other, every human being, and our holy days. The —"

Maish's pudgy hand was up. Bess cringed in the back, determined to move up to her brother-in-law's side if things got too bad. Where was Maish's wife, Yetta? Did she even know he was here?

The other eleven people who had gathered, most of them younger members of the congregation with families, most of them professional — doctors, lawyers, businessmen and women — turned toward the overweight man with the sad eyes whose hand was up.

"Morris Lieberman?" Rabbi Wass said, adjusting his glasses.

"Why did God let my son and grandchild die?" Maish asked.

Bess quietly rose and began to ease her way toward the empty seat next to Maish.

"God created man and gave man free will." Rabbi Wass was ready for this one. "Men are free to act with compassion and goodness or with evil. God watches. If we destroy each other, He watches. If we honor Him and perform acts of contrition and decency, He watches. God takes the dead unto Himself, but He leaves us free to plot our own destinies."

"I don't see that anywhere in the Torah," said Maish. "I read it twice, once last night. The Bible is not full of wisdom. It is full of contradiction, mistakes, and nonsense. And it is full of evil. Abraham and others pretend their wives are not their wives and turn them over as whores to protect their own lives. God gives commandments and then creates so many rituals that we can't keep up with them. Offer flour, kill rams and sheep, spread blood on the altar and you're forgiven for stealing if you pay back twenty percent extra. Don't eat animals that have cloven hooves. In Leviticus, a hare is named as an animal that chews cud and has a cloven hoof. Aaron's sons make the wrong kind of fire at the altar and God immediately burns them to death. Where was their chance to make offerings and atone? And He goes on and on about lepers? We don't have any lepers.

"Cain kills Abel," Maish went on, checking the scrawling words on his pad. "He's forgiven. Jacob and his mother cheat Esau out of his inheritance simply because he is hairy. Isaac refuses Miriam because she isn't pretty enough for a wife, but he has no trouble taking her to bed and having children."

"We'll discuss all that," Rabbi Wass said, looking at the interested faces of the small group. It was clear that a number of them regarded Maish as slightly mad. A few knew something about what had happened to his son. Most did not want to know.

115

"God is evil," said Maish. "That's that. God is selfish. Sits there demanding we spend our lives thanking Him, praising Him, and what does He do for us? Persecution, the Holocaust, the murder of innocent people like my David."

It was definitely the longest speech Bess had ever heard from her brother-in-law, and though he had a pad in his ample lap he had only referred to it once. Now he sat back, lips tight, waiting for the slightly flustered rabbi to respond so he could attack again.

Bess was at her brother-in-law's side now. He didn't seem to notice. Was he really going mad? He had been close to something like it when David had died. She was torn between trying to usher him out of the sanctuary and letting him speak. Maybe there was something cathartic in Maish's coming tonight. Maybe he had to get it out. She touched his arm. He looked at her as if she weren't there and turned back to Rabbi Wass.

"God's ways are difficult to know," Rabbi Wass admitted.

"Difficult?" responded Maish. "In Leviticus, He says to Moses that even those who commit a sin and don't know it should repent and present a sacrifice. How do you repent if you don't know you've committed a sin? Is God crazy? The answer is clear. God is crazy.

116

Madness rules the universe."

This was not what the small gathering had expected. From their faces, Rabbi Wass could see that the group was about divided between those who were riveted by this performance and others who were exasperated by the ravings of this fat man whose voice sounded as if it were about to break.

"If you —" Rabbi Wass began, and was cut off again by Maish.

"The plagues. God tells Moses to go to Pharaoh and tell him to let the Jews go or something terrible will happen. Pharaoh says okay, hunky dory, and then God — it says right there in Exodus — hardened the Pharaoh's heart and Pharaoh changed his mind. Pharaoh keeps saying yes and God hardens his heart. What sense are we talking here? People are dying. Moses does what he's told but unless he's some kind of idiot, he's got to be wondering what's going on. What's God doing here? Having fun? God is crazy."

"There are many, including me," Rabbi Wass tried, "who believe that much in the Bible is not so much simple fact as enigmatic lesson, mysterious ideas to be explored and discussed. The one solid irrefutable fact is that God tells us to be good to each other, Jew or Gentile."

"And in return," said Maish, "He goes

around, at least during the Torah times, killing the enemies of the Jews and throwing them off of their land. You ask me, the Bible was written by a lot of different people who made it up as they went along, not knowing what it meant, not knowing if they were contradicting or talking nonsense. And mostly they talk nonsense. Were there no innocent people in the world but Noah and his family when God drowned everyone?"

"You've given us a lot to consider," said Rabbi Wass, "maybe the cornerstone of our discussions. Your question is not 'Does God exist?' but 'Is God good or evil or both and how can we understand and live with his capriciousness?' "

"David is dead," Maish said, standing, the frayed sheets of his yellow pad flapping. "My grandchild is dead before leaving his mother's womb. My aunts, uncles, cousins died in concentration camps. I want nothing to do with your *meshugena* God. If he wants to burn me like the sons of Aaron, here I'm standing. I've blasphemed. I live. God plays sick jokes."

With this Maish eased his way past Bess and went slowly up the aisle of the sanctuary and out the door. Bess exchanged a quick look with Rabbi Wass who was trying his best not to look flustered by the attack. Then Bess got up and followed Maish. It was going to be a very, very, long day and night.

Until now they had never hit a convenience store before dark. It was Antoine's idea. He had paced back and forth in their small room rubbing the top of his shaved brown head thinking out loud.

"They expect us at night, right?" he said.

Irwin Saviello shrugged. It was true. Antoine had turned off the television set so he had no choice but to listen or pretend to listen.

"Okay," said Antoine. "We been hitting places in the same area, this side of Ridge, right?"

"Right," said Irwin.

"So, some time they're gonna start laying for us, maybe cruising by, getting lucky," said Antoine.

Irwin said nothing. Antoine needed nothing said to keep pacing and talking.

"Why don't we just go to Milwaukee?" asked Irwin. "Where they don't know us?"

"So, we hit someplace further north like," Antoine said, ignoring the big man. "Maybe right on Howard Street, other side of Western, and we do it before it gets dark."

"Okay," said Irwin.

"And then we start hitting places on the South Side," said Antoine. "Or maybe if we

119

have enough, we drive to St. Louis, stay with my brother and work there."

"Okay," Irwin repeated.

If he got all he wanted to eat and could watch television, then it didn't matter to Irwin where they went, Milwaukee, St. Louis, the South Side. If he could also get the chance to hit some people hard, watch their noses or cheek bones break, or cut them open with his knuckles and then take the money from the register and a big bag of sweet things and some sandwiches, that would be fine. He had no other ambitions. He knew Antoine spent most of what they made on drugs, but there was always enough for what Irwin wanted and needed and he needed someone like Antoine to tell him what to do. It didn't matter to Irwin that Antoine was black. Irwin didn't have a prejudiced cell in his body. People were people. Except the Pakistanis and Indians who often owned or ran the convenience stores they hit. He didn't know why, but Irwin hated Indians and Pakistanis. He didn't like the way they talked, the way they drove, the looks they gave him as if he was something to get away from. He liked hitting them.

And so they had risen and cruised the neighborhood up and down Howard Street. The places too close to the lake were not prime targets. They were at the edge of the

Jungle, black people with no money, a lot of fear and hate walked the streets, and the 7-Eleven clerks probably had shotguns strapped under the counter aiming at each customer as they paid. They drove farther out and spotted a place near California, a small place, not one of the chains, a good four or five blocks beyond Western.

Irwin sat in the car while Antoine went in and bought a pack of Kools and a Hershey's with almonds. He gave the candy bar to Irwin when he came out and started the car.

"Perfect," Antoine said with a smile backing out.

Antoine was looking jumpy. He was in a hurry to spend some of their money on drugs. That was okay with Irwin. Later they would go back to the convenience store.

"Indian?" asked Irwin.

"I think so," Antoine said, trying to drive and open his pack of cigarettes. "Mighta been some kinda Spic. Little mustache. You know?"

Irwin nodded and ate his candy bar. He was content.

CHAPTER 5

"No crime," he repeated in the interrogation room, his huge arms folded.

Abe and Bill had found the man known as Clarence Millthorpe very easily. They knew he had some cellar or vacant apartment where he could hide, but they hadn't had to take the time to search. They had found the big man right on the hood of a pickup truck eating a couple of pieces of bread with something between them.

"Look up at that window" had been the man's first words as he pointed toward a window in the apartment behind him. "Big guy, wears one of those baseball caps with DIESEL or some such shit written on it, red beard, tough. Afraid to come down here and tell me to get off his truck."

Abe and Bill had pulled right next to the truck blocking one lane of traffic on Lunt. They had gotten out slowly, ready for trouble. Hanrahan was not only ready. He almost prayed for it.

"We would like to talk to you," said Lieberman. "Could you get down off that hood?"

Millthorpe slid off the hood still eating and said, "Talk to me about what?"

"Last night you threatened a woman, called her names, scared her," said Hanrahan.

Millthorpe shrugged, stuffed what was left of his sandwich in his mouth, and wiped his hands on his scruffy trousers.

"You gonna take me in? Give me something to eat?" Millthorpe asked. "You take me in, you gotta feed me somethin'."

"Let's go," said Lieberman as Hanrahan stepped very close to the big man, definitely invading his space. Millthorpe had inched past him and into the backseat of Abe's car. He couldn't have been more cooperative.

"I remember you," Millthorpe had said. "Name's . . . Jew name . . . Liebowitz . . . no, Lieberman."

Lieberman driving hadn't answered and when Millthorpe, with a pleased look on his face, turned to Hanrahan, who sat next to him, the policeman didn't even look at him.

Now they sat in the small interrogation room, Millthorpe on one side, the two policemen on the other. On one wall was the traditional one-way mirror. The mirror was scratched and stained. Behind it was a tiny room, barely big enough for three people standing. Whoever was in that room could see and hear everything that went on. Abe knew it. Bill knew it, and ninety-nine percent of the witnesses, victims, and suspects questioned in the room knew they might well be watched and listened to by people beyond the mirror. Millthorpe had glanced at the mirror once, shook his head, and turned in real or feigned boredom back to the two policemen.

"No crime," he repeated. "Like all the other times. I didn't threaten, didn't throw anything at the lady. Threw a can down the street. Picked it up later and put it where I'd found it. Said a lot of bad words. That I rightly admit, but not at the lady. At the world. Not been treated kindly by the world, gentlemen, not been treated kindly at all. So, if you're gonna arrest me, get me a public defender. If you're gonna turn me over for another psycho-this or psycho-that evaluation, let's get to it. If not, take me back home. Either way, I'm hungry."

"Where's home?" asked Hanrahan.

Someone screamed in the squad room behind the closed door. None of the three men knew if the scream had come from a male or female voice. Millthorpe looked at the door for about ten seconds, lost in some thought or memory, and then turned back.

124

"Where's home?" asked Hanrahan again.

"Where you found me."

"The hood of a red pickup truck on Lunt?" asked Hanrahan.

Millthorpe shrugged and said, "Round abouts there."

"This is the seventh time you've been brought in for questioning," said Lieberman, looking at the file open in front of him.

"I think it's eight," Millthorpe said with satisfaction.

"Right," Lieberman amended. "This makes eight."

"What's your real name?" asked Lieberman.

"Clarence Millthorpe. We gonna do all this again? If we are, I'd like something to eat. I told you. No candy bar and coffee or a Pepsi or some such shit. A bowl of chili, a burger."

At that point the door to the room opened and a young uniformed officer who was, basically, running errands and answering phones for a month or two of penance came in. He was stocky, Hispanic, perfectly groomed, and obviously nervous about intruding on an interrogation.

"Yes?" said Abe.

"Sorry," said the young officer whose name was James Guttierez. "But Detective Hanrahan is needed out here."

Hanrahan shrugged and Lieberman nodded.

"Maybe with the big man gone," said Millthorpe with a smile, "someone might misbehave and tear this little Jew into tiny pieces."

Hanrahan didn't pause. He wasn't worried about his partner.

When Hanrahan had followed Guttierez out and closed the door, Lieberman wearily said, "Look under the table. Big surprise."

Millthorpe cocked his head again, hesitated, pushed his chair back about a foot, and looked under the table where Lieberman was holding an army .45 in his hand.

"You even talk that kind of garbage again," said Lieberman, "and the cleaning crew will be picking up big pieces of chopped Millthorpe. They'll put the parts in a Hefty bag and throw it in the incinerator and no one will ever even ask about you."

Millthorpe sat back, folded his arms, and tried to decide if the skinny little old fart of a detective was telling the truth.

"You're shittin'," he said.

"No," said Lieberman. "I'm tired. I've got a family to take care of, responsibilities. There is no way I would allow myself to be murdered when I have a gun in my hand and you have nothing but a big mouth."

"You got a point," said Millthorpe.

"Good," said Abe. "We can start again with that point of agreement."

Outside the interrogation room Hanrahan found himself facing a black man in his thirties. The man was handsome, athletic looking, close-cropped hair and wearing jeans, a white shirt, and a heavy denim jacket.

"Father Parker?" said Hanrahan, holding out his hand.

Guttierez had fled for a ringing phone and a shout from one of the detectives across the squad room.

"I know that's not a question about my identity," said the priest. "I'll assume it's a sign that you didn't expect to see me here."

Sam "Whiz" Parker had been a star running back at the University of Illinois and could, unlike Bill Hanrahan who had bad knees, have been drafted within the third round when he graduated. Instead, he had received the calling and now was in charge of St. Bartholomew's Catholic Church in Edgewater whose parishioners were primarily Vietnamese, Korean, and poor whites. St. Bart's was well within the province of the Clark Street station in which they were now standing.

"Can I get you . . . ?" Hanrahan began.

"Nothing," said Father Parker. "I heard about what happened in Ohio."

"Yeah," Hanrahan said, looking around the squad room.

"Thought you might like to go out for coffee or something and talk about it."

"I don't know," said Hanrahan.

"We both remember last time," said Parker.

"Vividly." Hanrahan rubbed the back of his left hand with the palm of his right. "It won't happen again."

Actually, Hanrahan had suffered major losses of faith in his job: his sobriety, his family, and his religion. He had gone to St. Bart's during an investigation and met "Whiz" Parker, who knew instantly who Bill was. Bill Hanrahan had been one of his football heroes. Together the priest and the cop had begun to work things out, to put Hanrahan's life back together. It was gradual, no push to rejoin the Mother Church, but he was headed well back in that direction. At least he had been until he saw the woman with her head blown off in a Dayton motel.

"A coffee," Hanrahan agreed. "Maybe a burger. After we finish with the guy we're working on."

"Clark Mills," said the priest.

"What?"

"The uniformed officer took me into the little room with the one-way mirror. I've heard about them, but I've never been behind one. Strange feeling. Like the confessional."

"You said . . ."

"Clark Mills," said Parker. "Left Michigan State his third year to go into the NFL draft. Great lineman. All–Big Ten. Came out about five years before I graduated, between you and me. As I recall, he was injured in some kind of car crash before he even signed with the Packers, who drafted him second round."

"You sure that's Mills?"

"I'm sure," said Parker. "What's he done, if I can ask?"

"You can ask," Hanrahan said. "Maybe you can even help if you want to."

"If I can," said Parker. "Mills was a great player."

"Now he's homeless and harassing people over on Lunt."

"Mills?" Parker looked at the interrogation room door. "He's the one who's been doing that? I've heard about him. Has he hurt anyone?"

"Not yet," said Hanrahan, "but it's just a question of how long if we don't do something, and he doesn't show any sign of cooperating. He scared the hell out of a woman last night. She's more than just shaken up."

"What do you want me to do?"

"Go back in the room with the one-way

mirror and come in the interrogation room if I call."

"That's it?"

"That'll do," said Hanrahan.

"Then coffee and talk," Parker reminded him.

"Coffee, a couple of Dunkin' Donuts, and talk," said Hanrahan.

Parker headed back to the little room with the one-way mirror and Hanrahan opened the door to the interrogation room where Lieberman was saying ". . . a one-way bus ticket to a destination of your choice. And you don't come back."

Hanrahan closed the door and moved to the chair he had been sitting in. Mills didn't even look at him.

"Not interested," said Mills.

"Well," said Lieberman. "Maybe we can persuade you."

"Nope."

"Maybe we can, Clark," said Hanrahan.

Lieberman turned slowly to his partner. The big black man across the table stood up suddenly, his chair falling back against the wall.

"Behind that mirror is a man who recognized you," said Hanrahan. "He used to respect you. He's watching to see how you handle this."

"Who?" said the huge man, leaning forward toward the detective.

"I don't feel like telling you right this minute," said Hanrahan. "Not till you sit down, behave like a reasonably sane human being, and we come to some agreement."

"No." Mills looked at the mirror.

"Pick up the chair, Clark," said Lieberman. "Sit in it. Do you know what happens now that we know who you are?"

Mills looked down at Lieberman.

"Pick up the chair and sit down," said Lieberman.

There was a long pause while the sound of voices from the squad room came through the door and into the small room. Two people out there were crying at the same time. It sounded like a contest to determine who could be more annoying.

Sullenly, reluctantly, Clark Mills picked up the wooden chair, sat, and crossed his arms.

"I'm sure," said Lieberman, "my partner has already asked that your records be sent to us by e-mail or fax immediately."

Lieberman was less than sure, but he said it anyway. They could probably handle Mills without expense to the department, and it was doubtful even if they tried to get it that they could get much information that day.

"That's confidential," said Mills. "I want a lawyer."

Hanrahan folded his hands on the table. Lieberman slipped his .45 into the right pocket of his trousers, out of sight of anyone who might be looking.

"We will inform your college, Michigan State, about what you've turned into," said Hanrahan. "Your coach. Your teammates. Probably they'll publish a little article asking former fans and teammates to kick in twenty cents each to send you. A fund for a homeless bully, a former MSU All-American."

"You're shittin' me," said Mills, not at all sure if Hanrahan were telling the truth. "Who's behind that mirror?"

"You have family, Clark?" asked Lieberman. "We'd better find out who they are and where they are and tell them what you've turned into. They may want to help. Then again, they might just be humiliated. They still might want to help. Your parents alive?"

"Don't know," said Mills. "My mother was last time I knew."

"Sisters, brothers, aunts, uncles, high school coach and teachers, friends?" asked Hanrahan.

Mills was sweating now and breathing deeply. Hanrahan was ready to stop him if he came over the table at the two detectives.

Hanrahan wanted him to come over the table.

"Want to tell us where you're from?" asked Lieberman. "We can still stop the people back home from finding out what happened to their hero."

"Albany, Georgia," Mills said with a sigh.

"How'd you like a ticket back there?" asked Hanrahan.

Mills was silent. He unfolded his arms, didn't know what to do with his hands, and finally placed them nervously on his lap.

"No," said Mills. "You bastards think I got a family living in some shack with dirt floors. My father's a professor of economics at Albany State College. My mother's a lawyer. My sister manages a doctor's office in Albany. My brother . . . There are no failures in my family but me. I'm not going back. But I'll think about going somewhere if you stop those calls to Michigan State and you keep this away from my family."

Hanrahan and Lieberman looked at each other.

"How about Dallas?" asked Lieberman. "Warmer there. Know someone there who could try you out on a job. Not much of a job, but . . ."

"I'll think about it," Mills said, looking at the mirror again.

"About Dallas or the job?" asked Hanrahan.

"The job," said Mills, defeated.

"We'll take you down to the Greyhound station and put you on a bus. We'll even give you twenty-five bucks," said Lieberman. "You don't come back to Chicago. Never. I don't care if you become governor of Texas, Georgia, and Arkansas combined."

Mills nodded and said softly, "I gotta pick up a few things I've got stashed."

"Whoever takes you to the bus will stop with you," said Hanrahan.

"Want to go alone," said Mills. "I . . . I got a cat I've got to do something with."

"Take him to Dallas," said Lieberman.

"Her," said Mills.

"Her," Lieberman conceded.

"I want to think about that and I've got some things to pick up. I can't run. I don't want my people to know about me. They think I'm a regional sales manager for Budweiser. Probably wonder why they haven't heard from me in . . . I don't know how many years."

A look between the two detectives and Hanrahan said, "Okay. But not overnight. We pick you up with whatever you've got in the park on Lunt and Sheridan. You have three hours. Find a bench near the street and wait. You're not there, we find you and make those calls."

"I'll be there," said Mills. "I gotta know. Who's behind that mirror?"

The truth was that Lieberman was almost as curious as Mills. He looked at Hanrahan, who said, "Come in, Father."

No more than five seconds later Father Parker came into the small room. Mills looked up without immediate recognition though something in his eyes seemed to . . .

"Whiz Parker," said Mills.

"Father Samuel Parker," Hanrahan amended.

"You recognized me?" said Mills, looking up at the priest.

Parker nodded and said, "You were a pleasure to watch play."

"I didn't think anyone would recognize me, not ever," said Mills.

"You a Catholic?" asked Parker.

"I'm nothing. Family is Baptist, but mostly for show. Small college town. I don't think my mother and father believe in God. Don't know about my brother and sisters. They go to church."

"I saw your last game," said Parker. "Michigan State, Illinois. Never saw a quarterback protected so well by one lineman."

Mills shook his head, remembering. "Wanted to impress the scouts."

"No," said Parker. "That was the only way

you knew how to play. You take care of your-self and trust these two policemen."

Mills nodded, sitting up a little straighter as Parker left the room.

It was Lieberman's turn to get up. He went out into the squad room in search of a uni-form to take Mills back to his neighborhood. Father Parker was looking at the madness of the squad room, his hands in his pockets. Lieberman went to his desk where he found four messages. One was from Bess saying call immediately. One was from someone who called himself Aztec, one of the many names of Emiliano "El Perro" Del Sol. Aztec had left a number. The third call was from his daugh-ter, Lisa, who was at the house and wanted to talk to him soon. "Soon" was underlined. So she hadn't left for Los Angeles yet. The last message wasn't a phone call. It was from Captain Kearney telling him to come to his office as soon as he could.

Lieberman called the uniform division assignment desk and asked Lieutenant Gib-son if he had someone who could make a brief run. Gibson said, "Sure. We're running slow this A.M. Four car accidents. Two bar fights with one in the hospital. The issue was Notre Dame football. Pawn shop robbery. Four drug pickups. Slow. Bring your man down. How's the Gornitz business coming?"

"I'm getting back on that right now," said Lieberman. "Thanks, Mike."

"We serve and protect," said Gibson as he did at the end of every conversation with a fellow officer and had for more than twenty years.

Lieberman ignored his messages for a while and went into the interrogation room where he told Hanrahan that everything was ready. A definitely defeated, slouch-shouldered Clark Mills came out and looked at Sam Parker.

"I was good that day," said Mills.

"You were *great* that day, Clark," said the priest. "If I had a photograph, I'd ask you to autograph it."

"That's my desk," said Lieberman, pointing to his desk near the window. "Go have a seat. I'll be right with you."

Mills made his way slowly through the crowd and maze of desks and chairs and sat next to Lieberman's desk.

"Father Parker wants to go out for a cup of coffee and some talk," said Hanrahan. "So do I."

"Enjoy," Lieberman said.

"What about Stashall?" asked Hanrahan.

"I'll go pay him a visit," said Lieberman. "We'll talk later."

His partner and the priest worked their way to the squad room door and out. Lieberman ushered Clark Mills down to the uniformed assignment room and turned him over to Gibson.

"Three hours, Clark," Lieberman reminded him.

"Three hours," the big man repeated. "I'll be there."

Lieberman went back upstairs checking his watch. It wasn't even eleven and he was starving. The memory of chopped liver in front of his partner suddenly came over him. It was almost worth the damage to his cholesterol count. Fortunately, there wasn't enough time to fall off the wagon. He made his way back upstairs and knocked at Kearney's office. Kearney called "come in," and he did. Kearney sat at his small conference table along with Assistant State Attorney Eugene Carbin, who wore a frown and greeted Lieberman with a nearly disgusted shake of his head.

"Have a seat, Abe," Kearney said.

Lieberman sat. Something was definitely about to happen. There was an open box on the desk. Next to the box was a rolled-up paper towel that looked as if it had come out of the box. Next to that was a piece of paper with printing on it.

"Message was in the box. It's for you," said Carbin, looking at the piece of paper.

Had the lawyer been white, Lieberman

thought, his face would be bright red.

"Box came to me," said Kearney. "Delivery service. Already checked. Sender paid cash, dropped the package at the delivery office. Left enough money. No one saw or remembers seeing who left the package."

Lieberman sat silently as Kearney turned the sheet of paper toward Abe so he could read it.

"I already touched it," said Kearney. "It was addressed to me. Don't touch it. We'll check it for prints when we're done."

Lieberman considered trying to read the note without his glasses. Carbin wore glasses. What the hell. He took his glasses from his pocket and read the note without touching it.

To Detective Abraham Lieberman:
This is a warning about what might happen next. Gornitz doesn't testify. Tell him what you've got in the box. There'll be more little gifts till Gornitz proves he doesn't plan to talk. He knows how to prove it. The boy walks when we know Gornitz isn't going to talk.

There was no signature.

"What do you think it means?" asked Carbin, making it clear that he had his own ideas about what it meant.

"For some reason," Lieberman said, "I've been picked to tell Mickey Gornitz that if he doesn't commit suicide, whoever has his son will kill the boy. Which leads me to the next conclusion which is that there's something wrapped in that towel meant to convince me and Mickey that they mean what they say."

With that Kearney carefully peeled back the folds of the paper towel to reveal what Lieberman recognized as the neatly severed section of a finger.

"What do you make of that?" asked Carbin.

Lieberman took off his glasses and examined the finger joint without touching it. It was bloody at both ends, nearly white. The tip of the finger was missing. Lieberman looked closely and leaned back.

"Middle joint," he said. "No fingertip, no fingerprint. May not be from the boy. Looks a little puffy to be from a seventeen-year-old. Forensics can tell us."

"Why not send us one of the boy's real fingers?" asked Carbin.

"Don't want to risk killing him," Lieberman guessed, "or making him so sick that they'll need a doctor, a hospital, to keep him alive."

"And?" Carbin asked, listening closely.

"Seems like a dumb move by Stashall," said

140

Abe, looking at the note and finger joint. "He's no Sam Giancanna, but he's no fool. He probably figures that we'll know it's not the kid's. Maybe he's giving us a chance to convince Mickey. Maybe the next package will be a piece of the kid."

"The way you figure it?" Carbin asked Kearney.

"Yeah," said Kearney, sitting back.

All three men were looking at the box, the note and the finger joint, hoping they'd give them an answer to what they should do next.

"I wonder whose it is," Carbin said, looking at the center slice of finger.

"Forensics," said Lieberman standing.

"I want you to talk to Gornitz," said Carbin.

"You mean he wants to talk to me."

"Whatever," said the weary attorney. "Nothing about this. Tell him we plan to find his son alive. Stall while we put pressure on Stashall."

"Pressure?" Lieberman repeated. "Stashall's facing prison. Maybe worse. There are mob people out there who might think Jimmy Stashall would talk and go into witness protection. They might want him dead. It wouldn't be the first."

"Fifteen in the last five years," said Carbin. "All dead. All mob. All unsolved."

"I don't see what he's got to lose by trying

to get to Mickey," said Lieberman. "And I don't see much we've got to pressure him with. Can I go now? I've got a family problem I've got to take care of."

Kearney nodded. Lieberman got up and left the room. He would check with forensics later when they had time to look at the items on Kearney's desk. In the squad room, Lieberman moved his .45 from his pocket to the holster under his jacket. Then he headed for his desk. He would pay a visit to Johnny Stashall, go see Mickey Gornitz again, and do what he could to take care of those family problems.

CHAPTER 6

Huang Chen counted the fortune cookies to be sure each box contained the one hundred promised on the label. He had been buying them for the last year from a family of recent Korean immigrants. They charged little for the fortune cookies but shorted him on the allotted number frequently. Where was honor in this generation?

People did not notice Huang Chen and that was what he wished. He was small, wore dark slacks and a slightly frayed but always clean and well-pressed matching jacket over one of his off-white shirts. He seldom spoke unless spoken to and was content to run his restaurant and barely exist.

Huang Chen loved his daughter, though he never told her so.

Huang Chen did not like the idea that Iris was determined to marry the big American policeman. Not only was he white, but Hanrahan carried a heavy burden of guilt and tragedy that Huang Chen could feel in his presence.

Though he would never say so, he would far prefer that Iris marry Liao Woo, who was very rich and very old. He would take care of Iris. He would respect her. But this was America, and Huang Chen had learned long ago that the word of a father was of value only if his children agreed with him. It was a hollow respect.

Liao Woo had hinted that if Huang Chen wished it, the American could be persuaded to cease his attention to Iris. Iris's father had indicated politely that he did not favor this approach. Yet the more he saw of the brooding Hanrahan, the more he considered that it might be his duty to protect his daughter whatever the consequences.

He finished counting. There were only ninety-seven cookies in the box.

Jimmy Stashall wasn't hiding. He could usually be found in his home in Northbrook or his office on Montrose. His office on Montrose, not far from the El, was four rooms including a modern, well-furnished reception area where various members of Stashall's operation, covering a good part of the near North Side, could be found sitting, talking, smoking. Lieberman knew them all and they knew him. The room behind the reception area was that of Stashall's secretary-receptionist. She was young, though not as young as she looked, clean-looking with little makeup and darkly pretty. She had her own desk and computer and chairs for those who were going in to see her boss, who also was her mother's brother and, thus, her uncle. Jimmy's office was old wood, antiques, bookcases, photographs, and real paintings on the wall of scenes of the Mediterranean. The entire office suite was modeled after Clark Gable's in *Boom Town*, though Jimmy had forgotten most of the details of the movie, which he hadn't seen for at least fifteen years before he had the office decorated.

Jimmy Stashall's more-or-less-honest job was running the J.S. Office and Factory Cleaning Service, a service that sent out crews at night to clean office buildings and factories that didn't require a full-time staff. Both sides of his operation had employed Mickey Gornitz as bookkeeper and memory.

Lieberman tried to focus on Stashall as he headed south toward Montrose on the Outer Drive. He'd probably only have one good shot at Stashall, who would have his lawyer call Carbin's office and complain about police harassment.

Before he had left the squad room, Lieberman had called home. Bess answered. He knew Lisa was probably home, but wouldn't want to answer in case it was her ex-husband, Todd, or her current husband, Marvin.

"Everyone in the world suddenly seems to have a *loch en kopf,* a hole in the head," said Bess. "I was just going out the door when the phone rang. I've got to run. Shirley Ovitz is waiting outside for me."

Bess made it fast. She told him what Maish had done at the temple and urged Abe to go see his brother as soon as possible.

"Yetta is frantic," Bess said. "Try to make it soon. And Lisa isn't going back to California today. She wants to talk to you."

"I look forward to it with great anticipation," said Lieberman.

"Maish," she reminded him. "Talk to him."

That left only the call to El Perro. He recognized the number, the office of the bingo parlor Los Tentaculos had taken over. El Perro liked to call numbers himself at least two nights a week. He also liked to shoot and stab people who irritated him or got in the way of his illegal activities. It was less the money that motivated El Perro than the excuse to inflict pain. He had been known to go either loudly and violently mad or calmly and sadistically murderous toward perfectly innocent people who simply had the misfortune to have faces that irritated El Perro.

The oddity was that Emiliano "El Perro"

Del Sol respected no one except his mother, who had fled from him five years earlier, and Abe Lieberman, whom he found tough, unafraid, and as good as his word. It amused the semi-mad gang leader that El Viejo was such a thin little man with such *cajones*. Their relationship was symbiotic. El Perro gave Lieberman information or got it for him when he needed it, and El Perro would take care of problems for El Viejo when the law was not sufficient to do it. In return, Lieberman offered El Perro and his gang a certain degree of protection. There was a line Emiliano was not allowed to cross, but he had mastered the art of walking its length with a smile on his scarred face. El Perro was crazy. He was not stupid.

"Emiliano Del Sol," Lieberman had said when someone answered the phone at the bingo office.

"*¿Quien es?*"

"*El Viejo.*"

"*Bueno.*"

The person who had answered put the phone down and Lieberman had looked around the squad room. He didn't have a hell of a lot of time if he and Hanrahan were going to pick Clark Mills up at three and get him downtown to the Greyhound station.

"*¿Viejo?*" came El Perro's happy voice,

which might mean that he was happy to talk to the detective or had just maimed a store-keeper who had paid his protection money too slowly.

"*Sí,*" said Lieberman.

"The Cubs. They gonna to the World Series this year?"

"This'll be the year," said Lieberman.

"*Por supuesto.* They got Mexicans, Venezuelans, more Hispanics than ever. They got Sammy. They gotta win."

"We'll go to opening day," said Lieberman.

"You got a date. Wear your best dress."

"If you wear yours, the one that shows your knees."

El Perro laughed. It wasn't exactly a laugh, more like the cackle of a mad rooster that knew his time was at hand and didn't give a damn.

"I got business to go to," said El Perro. "I'm talkin' to you about the Korean, Kim."

"I think I better call you back," said Lieberman. "I'm at my desk and I'm swamped."

"*Yo comprendo,*" said El Perro.

Lieberman was well aware that the madman might say he had just murdered the one-armed Korean who was stalking Lieberman, or might propose that he do so or maybe remove Kim's other arm. It was not the kind of thing Lieberman wanted to discuss on a police department phone.

"I'll call you as soon as I can. Don't do anything till we talk."

"I'll sit here on my ass and listen to CDs," said El Perro. "When we talk, I need a favor maybe."

"When we talk," Lieberman had said.

Now the detective was parking illegally on Montrose, his sun visor with his police card showing. It was starting to get dark, but Lieberman thought that Stashall had a lot on his mind and probably would be brooding behind his desk. He didn't know what, if anything, he could get from Stashall, but his partner was on the line, a woman had been killed, and a boy was being used to blackmail Mickey Gornitz into killing himself. As Lieberman often said, he took umbrage at this and wanted very much to talk to the most likely suspect, Jimmy Stashall.

Lieberman entered the door to the faded yellow-brick office building wedged between a supermarket and an electronics repair shop. There were names on the board in the clean white-tiled entry hall. Lieberman didn't look at the board. He knew where he was going.

"You believe in curses, Sam?" Hanrahan said, looking at the last of his mug of coffee at

Dunkin' Donuts where they sat in a booth. The place wasn't busy. A postman sat at the counter telling the old man serving coffee and doughnuts some of his adventures. Two women, an old woman, and an equally old man sat in another booth drinking coffee and talking softly.

"I believe that people can believe they're cursed and that things will happen to confirm it if they believe," said the priest, ignoring the plain doughnut on the plate before him and taking a drink from the first refill of coffee the old waitress had brought him.

"But no real curses?" Hanrahan pushed.

Father Parker shrugged. "Once in a while . . . who knows? Believe in God. Believe in the Devil. I don't think you're cursed, Bill."

"My wife left me," Hanrahan said, eyeing his second doughnut, chocolate frosted. "My kids left me. A woman died because I was drunk when I was supposed to be watching her. I murdered a man, tricked him into trying to break into my house, and then killed him. One of my boys is an alcoholic. And a day ago a woman I was supposed to be guarding had half her face blown into pulp and her son kidnapped with me in the next room."

Sam Parker knew all this. After thirty years of falling away from the church, Hanrahan seemed to be returning cautiously and with some continued skepticism. He had confessed to all of this at length.

"What's next? I'll probably get my partner killed."

"Or you might be there to save his life," said the priest. "That's happened too, hasn't it? Saying you're cursed is usually just an excuse for mistakes, bad decisions, and bad luck. A policeman's bound to have all three. And, depending on how you look at it, you could also say you're blessed. You're going to get married. You're no longer estranged from your son Michael. You've stopped drinking. You're got your health, give or take a bad knee or two, and you're relatively sane. Many who walk around with a smile can't say as much."

Hanrahan took a bite of the doughnut. Since he stopped drinking, chocolate had become almost irresistible. He had gained almost twenty pounds. Because there was a lot of Bill Hanrahan, it didn't show yet, but it would. He could feel it when he had to run or climb a lot of stairs. He should get to the gym again.

"I'm convinced. Probably was before we had this talk. I don't believe in curses," Hanrahan said after finishing his mouthful of doughnut. "I believe I'm just a foulup."

"Well, that's a start. You're not blaming

others. Line up the good with the bad in your life. It probably balances pretty well, as it does for most of us. By the way, I've noticed that neither you nor Abe use obscenities," said Sam. "I thought it was mandatory for cops. Or are you just careful around me?"

"No," said Bill, recognizing that the priest was changing the subject. "Abe and I are called the Street Angels behind our backs and sometimes to our faces. We're no angels. Just our backgrounds. Father, I'm thinkin' about quitting the force."

Traffic was backed up on the street. The clanging of a bell let the two men know that the train gates were down a block away.

"Seriously thinking?" asked the priest.

"Maybe. Probably not."

Hanrahan pushed the plate with the remains of the doughnut away from him.

"I'm sitting here wondering what's happening to Abe," said Hanrahan. "Is he in trouble because I'm not with him? Is he safer because I'm not with him? It's hard to make decisions when you think you're cursed."

"I thought you didn't believe in curses," said Parker, breaking his doughnut and dunking it.

"Hedging my bets," the policeman replied. "I've got to find the kidnapped kid before they kill him. If they kill the kid, I'm quitting."

"You mean you're quitting after you get the people who kill him," said Parker.

"Hadn't thought that far," Hanrahan said with a shrug, his eyes aiming at the doughnut he had pushed away. "Maybe."

"No more murder," Sam Parker said seriously, looking into the eyes of the big man across the table. "That's not how you free yourself."

"Maybe not," said Hanrahan. "You're probably right."

"Probably? You know how long I trained to answer questions like that? I'm still working on them. You catch criminals and help people in trouble and I deal with moral problems. I promise to come to you when someone I know is in trouble with the law or I'm aware of a criminal act and you promise to let the Lord take care of the moral problems."

"Don't trust your Lord yet," said Hanrahan, rising and dropping three dollars on the table. "Wish I did. Thanks for listening to me, Sam."

"It's what I get paid for," said the priest, wiping his mouth and starting to stand.

"No," said Bill. "I'll think about it on my own. I guess the real question is whether I should go ahead and marry Iris, take a chance on what might happen to her because of me."

"You've got two weddings scheduled," said

Sam Parker, sitting back down. "Chinese and Unitarian. Think long and hard. Spend a few hours at the zoo or a movie. No decisions till we talk again."

"No decisions."

The two men shook hands and Hanrahan got out of the booth and moved slowly to the door. He wanted to run. He wanted to get to Jimmy Stashall's to back up his partner. He wanted to find Mickey Gornitz's boy alive.

It was almost six at night. Irwin and Antoine, Salt and Pepper, sat in the parking lot of the small convenience store on Howard Street less than three miles from the home of Abraham Lieberman. People came and went. The sky was gray and there was a definite chill in the air that said it would be a good idea to wear at least a light jacket. Antoine and Irwin wore matching University of Illinois orange sweat shirts they had picked up at Goodwill. It was Antoine's idea to keep the cops guessing. It was the only time they had dressed alike and the only time they planned to work that day.

"If it don't clear out in three more minutes, we try some other time," said Antoine, running his hand over his freshly shaved head.

"I say we go in," said Irwin, his hands folded in his lap. "So some customer's in there. Fuck it. We take his wallet too. I'm gettin' hungry and I'd really like to bop an Indian."

Two kids, young black girls, came out of the convenience store and walked past the parked car laughing.

"Can't understand them people," said one little girl. "They talk so damned funny."

"In what way can I be of assistance," a girl of no more than ten said in a near-perfect imitation of an Indian or Pakistani.

The two girls laughed and moved away sharing a small brown paper bag of candy.

"Let's do it now," said Irwin, opening the door before Antoine could stop him.

"You dumb —" Antoine said, getting out and following his partner who was walking very fast toward the door of the convenience store.

When Irwin entered, Antoine slowed down and put on his ski mask. He hated the damned itchy thing but it would surely improve their chances. When he had told Irwin about his plan, Irwin refused to wear a mask. Ripping out the video monitor was enough for him, and, besides, he panicked at the idea of wearing something over his face. And, he had told Antoine, what good would it do? They had committed so many robberies that the police probably already had full descrip-

155

tions of them. Antoine had blown up. Irwin Saviello was not supposed to think. Antoine was the thinker; besides, Antoine conceded in what there was of his heart of hearts, Irwin might be right.

As soon as he entered, gun in his pocket, Antoine saw that Irwin was standing in front of the counter behind which stood a dark, foreign-looking woman about fifty years old. Her hair was long and tied back and she wore a no-nonsense dress and apron. She was also pretty and wearing a smile that ended the moment Antoine entered.

"Do it!" Antoine shouted, heading for the camera.

Irwin was frozen across the counter from the woman. He hadn't had to hit a woman before. It had always been men, dark men who talked funny and had more money than he did. That had been fun, but this . . .

Antoine leaped up and tore at the video camera, it came lose and clattered to the floor.

Irwin came to life reluctantly, realizing that something had to be done. He threw his always effective short right-hand punch at the woman's face, a punch that regularly broke bones and often led to plastic surgery and near death. He knew his punch was fast. He prided himself on it. Somewhere rushing through his being was the feeling that he might enjoy hitting a woman and that would start him down a new and more dangerous road than the one he had been traveling. We should have checked, he thought. We should have checked it out.

The problem was that the punch didn't land. For the first time, Irwin Saviello had not connected. At first he thought he had simply somehow missed, and then he realized that the woman had ducked to one side. His still-extended right arm suddenly experienced great pain and in the instant it took him to realize that he had been hit with something hard, Antoine behind him was firing. Irwin stood stunned for an instant and ducked as the bullets whined past him. Now the woman was screaming in a foreign language. Antoine stepped forward toward the counter continuing to fire.

The woman ducked behind the counter screaming and chattering in some nutsy language. Antoine was almost at the counter now. His plan was to reach over and shoot her in the goddamn head. As he started to lean over past Irwin, who was holding his arm, he heard the blast. Irwin was on the floor in pain. Then Antoine heard a shot. For an instant, he thought the cops had come, and then he felt the pain in his left leg. He staggered back and looked down. There was a hole, jagged though generally round, in the front of the counter, and Antoine's leg was definitely bleeding.

The woman suddenly stood up, still screaming, a shotgun in her hands, a pump gun with a lot more power than Antoine's weapon. Before she got off the second shot, Antoine made a dive behind a row of potato chips and snacks. Irwin, meanwhile, was crawling toward the door unsure of whether he was going to get the hell out of there or go around the counter and make a move on the ranting woman. He was angry and hurting. He'd go for the woman.

"Let's go," shouted Antoine.

Irwin kept crawling. The woman with the shotgun fired again. This time she sent snacks flying. Antoine was on the floor now too, doing a snake-crawl toward the front door, dragging his wounded leg behind him.

Suddenly the screaming woman ran out from behind the counter with Irwin lunging toward her. She didn't have time to turn and fire again. Instead she ran for the door in the rear and just made it through as Irwin grabbed for her, got his hand on the shotgun, and pulled it from her hands. The woman ran screaming through the alley. Irwin didn't know that much about shotguns, but he knew this one was simply pump and shoot. He stepped into the alley prepared to do just that. The woman was no more than fifteen or twenty feet away. Close enough. That's when he realized that he couldn't raise his right hand. He let out a moan of pain and anger and raised the shotgun with his left hand, trying to level it at the fleeing woman, hoping it was ready to fire.

It did, but the blast hit a rusty garbage can across the alley. The woman turned the corner at the end of the alley and he couldn't see her, but he could hear her screaming.

Irwin kept the shotgun in his left hand, his right arm dangling at his side. Something was probably broken. It didn't quite hurt. It was more like an irritating throb. He went back into the convenience store and called "Antoine."

He stepped on a pile of potato chips and bags. No answer. Irwin looked out the window and saw Antoine limping slowly, very slowly, toward the car. His left leg was covered with blood.

Irwin moved behind the counter imagining — or possibly it was real — the woman running down the street screaming for help. The cash register was open. There was a trail of blood running through the floor full of snacks and behind the counter. Antoine had managed to get to the register.

Irwin hurried after his partner who was just climbing into the driver's seat, a look of agonizing pain on his face. The gun was still in his hand. Irwin was almost at the car door when Antoine started the engine, lifted his gun, shouted something, and fired at his partner. The shot shattered the passenger-side window, spraying glass, and barely missed Irwin's head. Before the bewildered Irwin could react, Antoine, letting out a massive groan of pain, sped out of the parking lot.

Irwin Saviello, not really sure of where he was and with only four dollars and eighty cents in his pocket, stood in the middle of the small convenience store parking lot. His right arm was definitely broken. In his left, he carried a shotgun he couldn't use. Somewhere the screaming woman was getting the police.

Irwin went back into the convenience store, got a bag from behind the counter, came out, and put down the shotgun so he could, awkwardly, fill the paper bag with Ding-Dongs, Twinkies, Little Debbie Chocolate Cup Cakes, and candy bars, mostly Snickers. He tucked the bag under his arm and picked up the shotgun. He could have and probably should have left the weapon. Even he knew that. But he had the feeling that he would want to use it soon, probably against Antoine, providing he could get out of this. He found a sweater behind the counter, used it to cover the shotgun somewhat, and hurried out the back door and into the alley, turning in the opposite direction from the one in which the woman had run.

A barrel of a man wearing a white turtleneck sweater above a pair of black slacks stood in front of Abe Lieberman. The man, who was known as Heinie Manush, did not tower over Lieberman. It was more like he surrounded the detective. Heinie who was perhaps forty years old, weighed significantly over 300 pounds and never wore any expression on his less-than-happy face.

"Got a warrant?" Heinie asked as a woman behind the reception desk looked up at the confrontation.

"Heinie," Lieberman said with an exasperated sigh. "You've been watching too much television. I don't need a warrant to interview a potential witness."

"Jimmy ain't a witness," said Heinie.

"To what?" asked Lieberman.

"To anything."

"I'm really enjoying our conversation," said Lieberman, "but now I see Stashall."

"Not possible."

"Is possible. I'll see him here or bring him

all the way out to the Clark Street station."

"State attorney already talked to Jimmy," said Heinie. "Came up empty."

"Thanks for sharing that with me," Lieberman said with a weary hound of a smile. "Now I'm going in to see Stashall."

Lieberman tried to walk around the wide man who stepped in front of him.

"Ain't here," said Heinie.

"If he wasn't here, you wouldn't be trying to stop me from going in there. Step out of the way or announce me."

"Or what?"

"Or you're obstructing justice," said Lieberman. "I'll charge you. With your record, your lawyer will be lucky to plea bargain you down to a couple of years. That's at least six months more time on your record. History is moving quickly, Heinie. You'll come out to a different world, a world that doesn't need you, and what for?"

The woman at the desk was white-haired, almost stereotypically matronly in a brown suit. She had once been Jimmy Stashall's secretary. Now she was filling in for her daughter, who had replaced her when she had had enough. The daughter had a small cyst in her breast. It was being removed. The woman behind the desk would only be here a day or two, but every minute was a bad memory. She picked up the phone on her desk, pressed a button, and said, "Mr. Stashall, there's a policeman here to talk to you."

She looked up and said, "What's your name?"

"You don't remember me? Abe Lieberman."

"Abe Lieberman," the woman said into the phone. "Yes."

She hung up the phone and said to Heinie, "Let Detective Lieberman by."

Heinie grunted and stepped aside.

"Heinie," Lieberman whispered, "you need a diet. You want a good one, give me a call."

Lieberman walked to the door and opened it without knocking. Heinie started to follow him in, but the man behind the desk in front of Lieberman said, "Wait out there, Heinie. I'll call if I want you. Abe and I are old enemies."

Reluctantly Manush closed the door.

Jimmy Stashall was thin. His hair was black and thin. His nose was thin. His trademark was the suspenders he wore to keep his pants up. They were black and thin. A belt just wasn't good enough. Jimmy was fifty-seven and had a record even longer than Heinie's. He wasn't on his way up or down in the mob.

He had some territory and if he wanted to

do other business outside that territory, he checked with the right people to be sure it was okay. He played the game, took the raps, and had scars like a common eighteenth-century seaman.

"Nothing to tell you, Abe," he said without rising.

The office looked as if it had just been moved into. The furniture, solid, like a lawyer trying to make the right impression, was dark wood and antique. The view from the window behind Stashall was the traffic going down Montrose. There were pictures on the walls, about a dozen of them with Jimmy and various movie stars and Vegas entertainers. In all the pictures, Jimmy and the stars were arms around the neck or shaking hands and grinning.

Lieberman shrugged and took a seat across the desk from Stashall.

"Then we schmooze a few minutes, crack wise a few times, mention a few names from back when," said the detective.

"I talked to Carbin," said Stashall. "We can pass a few minutes. Then I've got a meeting. I've got nothin' to say."

Lieberman could bring him back to the station, but both of them knew he wouldn't. Stashall would ask for his lawyer and clam up. The lawyer would come and get him out, probably file a complaint, which might or might not get Lieberman in trouble.

"Lost any fingers recently?" asked Lieberman.

Stashall held up both hands and looked at them.

"Other people's fingers," said Lieberman.

"No. You been drinking, Lieberman?"

"No."

"You're not making sense," Stashall said, shifting in his swivel chair and looking at his watch.

"Mickey Gornitz," said Lieberman.

"Used to work for me. No more."

"You'd be happy if he were dead."

Stashall shrugged and looked at his watch. "Lieberman, score a point here or I'll tell you about the dinner I had with Wayne Newton in Vegas."

"You told me about that more than five years ago."

"I did? We're getting old, Abe. Don't remember things."

"I want the boy," said Lieberman.

"I know," said Stashall. "Gornitz's kid is missing. Carbin thinks I snatched him. You think I snatched him. I didn't snatch him. I don't know where he is and I don't know who to ask. Period. Zip. That's it. Ever tell you about meeting Liberace? He's over there on the wall, right over me and Jack Jones."

"I didn't really come for information," said Lieberman, lowering his voice. "Or to sit in awe of photographs of entertainers who probably have no idea of who you are."

Stashall leaned over the desk. "Then why're you here?"

"To tell you that if the boy dies, you die."

"You're shovelin' bullshit," Stashall said with an uncertain smile, not at all like the ones in the photographs.

"I'm not," said Lieberman. "And you know I'm not."

"I don't have the kid," Stashall shouted. "And if you want to piss out threats, even cops can have accidents."

"Okay, we've scared the hell out of each other," said Lieberman. "But I meant what I said and you're not going to go after a cop. You've got enough on your mind, and it's going to get worse."

"Look, Lieberman," Stashall said, reaching into his pocket for a breath mint. He offered one to the detective. Abe took it. "I could swear to you on the soul of my mother and my grandmother, the one on my mother's side. The other one, we didn't get along. Problem is that if I swear this time, the next time we have business, you ask me to swear on my mother and grandmother's soul, and I can't

166

do it. See my dilemma on this one?"

"I'm torn by it," said Lieberman. "Jimmy, I wouldn't believe you if you swore by your right hand and cut it off right now. Gornitz is going to talk and you are going to do time."

Stashall shook his head.

"Lawyers, courts, grand juries," he said with a sad smile. "So much can happen. It costs, but sometimes it's worth the price. Know what I mean?"

"The kid, Jimmy," Lieberman said.

"Don't have him," Jimmy Stashall replied. "Don't know who does. That's all you'll get from me. Even if you took me in and had a chance to play games with me, you wouldn't get more. Even if there was more. Which there isn't."

Lieberman got up slowly. "Thanks for the mint."

"I got a few minutes," Stashall said, rising. "You want a coffee, Dr Pepper?"

"No, thanks."

Lieberman walked to the door.

"I can't say the Gornitz business doesn't bother me," Stashall said behind him. "I trusted him like you trust your partner. It's gonna cost me. It's gonna cost him. But I didn't kill his ex-wife or have her hit and I didn't take the kid. I don't need you all over me now and that's what I've got. There are better ways of dealing with Gornitz. Besides, I didn't even know where his ex-wife and kid were. I've got friends and people who owe me favors, but, between you and me, we're not talkin' Einsteins here. I don't know if I could have found them if I tried, and I didn't try. Have a nice day and close the door on your way out."

Lieberman went out, closing the office door behind him.

Heinie was standing, hands clasped before him, five feet in front of the door facing Lieberman.

"I'll tell you in all honesty, Heinie, I like your white turtleneck."

"Thanks."

"It would help if you had a neck, but you can't have everything."

Heinie stepped back to let Lieberman pass. Then Heinie went into Stashall's office and closed the door.

Mistake, thought Lieberman. He had been left alone, probably only for a few seconds, with the matronly secretary, who was standing in front of an open file cabinet putting files away.

"You know my name," said Lieberman. "And I remember yours. Grace . . ."

"Grace Frasco," the woman said without looking away from her work.

"You've been away a long time," he said.

"I'm just filling in for my daughter for a day or two."

"She like the work?"

"She'd like to be busier, but it pays well and we've got bills to pay and no one to count on but each other," she said. "Mr. Stashall knew my uncle, Anthony Visconti. Remember him?"

"Someone blew him up in his car in Miami," said Lieberman.

"Mr. Stashall married my sister. She's dead now and . . . I'm sorry, Detective, but that's all I've got to say."

"A woman's been murdered," he went on. "Shot in the face. Her son has been kidnapped. You know Mickey Gornitz?"

"No," she said. "My daughter knows him, but there's no point in talking to her. She won't answer."

She stopped, file in hand, and turned to Lieberman. People liked to talk to Lieberman. He was a good listener. He liked to listen.

"I know things are not always savory in Mr. Stashall's business dealings. God knows they weren't in my uncle's."

Lieberman nodded, attentive.

"But," she went on, "I don't believe that Mr. Stashall killed that woman and took her son. I'm not saying he doesn't want to deal with the problem created by Mr. Gornitz, but he doesn't have that boy and I pray to God and the Holy Virgin that you find him alive and well."

The door to Stashall's office started to open. Grace Frasco looked anxious. Lieberman got out before Stashall and Manush emerged.

It wasn't raining when he hit the street, but it felt like it and the sky was Chicago October gray. The gray he could take. The summer heat he could take. The winters were the problem. Lieberman loved his city, but he hated the deep snows that trapped his car and he hated the deep cold. The normal cold, zero weather, he could take, but in recent winters January and February were bringing wind chills forty below and lower. Such temperatures froze his car battery in spite of the garage, which wasn't heated and which he couldn't use when there had been a big snow. He wouldn't move. Neither he nor Bess wanted to move, but they talked about northern California and the Gulf coast of Florida from time to time.

Bill Hanrahan was leaning against Lieberman's car, arms folded. A few kids who should have been in school moved by laughing. A woman pushing a baby carriage with a friend at her side were carrying on an animated conversation in what Lieberman thought was Russian.

"How'd it go?" asked Hanrahan.

"Stashall says he didn't do it," said Lieberman.

"What'd you expect?" asked Lieberman's partner.

"I didn't expect that I might believe him."

CHAPTER 7

Stashall watched the two detectives from his window. Someone knocked at the door behind him. He told them to go away. The cops were talking but nothing in their faces gave away what they were thinking.

What Stashall was thinking was that life was unfair. He had worked hard, with his bare hands, all the dirty jobs Anthony Visconti had thrown at him. Visconti had taken him in like a son. Visconti had protected him and then Visconti had died and Jimmy had worked even harder and, he thought, gained more than a little respect.

He was a good family man. He paid his people well and on time. He always gave the buyer or victim a chance before he allowed violence.

Yes, he committed crimes, crimes for the mob, crimes for himself, to take care of his family, his mother who was eighty-five damn years old, the sweetest . . . Shit, it was Gornitz. He had made a mistake in hiring that

Jew bastard. That's what you get for being liberal.

It was getting late so they decided not to leave a car in front of Stashall's and have to come back for it. Hanrahan and Lieberman drove separately to North Avenue and Emiliano "El Perro" Del Sol's bingo parlor. Lieberman listened to the radio humming along to the golden oldies. That was one of the great things about having the big brooding Hanrahan as a partner. They both liked the same 1950s music. Lieberman knew vaguely that Elvis was singing. He liked Elvis. Bess did not. Bess liked the Beach Boys. Abe did not. Since they seldom listened to music together, it wasn't much of an issue in their marriage.

Lieberman went over his conversation with Jimmy Stashall and Grace Frasco. Stashall could lie. So could Grace Frasco, whom he didn't know very well. The woman had aged gracefully. She was probably younger than Lieberman, who seemed, according to his mirror, to have been born looking weary and old. But weary or not, Lieberman had something in his gut like most cops with his years on the job. It told him when people were lying. It wasn't always accurate, but it was enough of the time to make him listen to the rumbling inside him.

Driving behind him, Bill Hanrahan listened to nothing. He tried not to think about what he could have done and maybe should have done to save the woman and keep the kid from being taken. He had spent most of his waking time since the murder trying not to think about it. He was monumentally unsuccessful. Maybe he should have sensed what might happen in Ohio. Maybe he should have assumed the possibility and stood guard outside the window or dozed in his car from where he could see the window, but they could have come through the motel room door too. He couldn't watch them both. Besides, he wasn't violating procedure. He had been listening. He had been in the room seconds after the shot. He had seen the car take off, missed it by seconds. Still, as he had told Sam Parker, he seemed to be one hell of a jinx. He decided to dig out the crucifix his mother had given him when he was confirmed. He would find a chain, wear the image of Christ against his heart. It might help. Probably wouldn't. What was it Lieberman had said awhile ago? Myths can be comforting.

There were parking spaces in the new parking lot next to the bingo parlor. There had been a small bodega, a mom-and-pop grocery there only months ago. El Perro had persuaded them to sell the business to him at what he considered a reasonable price. The old couple had accepted without an argument. Then El Perro had called Father Marielli at Holy Angels and told him he could send someone to take what was in the grocery and give it to the poor. That was after he and his men took what they wanted, which turned out to be very little.

As violent as he was, as feared as he was, El Perro wouldn't have survived if he didn't have support from the community from which he was stealing. When he could buy the gratitude of the neighborhood and the church without any cost to him, he did. To many he had become a hero — a hero to stay away from, but a hero nonetheless. To many others who had seen him in a moment of madness or heard about it, he was not a hero but a demon God had unleashed on North Avenue to remind them of his power. God was good, but God needed to remind people that evil existed, and El Perro was certainly unpredictable, violent evil sent by God to test their ability to suffer through life.

Lieberman had waited in his car for his partner to park. Together they had walked into the bingo parlor. Hanrahan had said only "We've got an hour before Mills is supposed to be sitting on that bench in Lunt Park. How long you think he'll sit there?"

"He'll sit," Lieberman said opening the bingo parlor door.

Inside, leaning against a wall in the alcove whose walls were covered with colorful posters in Spanish, was El Chuculo, the Knife, a skinny, good-looking, and very lethal young man. He was good for at least three killings that Lieberman knew about. On two occasions, not murders, Lieberman had helped let El Chuculo walk as a payback to El Perro.

"Buenos tardes, Viejo," the young man said, standing up.

In the past, till about the time El Perro took over the bingo parlor and started calling the numbers himself, every member of the gang had worn black jackets with a painting of an octopus on the back. Now Los Tentaculos wore slacks and jackets that didn't match and often ties that contributed even more to the chaos of mingled purposes. Dressing very badly had become Los Tentaculos' new uniform. Everyone in the broad circle in which they traveled knew who they were. Now even Piedras, the enforcer whose I.Q. was probably too low to register in a test but whose loyalty to El Perro was unquestionable, wore the slacks, jacket, and hideous tie combination.

"¿Porque usted no esta in la calle?" asked Lieberman.

"Hace frio, Viejo. Yo puede a ver todos aqui,"

said the young man who, the two detectives knew, had a folding knife with a very long blade somewhere he could get to it quickly.

The policemen walked into the bingo parlor through the door next to Fernandez. The room was large, filled with long tables and chairs. On a raised platform, a thick wire sphere filled with bingo numbers on the table in front of him, sat Emiliano "El Perro" Del Sol, smiling at the two policemen. At least it seemed to be a smile. The white scar that ran down his face made it difficult to be certain. Behind El Perro stood the solid Piedras and another young member of the gang named Ramon Tijas, who had not yet acquired a nickname. As soon as he did something particularly gory and vicious, El Perro would dub him. El Perro was the only one not wearing a sports jacket. He wore a silk Cubs jacket with a matching blue silk tie.

"*Viejo,* Irish," El Perro said, motioning to chairs in front of him on the platform. "*¿Que pasa?*"

El Perro had abandoned his office at the front of the bingo parlor in favor of the platform where he ruled like a bandit king. The bingo parlor was not the most lucrative part of El Perro's enterprises. After extortion came a variety of things, arson for insurance, beatings or even murders paid for on a sliding scale, a little cocaine dealing but no other drug, and car theft, but the bingo parlor had taken what existed of El Perro's imagination.

"You called," Lieberman said in English so his partner could understand the conversation.

The detectives mounted the platform and stood in front of the gang leader.

"*Sientase,*" said El Perro.

"We've got an appointment," said Lieberman. "Can't stay long."

El Perro looked at Hanrahan. "*Viejo,* your partner still hates me."

"He's funny that way," said Lieberman.

"But you, *Viejo,* you and I are friends."

"I suppose in a crazy sort of way, we are," said Lieberman. "I'll ask you the same question you asked me Emiliano, *que pasa?*"

"*Quiero a hablar solamente con usted,*" El Perro said, looking at Hanrahan.

"*No es —*" Lieberman said.

"I got enough of what he said," Hanrahan said. "I'll go out and talk about capital gains taxes with Chuculo."

"*Gracias,* Irish," said El Perro.

"*De nada,*" said Hanrahan, stepping down from the platform and heading between the chairs and tables and through the doors.

"He's learning Spanish," said El Perro, obviously pleased.

"Picking up a little here and there." Lieberman continued to speak in English in case Hanrahan was listening at the door. "Comes with the job. Some cops pick up a little Vietnamese, Russian, Creole. What did you want to talk about?"

"Kim," said El Perro. "That Korean is loco."

And you, thought Lieberman, are a model of sanity.

"Kim," Lieberman repeated.

"I think he should disappear *por siempre.* He's gonna keep coming after you, your *familia, todos.* I can hurt that one-armed motherfucker but he won't stop. Never seen anything like him. Those people are smart, but they can be crazy nuts. I think maybe I should —"

"I'll have another talk with him," said Lieberman.

"Won't do no good," El Perro said with a shrug. "I say just go in there and shoot the bastard."

"In there?"

"Mi officina. " El Perro nodded at the office.

Lieberman knew there were no windows in there. That was one of the things El Perro had liked about it. There was only the one solid oak door to which Emiliano kept the only key. He nodded in agreement.

"Bueno," said El Perro, fishing the office key out of his pocket and handing it to Lieberman.

"Cinco minutos, no mas," said Lieberman.

"Take your time," said El Perro. "I got numbers to weigh and mark. New numbers. You wanna call numbers some night, *Viejo?* It's fun."

"I'll think about it," Lieberman said over his shoulder as he headed for the office.

"It's fun," El Perro repeated. *"¿Verdad, Piedras?"*

"Sí," said the stone-faced enforcer.

"Almost as good as having a woman," said El Perro.

Lieberman didn't comment on that one. When he got to the office, he put the key in the lock, turned it, walked through the open door, and closed the door behind him. Kim was sitting on the floor in the corner of the room. Every bit of furniture had been moved out. The office had been turned into a windowless cell. The Korean was hugging his knees with his one arm and his head was down. He looked up and saw Lieberman. Hatred burned. Kim's face was puffed, bruised, and his right cheek looked odd and was probably broken.

"They won't stop me," he said. "That crazy Spic won't stop me from killing you."

In the reverse situation, Lieberman was sure El Perro would have referred to Kim as a gook.

Lieberman was hungry. Lieberman was not looking forward to going home and dealing with his daughter and his brother. Lieberman was, he realized, in a very bad mood.

"Kim," he said, "you lost your arm because you were a criminal extorting from your own people and one of them shot you in self-defense. You lost your gang. Your family disowned you. I didn't do anything but my job."

"You hounded me," said Kim, still seated in the corner. "You made me lose my people, my family, my work, my arm, my self-respect. That cannot be forgiven."

"Let's say you kill me," said Lieberman. "Then what? Who do you hate next? What do you live on?"

"I will worry about that when I am relieved of your presence on this earth," said Kim.

"El Perro suggested strongly that I kill you," said Lieberman. "Or that he do it."

"His moron has already come close to doing that," said Kim. "I am sure I have some broken ribs and a broken bone in my face."

"I'm sorry," said Lieberman.

"Do not be. It strengthens my hatred of you."

"How much do you want to live, Kim?"

No answer.

"I'm going to give you two choices," the detective said softly. "You walk out of here with me, we pick up your things, and then we take you to the Greyhound station where we buy you a ticket to anywhere and you don't come back. You'll have company while you wait. A gentleman named Clark Mills. If you don't come with me and promise to get on a bus, I just leave here and you stay with El Perro. You're not giving me much of a choice."

There was silence in the room. In the hall behind Lieberman, El Perro shouted, *"Diez y ocho"* and began to laugh.

Lieberman checked his watch and stood waiting.

"I could come back," said Kim.

"You are a man of your word," said Lieberman. "That's about all you have left. Walk out with me and I'll believe you. Stay and —"

"I've already given my word that I would kill you," Kim said, getting to his feet with the help of the wall and his one arm.

"No, technically you've *vowed* to kill me," said Lieberman. "You haven't given your word to anyone."

Kim closed his eyes in pain. Discretion was the better part of painful death.

"I will go with you," he said. "But that will not end my hatred."

"Hate away. Just get out of town and stay out. You want to write me a hate letter once in a while, feel free. You know where I live. Let me give you a hand." Lieberman stepped forward to help the injured man.

"Would that you could along with an arm," said Kim.

"The doctors said you could be fitted for a prosthetic arm," said Lieberman. "Follow up on that when you get where you're going."

Kim nodded and refused the detective's outstretched hand.

"Remember, you will live with my eternal curse and hatred," said Kim.

"I'll just have to learn to live with that," Lieberman said. "Let's go."

Kim almost fell as they walked out, but Lieberman didn't touch him.

"You takin' him, *Viejo?*" El Perro shouted. "Bueno. But you can just kill him in the office. I'll have someone get rid of the body."

"I'll take him, Emiliano," Lieberman said.

El Perro nodded, satisfied. Now El Viejo owed him another favor, not that they were counting.

Kim staggered into the alcove where Hanrahan grabbed him before he could fall. Kim, for some reason, didn't blame Hanrahan for his woes, though Lieberman and Hanrahan had both been on his case. Maybe Kim couldn't handle two hatreds at the same time.

El Chuculo seemed disinterested as the two policemen took the Korean out the front door of the bingo parlor.

"I'll take him," said Hanrahan.

Lieberman nodded. He had nothing more to say to Kim, and he didn't think a conversation would be a good idea.

It was raining lightly, but thunder cracked somewhere west.

Soon Abe would have to face his family. It was going to be a very long day. He deserved something to eat, something fat and full of calories. He would try to resist.

Irwin Saviello, shotgun in his lap, ate two more Little Debbies as he faced the door in the only chair with arms in the room he shared with Antoine Dodson.

Irwin was angry, an anger so deep and burning that he didn't even think about it. It just roared inside him. He was sure he had a temperature. That, he knew, might well come from the fact that he had a broken arm, but he preferred to think that it was a result of the rage he felt against his partner and supposed friend.

Antoine had abandoned him, left him

standing with one arm broken and holding a shotgun in the parking lot of that convenience store. There was no reason Antoine couldn't have waited another few seconds, no reason to leave him for the police to come with the screaming woman.

But Irwin had fooled them and himself. Somehow he had managed to get away. Irwin was not smart. He knew that. He had always been dependent on others. First, there had been his brother Salvatore, who had taught him breaking and entering and fought at his side in bars and alleys. They had been a good team. Then Sal had been killed by a broken grape juice bottle in one of those alleys. His face had been slashed, his throat ripped open. Irwin had tried to make it on his own, being used as a bodyguard or backup by a series of small-time drug dealers and armed muggers till he had tried to go off on his own and had been quickly caught. Then, in prison, he had met Antoine Dodson. He had been taught by Sal not to trust niggers, but Antoine was smart. They had done well in prison and after. Well, they had done well enough for Irwin Saviello. Then this.

His father had betrayed him by leaving home when he was a baby. His mother had betrayed him by dying. Only his brother, only Sal, had never betrayed him. He knew that now. There wasn't anyone alive who wouldn't betray him.

Irwin had walked quickly from the convenience store parking lot, crossed Howard, hurrying past the smells of a pizza parlor and into a narrow walkway between two apartment buildings. Then, shotgun in hand under the sweater and clutching his bag of sweets, he had run, run as fast as the gun and his screaming arm would let him. He didn't know how long he had run through alleys and down streets, past kids and couples, men sweeping sidewalks, mothers out with babies.

Then he had found himself in the parking lot of a strip mall. The mall was fairly large and full. There was a Walgreen's, a deli, and a dollar store. Irwin thought he heard a siren. It wasn't the first time since he had begun running, but this was close.

He had looked around, breathing hard, and saw a woman putting groceries in the trunk of her car from a supermarket cart. She wasn't young, but she wasn't old either. He thought from her face that she was pretty and probably Mexican. He didn't care. He moved slowly behind her, looked around as she closed the trunk, and said, "I got a gun."

The woman had turned quickly in fear to look at him. He had let the sweater slip back to reveal the shotgun.

"Get in. Drive where I say. I won't hurt you. I won't even punch you."

"Don't kill me." The woman whimpered, looking around for help.

"Get in. Now. Drive where I say and I won't hurt you. I just want to get away from here."

She shook her head as he nudged her to the passenger side of the car. She opened the door and slid in, going awkwardly over the gear shift lever into the driver's seat. Irwin got in after her, let the gun rest on his lap, and closed the door.

"Where?" she had said.

"Just drive," he said, pushing his bag of stolen sweets on the floor between his legs. "Drive that way."

He had pointed in what he thought was the direction of uptown, hoping to recognize something.

"Down that big street," he said.

She drove south on Western Avenue. He ate Twinkies and packages of Oreo cookies, carefully putting the crinkly wrappers and pieces of cardboard with clinging remains of the small cakes into the small paper bag. He tried to think. All he could do was focus on getting to the apartment, hoping that Antoine was there so he could blow his head off, providing he could level the shotgun and fire with his left hand. He was reasonably sure he could. The worst that could happen would be that he would strangle his partner with one hand. Even if Antoine had his gun and shot him, Irwin would get to him. Of that he was sure.

He offered the woman a Snickers bar. She shook her head no.

They had driven saying nothing. She had breathed heavily, trying, he knew, not to cry.

"I won't hurt you," he said.

They drove South on Western until they reached some things that Irwin thought he recognized — a Burger King, an Ace hardware, a martial arts studio with a painting of a man in white pajamas kicking his bare foot over his head.

"That shit never works," Irwin had said, pointing an Oreo at the sign. "You got a stick, a baseball bat, a gun, your hands if you're big like me. That shit never works."

The pretty Mexican woman nodded. She was afraid to speak. He knew she was thinking of just jumping out at a stoplight because his hand wasn't on the trigger, but she was afraid and she was right to be.

"Over there," he said. "By that house, between those two cars. That's where I live."

She pulled in. Traffic was a normal heavy on Western. It made her feel safer.

"Give me ten dollars," he said.

She fumbled for her purse, opened it, and came up with her wallet. There was more than sixty dollars in it. She took out two fives and handed them to Irwin, who took them in his one good hand and pocketed them in his jacket.

"Now I'm gettin' out. You drive. Forget you met me. They catch me and you I.D. me and I come for you. I blow your head off. You're scared and you lost ten bucks. That's all."

He got out and watched the woman speed away. He still had at least eight blocks to walk, but he was proud of the way he was handling things, proud of being able to do it on his own. Now all he had to do was get Antoine.

He had made it back to the apartment. If Antoine was there, he had decided to let him soft talk. Then he would get close and beat the bastard to death with the shotgun. Friends, partners don't leave each other in parking lots with broken arms. But Antoine wasn't there. His few clothes were still in the closet. The money he had hidden under the linoleum was still there. Somehow Irwin had gotten there first. Maybe Antoine had stopped somewhere to take care of his pellet-filled and bleeding leg. Maybe Antoine had died. That was as far as Irwin could think and much further than he was usually able to go in thought.

Now, his arm swollen and the broken bone trying to crack through the purple skin, he sat waiting. Checking to see that the shotgun was loaded had been difficult, painful, but he and the gun were both ready. If Antoine was alive, he would come. Neither he nor Irwin had anyplace else to go.

Antoine Dodson had driven away cursing his pain, his failure, the stupid white idiot he worked with. He had watched Irwin standing there, one arm limp, the other holding the shotgun. He'd probably stand there till the police came and picked him up or shot him on the cracked concrete. Who gave a shit? Antoine had to think of himself.

He drove: At first it wasn't so bad. He breathed deeply, thankful that it was his left leg in agony or he wouldn't have been able to drive. He considered driving down Broadway back to uptown, back to the apartment where he would pick up his clothes and his money and get the hell out of town. Irwin might turn him in, especially after being left alone to face the cops, but it would take awhile. If Antoine moved fast, he could get to the room, gather his few things, and be gone long before Irwin said anything. That was if things went well.

They didn't. The pain grew. Antoine touched his leg and his hand came back bloody.

"Shit, shit, shit, shit, fuck," he said, slamming a fist against the dashboard.

He needed doctoring. No doubt. He needed it and needed it fast or he would pass out and might well bleed to death in the car.

He'd have to go to a hospital, tell a story, hope they didn't match up the robbery with him. He had no choice. Bleeding to death wasn't an option. He'd tell a story and stick to it. That woman would never be able to identify him positively. He had worn his mask. And Irwin? A good lawyer could tear Irwin to pieces. Worst case, the state attorney's people would jump at a plea bargain. Antoine would have to give up on the idea of going to the apartment to pick up the cash there. He had a pocketful from the convenience store. He didn't know how far it would take him, but wherever it was, that's where he was going when he got his leg fixed up.

Antoine made it to Sheridan, cursed the traffic, groaned in pain, and kept driving, trying not to pass out. He turned onto the Outer Drive and almost missed the exit at Lawrence Avenue, but he caught it just in time and barely missed an oncoming car driven by a woman, a frightened black woman. He caught a glimpse of a couple of children in the backseat of the woman's car. But he didn't hit them.

He managed to make the next turn south, make it down the two blocks without hitting anything but the fender of a parked Buick, and turn into the emergency room driveway of Weiss Hospital. He tried to park the car reasonably close to the curb. The space was illegal, but he didn't have a choice. Only then did he remember that he was still carrying his gun. He should have wiped it for prints and pitched it out the car, but he had forgotten. He knew he was passing out, but he managed to wipe his prints from the gun. No one seemed to be watching as he stepped out and almost fell. He looked around frantically and saw a garbage can near the entrance. He fished out a sheet of newspaper. He wiped the gun again and, using the newspaper, flung the weapon toward a clump of bushes planted in front of the emergency room door. Though he was losing both strength and consciousness quickly, he managed to get the weapon into the closest bushes.

Then Antoine turned and limped toward the entrance. He took four steps and fell. He crawled the rest of the way to the glass and steel doors that opened automatically. Then, eyes closed, he managed a few more feet to get inside, not knowing if anyone was watching, wondering where the hell the doctors and nurses were.

That was it. He passed out.

When Antoine opened his eyes, he tried to sit up. Confused, he didn't recognize the room, the two men and the woman in white standing next to his bed. Then he remembered and lay back.

"Mr. Dodson." The nurse was calm, very black, and old enough to be Antoine's grandmother. "You are going to be fine. Eight pellets were removed from your leg. You've lost a lot of blood, but you are going to be fine. Are you up to talking to these men?"

"Who are they?" asked Antoine, mouth dry, leg throbbing, but the terrible pain gone.

"Police," she said.

"Too weak," said Antoine, closing his eyes.

"That's unfortunate," said one of the two men. "Without some answers soon, we're going to have to consider booking you for murder, robbery, and twenty other counts including reckless driving and take you in as soon as you can get up."

Antoine's eyes opened. "Murder? I didn't kill nobody. I got shot."

The two men in front of him were an unlikely pair. One was old, small with white curly hair and a little mustache. The other man was big, as big as Irwin. He looked powerful and he looked sad.

"You want to talk?" the nurse said. "You are capable."

"Maybe I'll talk a little," Antoine said in a whisper that sounded weaker than he was.

"I'll be at my station or with a patient," the nurse said, leaving the room.

"I'm Detective Lieberman. This is Detective Hanrahan. I'm going to read your rights and we'd like you to sign a statement that you've been read those rights and understand them."

"Okay," said Antoine. "But I didn't kill nobody."

Hanrahan began immediately to recite the Miranda warning, talking fast and not letting Antoine interrupt. Once Antoine asked for a lawyer, the questioning would stop. The trick was to keep him talking and any time it looked as if he might be about to ask for legal help to ask a new question.

"Let's talk about murder," Lieberman said, almost bored.

"Murder? I didn't kill nobody. I got shot over on Gunnison a few hours back or whatever time it is. Just walkin' down the street. Guy steps out, calls for my wallet, and shoots."

"He didn't get your wallet," said Hanrahan. "It was with your clothes. Forty-two dollars in it."

"I guess he got scared and ran," said Antoine. "I didn't kill anybody."

In fact, he was quite right. The Pakistani woman who had gone screaming down the alley was perfectly fine and remarkably able to give details of what had happened. She was sure she could identify both of the men who had robbed her and tried to kill her.

"We've got the gun," said Lieberman. "Found it in front of the hospital in the bushes."

"I don't know nothin' about a gun," he said. "I'm on parole. I don't carry guns."

"If you didn't do it, who did?" asked the big cop.

"I don't know. I wasn't anywhere near that store."

"What store?" asked Lieberman. "Who said anything about a store? Detective Hanrahan, did you mention a store?"

"No," said Hanrahan. "And you didn't either."

"Someone did," said Antoine. "Can I have some water?"

"I don't know," said Lieberman. "It might leak out of the holes in your leg and ruin the bandages."

"You've got a partner," said Hanrahan. "White guy, big. Maybe he knows about murder."

"I've got no —" Antoine started.

"We've been after you for two months," said Lieberman. "We've got store clerks lined up like opening day at Wrigley Field to identify the two of you. Now, if your partner knows about murder, maybe we can do something for you. We don't want you for anything but the robberies if you didn't kill anyone."

Antoine turned his head to the side.

It was a tense few seconds for the policemen who knew that Dodson might now ask for that lawyer. Amazingly, like so many criminals, Antoine didn't really know the law. Even if there had been a murder during the robbery and even if his partner had committed it, Antoine would still be eligible for a murder arrest as an accessory before the fact.

"Give us a hand," Hanrahan said reasonably, "and we'll give you one. All we want to do is clear this up, mark it solved, get our captain to say 'Job well done,' and go on with the next case."

"How much time will I get?" Antoine said.

"Don't know," said Lieberman. "We can put in a good word for you. Maybe you'll even walk if you turn in your partner."

The odds on Antoine Dodson walking away from this were nonexistent, as both detectives knew, but lying in that bed, Antoine might be ready to kiss the detectives' hands and believe anything they said.

"He left me in the parking lot," Antoine said. "Left me bleeding. I drove away. He must have killed her."

"Who is he?" asked Hanrahan.

"Where is he?" asked Lieberman.

"Irwin, maybe back at the room," Antoine said softly. "He ain't too bright. I don't know."

"Where's the room?" asked Hanrahan.

Antoine gave the address. It was less than eight blocks away. He gave the room number and the name, Irwin Saviello.

"That's all I got," said Antoine.

"You did the right thing," said Lieberman, believing, in fact, that Antoine Dodson had done the wrong thing if his goal had been to keep from going back to prison. "I think you should get a lawyer now. Want a public defender?"

Antoine shrugged and said, "I want some water."

"We'll tell the nurse on the way out," said Hanrahan. "And we'll call you a lawyer."

In the hall, Hanrahan said, "Warrant?"

"No time," said Lieberman. "We've got a felon with a lethal weapon who could flee at any second. I'll get Dodson a lawyer and then we go to the apartment."

Hanrahan nodded in agreement. He hoped

197

Saviello was in the room. He hoped, though he would never tell anyone, not even Lieberman, that Saviello tried to shoot it out. Bill Hanrahan needed closure on something.

Lieberman used a hospital phone and called the public defenders' office for Antoine Dodson. Whoever caught the case would be pissed as hell. With a stack on his or her desk, the lawyer would have little time to visit a defendant in the hospital. The hope was always for a plea bargain, quick, the best deal they could get. Their fear was a stubborn client who insisted he or she was innocent and wanted a trial.

Antoine Dodson would deal.

They had driven to the hospital in Lieberman's car, so Lieberman drove to the address on Magnolia near Lawrence and Broadway. The call from Weiss Hospital security had not gone specifically to the Clark Street station, but a report on the man with a leg full of shotgun pellets had been sent to all the stations in the city and suburbs.

Tying it in to the convenience store robbery had been obvious. Since the Salt and Pepper robberies belonged to Hanrahan and Lieberman, they had been handed the report, talked to the woman who had been robbed, and headed for the hospital. Considering the fact that she had probably broken the arm of one of the robbers and had definitely shot the other, not to mention that one of the robbers had come close to killing her, the woman had been remarkably calm.

All of this had taken place after three o'clock, when the two detectives and the one-armed Kim had gone to the bench in Lunt Park to pick up Clark Mills. Mills wasn't there. They tried other benches. They asked the few people they saw and the gas station attendant across the street if they had seen Mills, who was easy to spot and well known in the neighborhood. No one had seen him.

"Thought he'd show," said Lieberman.

"Makes two of us."

They had waited twenty minutes, then drove around the neighborhood. Nothing. Then they had taken Kim to the Greyhound station downtown and bought him a one-way ticket to San Francisco. Lieberman had also given him seventy-five dollars of his own money.

The bus was at five-fifteen.

"I suggest," Lieberman had said, "that you see a doctor as soon as you get to San Francisco."

Kim had said nothing.

"Remember," said Lieberman, "you don't come back to Chicago. You come back and I let El Perro have you."

"I keep my word," said Kim. "My honor, my word, are all I have remaining."

"More than a lot of people have," said Hanrahan.

They had helped Kim onto the bus, then watched it pull out.

"What you think?" Hanrahan had asked.

"Odds are even that he'll come back," said Lieberman. "He may decide that his honor requires revenge, retribution. And then again, he may find a job in San Francisco."

Now, after the stop at Weiss Hospital to talk to Antoine Dodson and wondering what had happened to Clark Mills to make him change his mind, they headed for the uptown address.

The transient three-story brick apartment building had about twenty single studio and one-bedroom apartments. The building looked pretty much like the other buildings on the block. Some were dark brick. Some were dirty yellow brick. The small plots of dirt between the street and sidewalk had no vegetation and looked as if someone had emptied garbage cans on them at least a year earlier and no one had bothered to pick up the garbage. There were some families, particularly from the rural South, who lived in the neighborhood and were trying to make a go of it and get into a better neighborhood, and there were a lot of people like Dodson and Saviello with no-where better to go.

The downstairs door was open, the lock long ago broken and not replaced. The same was true for the inner door beyond which the homeless probably gathered to sleep on the stairs where they would be kicked out by a building superintendent. The super might even feel sorry for them but fear the coming of the landlord. Bad job. The super probably was one of those poor whites from the South trying to make a living for his family. Such men, the detectives knew, sometimes found their lives unbearable and went violently mad.

Policy was to call for backup. Backup meant losing ten minutes or more. It meant marked cars that could be seen from a window. It meant possible noise from police or the curious. It was easier without help.

The routine was clear. The two detectives had been through it over a hundred times. Guns drawn, they stood one on each side of the door. Lieberman reached over and turned the doorknob slowly. It took only part of a turn for Lieberman to mouth across to his partner "Open."

Lieberman went back against the wall and Hanrahan knocked twice.

The knock was answered by a gunshot blast that sent pellets exploding through the door, making a dozen or more little holes. The wall across from the door took the dying blows of the pellets.

"Saviello," called Lieberman.

"Go away," said Irwin. "I'm waiting for someone."

"We're the police," said Hanrahan.

"Who gives a shit?" said Irwin.

"Antoine's not coming," said Lieberman. "He's in the hospital. How do you think we found you? He told us. He told us you made him commit those robberies, that he was afraid of you, that he never wanted to do it, but you beat him, raped him."

"He's a lyin' bastard," Saviello said angrily. "I don't rape anybody. I didn't hit him. He planned it all. Then he left me standing in that parking lot. I'm gonna kill him."

"I don't think so," said Lieberman. "But you can hurt him. Confess, make a statement about what he did."

"He's not coming?"

"In the hospital," said Hanrahan.

"He'll get sent back to prison?"

"No doubt," said Hanrahan.

"My arm's broke," said Saviello. "She broke my arm. I can see the bone under the skin ready to just pop out like that thing from space in *Alien*."

"Drop your gun, put your hands high, and

we'll get you to a doctor," said Lieberman.

"Same hospital where Antoine is?" Irwin asked eagerly.

"I don't think that would be a good idea," said Lieberman.

"I can't lift my bad arm," said Saviello. "Broke. I told you. I try to lift it and that bone'll pop through."

"Then just drop the gun on the floor," said Lieberman.

"You'll kill me," said Irwin. "I know."

"We won't kill you," said Lieberman. "We need you to help us put Antoine in prison. Antoine left you standing. We want to get him. You want to get him. We kill you and we have nothing. Drop the gun."

"I'm eating a Ho-Ho."

"You can bring it with you," said Lieberman.

"I got lots of stuff left to eat."

"Saviello," said Hanrahan, "drop the gun now."

Lieberman looked at his partner. That was not the way this was supposed to go down. Lieberman had been getting to the near halfwit inside the room beyond the door. Hanrahan was risking blowing it.

"Irwin —" Lieberman began again, but it was too late.

Hanrahan reached over with his left hand,

weapon in his right, and opened the door with a hard push. He went into a quick crouch aiming at the man seated in the chair facing the door. The shotgun was in Saviello's lap. He had a Ho-Ho in his one usable hand. The floor was littered with wrappers and small rectangles of cardboard with traces of chocolate cupcake and cream filling.

"Push the gun on the floor now," Hanrahan said, aiming at Saviello's chest. "Push or die."

Lieberman was in the doorway, weapon also leveled, backing his partner.

There was a moment, just an instant, in which both detectives and probably even Irwin Saviello thought the robber was going to go for the shotgun with his one good hand. He reached down, still holding the Ho-Ho, and pushed the gun on the floor.

It was over.

CHAPTER 8

The message from Captain Kearney to go to the new hotel room where Mickey Gornitz was being held in protective custody came just as Lieberman was about to sign out. The note also said "See me."

"I'll book Saviello," said Hanrahan.

They had brought Irwin to Edgewater Hospital, where his broken arm had been set and a cast applied. Irwin had shown no signs of pain or any further willingness to talk. Both detectives were sure that he would the next day, after a night in the lockup and the hint of special treatment if he turned on Antoine Dodson who had abandoned him in the parking lot.

In the waiting room of the hospital emergency room where they had taken Irwin Saviello, the two detectives had sat apart from those waiting.

"Father Murphy, what's going on?"

They both knew what Abe was talking about. Hanrahan had unnecessarily risked his life breaking into Saviello's room and facing him.

"Truth, Rabbi? I don't know."

"The cop's death wish?" Lieberman whispered, sipping bitter coffee from a plastic cup.

"Maybe," said Hanrahan.

"The usual. You feel guilty. You think you're getting people killed. You want to make up for it by getting yourself killed. I thought you were working all this out with Father Parker."

"You should have been a rabbi," said Hanrahan.

"Some rabbis have the insight of a telephone book," said Lieberman. "That's a secret. We tell outsiders like you and we risk getting picked up in the middle of the night and taken to a secret camp in Wisconsin where we're brainwashed into thinking all rabbis are brilliant."

"Same for priests," said Hanrahan.

"Sam Parker seems pretty sharp," said Lieberman.

"He is. And could he run. You ever see him play?"

"Don't think so," said Abe, working on his coffee. "I'm a baseball man, remember? Go talk to Sam again. Keep talking to him."

Hanrahan nodded. He had no coffee to play with. He had taken a cup from Abe and placed it on a table next to his metal-armed chair. The cup was growing cold on a two-year-old copy of *Harper's Bazaar*.

"Tonight," said Lieberman.

"Tomorrow morning," said Hanrahan. "First thing."

"Promise?"

"My word. If I fail to do so, I'll take lessons and convert to Judaism. Even have a Bar Mitzvah. Hell, at this point I must know a few hundred words in Yiddish from working with you."

"And every one of them of the utmost utility," said Abe.

It was almost time for dinner when they got back to the squad room and Lieberman found the message about Mickey Gornitz. Hanrahan was at his desk. He had agreed to write the reports on both Dodson and Saviello and go home. It had, all in all, been a pretty good day, and Hanrahan felt a sudden drain in his soul. It would be a struggle to finish the reports, drive home, and go to bed. He would call Iris, tell her he'd see her tomorrow, and hope that he had no dreams. Hanrahan had thought he had himself under control, but when Saviello had hesitated in that apartment, he had lost it and risked his and his partner's life.

When Lieberman had gone into Captain

Kearney's office, Kearney, eyes dark from lack of sleep, had moved from the window where he had been standing to the small conference table where he sat, brushing his straight black hair back from his eyes and returning to the world. He looked even more weary than Hanrahan. He pointed to a chair and Lieberman sat.

"Good work on the Salt and Pepper," Kearney said.

"Thanks," said Lieberman.

"Your partner all right?"

"Perfect," said Lieberman. "Tired. Been through a lot."

Kearney had nodded, looked up, and said, "Call came through to Carbin's office a few hours ago. Caller said Gornitz's son wanted to talk to him. Caller said if he didn't, the kid was going to suffer and die. Simple as that. Carbin gave him a cell phone number, told the guy at the other end to call in an hour. Carbin went to the room with the cell phone. About an hour ago, the same guy called back from a pay phone and said that Gornitz should come on the phone fast. No chitchat. Carbin taped the call. Gornitz took it. His son came on, voice breaking, afraid, and said if Mickey wasn't dead in twenty-four hours, Matthew would be killed. That was it. Phone went dead."

"Twenty-four-hour suicide watch on Gornitz?" said Lieberman.

"Of course," said Kearney. "But that could get the kid killed. Carbin told Gornitz that if they hurt Matthew, he would have all the more reason to testify and get Stashall. That didn't seem to make Gornitz feel any better. Gornitz wants to talk to you. Now."

Kearney handed Abe a sheet of paper with an address and room number written in pencil. Abe knew the hotel. Used to be a class hotel on Sheridan two decades ago when George Halas lived less than a mile away and some of the best weddings took place there. Now the place was hanging on and would have been leveled years ago if anyone had wanted to put something else up in its place.

Abe headed for the hotel, stopping at the drive-through window of a taco stand where he ordered two vegetarian tacos with sour cream. He drove the remaining few blocks to the hotel where Gornitz was being held and sat eating the tasteless tacos and feeling hungrier as he ate.

What the hell had happened to Clark Mills? What could he say to Mickey Gornitz? What would he do if one of his grandchildren were kidnapped and he was given the same demand?

Lieberman knew he wouldn't kill himself.

He knew he would stall, lie, work the twenty-four hours knowing that they probably would kill his grandchild no matter what he did. Then he would find them, find them and make his own law. Mickey Gornitz probably knew the same things, but it's hard to tell a man not to take his only chance to save his only son.

Lieberman had recognized the two men from the state attorney's office standing in the hall. They had been expecting him. One of the men knocked at the door of Room 654, two hard taps, two soft ones.

"Detective Lieberman's here," said the man.

The door opened and Lieberman entered. The door was immediately closed and locked, a metal bar placed under the doorknob.

There were two more people from the state attorney's office, one was the man who had opened the door. The other was a young woman in a skirt and sweater. Lieberman didn't know her. She had naturally curly hair and was reasonably pretty with a no-nonsense look on her face. She nodded and moved to a chair at the window. The man who had answered the door checked the iron bar and took a seat next to the door facing into the room in which Mickey Gornitz sat on a worn sofa, a plastic tray with barbecued ribs, fries, and cole slaw untouched in front of him.

"Abe," Mickey said, standing.

Mickey looked terrible. His eyes were set deep, sleepless and dark. He needed a shave and he definitely needed his remaining hair brushed.

Lieberman sat next to Gornitz on the sofa. The food looked and smelled good. Lieberman resisted.

"Abe," Gornitz whispered softly. "You heard?"

"I heard."

"What can I do?" Mickey pleaded, clapping his hands together. "Carbin was here. He told me they were bluffing. That they wouldn't dare kill Matt because it would be the one sure thing to make me talk. He said they'd call back and just keep holding him, maybe hurt him a little to make me suffer."

"He's probably right," said Lieberman.

"But that can't go on forever," Mickey said, rubbing his forehead with both hands.

"Well," Lieberman said very softly, "you could go through the window."

"Yes," Mickey said, looking up at Lieberman who was smoothing his mustache with a single finger.

"Problem is," said Lieberman, "you're dead and you'll never know if Stashall'll let your boy go. My guess is —"

"He won't," said Mickey, looking around the room in pain. "I know Stashall. I'm dead. My boy's dead, but I can save Matt from torture. You know the things they can do to people. And maybe, just maybe Stashall'll let him go if I'm dead. It's worth a chance, maybe, you know?"

Lieberman knew. He had seen the bodies in shallow graves in Indiana and the trunks of cars.

"Mickey," he said, "I think the only chance of your son staying alive is if you're alive. Carbin's right. They call back and you tell them that if anything happens to Matt, you tell everything. If they let him go, you'll think about holding back, at least on some things."

"Stashall won't buy it," Mickey said, starting to get up, then clasping his knees and sitting again. "If Carbin's thinking about putting me in a straitjacket or fill me with drugs to keep me quiet and to keep me from trying to kill myself and, so help me God, I won't talk."

"He won't do that," Lieberman said reassuringly, though he had no idea what Eugene Carbin could or would do. "We've got twenty-four hours. Let's use them. When they call back, one of us talks to them, says you're alive, and puts you on. You make the deal. They'll take it."

"They won't." Gornitz sobbed.

"You got a better idea, Mickey?"

Mickey didn't answer. He finally shook his head. He had no better idea.

"I'm just a bookkeeper," he said, holding his hands out for understanding. "A CPA. I don't know how all this happened. I don't want to die. It just —"

"You see the Crane game in forty-nine?" asked Lieberman.

Mickey paused, thought, and said, "Forty-nine? That's the one where your brother had fifty. Most outside jumpers. Picture of Maish, two columns and a big headline in the *Sun*."

"That's the one. Maish's biggest game."

"You had a bunch of assists," said Mickey, showing interest. "But they didn't count assists or rebounds back then. Only offense, scoring. Was Bosco coaching that year?"

"Perz," said Lieberman.

"It was great to be a Marshall Commando," said Mickey. "All *shvartza* now. Has been since the fifties. You even had them on your team."

"Yeah," said Lieberman, considering pointing out that of the three black players on his team, one had gone on to get a Ph.D. from Pepperdine and was now a full professor of psychology, another had started a soul food restaurant with his parents and brothers and branched out all over the country before selling out for millions and investing his part in a series of highly successful McDonald's franchises, and the last had become a lawyer and still worked for the ACLU. It was not the time to destroy Mickey's prejudices.

"Those were great days, Abe," Mickey said.

"Great days," Abe said, putting a hand on the man's sagging shoulder.

Abe did not remember them as great days, but it wasn't the time or place to go into the dangers of living in a Jewish ghetto surrounded by hostile Poles to the south, anti-Semitic Cicero to the west, blacks to the east, and an unknown commercial world of shops, movies, and neighborhood restaurants to the north, an area that was supposed to be neutral but never was. One night on Madison, on the way to the Marboro Theater, Abe and Maish had been surrounded by a gang of Irish kids who lived around St. Finnbar's Church. They had demanded money and Abe's new hat. Before he could consider turning over the hat, Maish had laid out two of the Irish kids. Abe had run head down into the face of the leader, and the four who were still standing rushed the brothers and may well have killed them if a crowd hadn't started to gather and the Irish kids hadn't run away. They got

Abe's hat. The great times.

"Mickey, you trust me?"

"Yeah, I guess."

"Stay alive."

Mickey shrugged.

"Promise," said Lieberman. "I'm counting on you."

"Okay," said Mickey. "But if they put Matt on the phone and hurt him . . ."

"We'll take care of it," said Lieberman. "Say, I'm seeing Maish tonight or tomorrow morning. I'll tell him you said hello and remind him about that Crane game."

Mickey's smile was full of pain, but it was a smile. Lieberman shook his hand, motioned at the woman near the window, who gave him a puzzled look and followed the detective out of the room and into the hall away from the two men at the door.

"I'm Lieberman," he said.

"I know," she said. "What do you want?"

"Your name."

"Ruth Tyro," she said.

"Used to be . . . ?"

"Tyronovitz," she said.

"Ruth Tyronovitz," he said. "I am going to make a sexist comment. You are the best-looking attorney in the state attorney's office. Also, given your age and gender, you must be very good to be in that room. You want to know what Mickey just told me? I'll tell you what Mickey told me. You tell Carbin any way you like. I suggest no one try to talk to Mickey about what's happening. I suggest you talk basketball, football, baseball, even soccer. Mickey's a sports nut. Keep him talking. Suggest poker, real money. Don't give him time to think."

Ruth Tyro was smart enough to say nothing and nod in understanding.

"Last thing," he said as he walked toward the elevator. "He's not going to eat those ribs. Eat them before they're cold. Eat them for the sake of a starving detective who'll dream about them if he thinks they're just sitting there waiting. Eat them."

"I'm a vegetarian," she said.

He turned to her. She was smiling. She had a great smile.

"But," she added, "I'll get the others to eat the ribs and I'll take the cole slaw and a few fries."

"Thanks," he said.

On the way home, Lieberman called in and told Kearney what had happened. Kearney was almost always in his office. He was there more than he was in his apartment. He slept on the three-pillow, less-than-comfortable lightweight sofa he had bought secondhand from Stavros the Greek less than a block away from the station. Kearney had his own troubles and memories, but he was a good cop. He just depressed the hell out of everybody.

One quick trip around Lunt Park and Lunt itself with a pause at the gas station to ask if anyone had seen Clark Mills. No one had.

He considered stopping at Maish and Yetta's, but he really didn't have it in him to cope with his brother's grief without a halfway decent night of something resembling sleep.

It was still early enough when he parked half a block away from his house so he would have a chance to say good night to Barry and Melisa. Barry had been complaining about having to go to bed early now that he was about to have his Bar Mitzvah. Melisa was eight and eight was her bedtime on school nights though the lights didn't go out till stories were read, water brought, imagined aches and problems dealt with. Bess and Abe had extended Barry's bedtime to ten, providing he was in his room at nine where he could listen to the music Lieberman hated and, they hoped, read a book.

Abe knew he was heading into trouble when he put his key in the lock and heard the voices inside. He recognized them all. It was too late to turn around, and, besides, it was his house and responsibility. He went in.

The living room was lighted, but the television was off and there was no one there. In the dining room beyond, however, under the bright overhead lights of the twenty-year-old fixture the chairs around the table were full. Bess sat at one end of the table, her end. Surrounding her was their daughter, Lisa, who glared up at her father as if he had done something particularly treacherous. At her side was Marvin Alexander, Lisa's husband. The smile on his dark-brown face was a bit sad but genuine. He stood, adjusted his rimless glasses, and shook Abe's hand.

"Flew in a few hours ago," he said.

"Good to see you, Doc," Lieberman said sincerely.

Marvin sat as Lieberman found himself looking at his ex-son-in-law Todd, the classics professor at Northwestern who had remarried and was basically out of the family except for the important fact that he was the father of Abe's grandchildren and that he retained a clinging dependency on both Bess and Abe.

There was a plate of food in front of Abe's place at the table with a bottle of opened and half-finished red wine nearby. The others were drinking coffee.

"I'll be right back," said Abe. "I want to say good night to the kids."

"Don't take too long, Avrum," Bess said in

a tone that brought visions of an all-night session to the detective.

Before going upstairs, Abe went to his and Bess's bedroom on the first floor, took off his his gun and holster, put them in the drawer of the table next to the bed, and locked the drawer with the key he always wore round his neck. Then, as he moved as silently as he could up the stairs, the voices behind him rose. The level of conversation was still civil, but Lieberman knew that could soon end. If anyone could hold it together, Bess could. Abe would let his wife handle this.

With Lisa present, the chances of her taking offense at anything her father said were almost assured. Yet she always came back for her father's input. It baffled Lieberman, who simply accepted it as he accepted most of what took place in his life. He addressed it, did what he could and felt he must, and went on.

Melisa was asleep in her small room. There was a night-light that cast enough light on her face for Abe to see her. He kissed her cheek and went softly out of the room, closing the door gently. The voices from below could be heard on the small landing though only a word or two came across.

The light was on in Barry's room. Lieberman knocked and his grandson told him to come in.

Barry, lean and an almost exact replica of Todd, his father, sat cross-legged on his bed with a book in his lap. The CD player was soft with a sound that Abe had learned to accept as music.

"Grandpa," he said. "You want to know what's going on down there?"

"It would help," said Abe, sitting on the only chair in the room, the one in front of the desk. This had been Lisa's room. Much of the furniture, to make it acceptable to a boy, had been played with, redone by Bess. And he had covered the walls with posters of rock stars caught in the act of screaming and basketball players caught in the act of flying.

"Well," said Barry, "my mother wants to go back to Los Angeles with Marvin, but she says he'll hold something against her. I'm not sure what, but it sounded like she was fooling around with some doctor where she works. Marvin says he won't hold it against her, that all she has to do is never do it again. He wants Melisa and me to come and live with them. My mother's not so sure that it's a good idea even if she agrees to go back. My father says he wants us to come live with him and his new wife. His new wife isn't bad, but I don't think she really wants us. Grandma is trying to work it out."

"Good report," Lieberman said. "What

would you and your sister like to do about all this?"

"I like Dr. Alexander. I like my father. I'm not sure either of us want to live with my mother and I don't think she really wants us. We'd both rather stay here with you."

"Anybody ask you?"

"No," he said.

"What are you reading?"

"A biography of Andrew Jackson."

"For school?"

"No. I'm gonna read a biography of every president," said Barry.

Abe got up wearily.

"Let me know when you get to Nixon," he said. "We'll talk."

"Okay," said Barry.

Lieberman gave his grandson a hug and said, "Back to the family trial."

"Mazel tov," said Barry.

"I'll need it," Abe said, closing the door as Barry went back to his book.

Abe was happy to escape the music in his grandson's room but not to face the music downstairs. The discussion continued as he entered the room and sat at his place looking down at a plate set on the table before his chair. It wasn't ribs, but it wasn't bad. Cucumber and onion salad, a lamb chop, and asparagus. He poured himself some wine as

Lisa and Todd began to speak at the same time.

"Let the man eat," said Bess. "We can talk about something else till he finishes."

"I'm a detective, remember," Abe said. "Let me guess what's going on. Deduction. Just like Sherlock Holmes or Poirot. Todd, you've decided you want the kids. Your wife now agrees. Marvin, for some reasons that elude me, you want my daughter back on condition that she not repeat the behavior that has resulted in my presently crowded dining room. You also want the kids. Lisa isn't sure of what she wants. My wife and I both want Barry and Melisa to stay with us. We think that's the best thing for them. But we're not disinterested parties."

"They aren't your children," said Lisa. "They're mine."

"And mine," added Todd. "You abandoned them to your parents."

"I always planned to send for them some-time," Lisa said.

"Women, by nature, it seems, were born to be a great impediment and bitterness in the lives of men," said Todd.

Lieberman had cut a piece of lamb and was about to bring it to his mouth. He paused and said, "No quotations from Greek tragedies. That was the rule when you were my son-in-law. It's the rule still. No hiding behind dead Greeks."

"*Orestes* by Euripides," said Marvin.

Todd looked up, surprised and pleased. "That's right."

"Provide yourself with friends as well as kin . . . One loyal friend is worth ten thousand relatives," said Marvin. "Also *Orestes*."

"Wonderful," said Lisa. "My ex-husband and my husband are going to be friends. Someone should call Jerry Springer. We'll all go sit on national television and the two of you can play dueling Euripides."

Lieberman had begun chewing the warm piece of lamb, but he paused again. He was unaware that his daughter had any sense of humor. It was his firm conviction that, with rare exceptions, she lived humorlessly in a recurring torrent of vocal and silent blame aimed at her father.

Maish, he thought, blames God. Lisa blames me, and these two sit here hiding behind the words of dead Greeks.

"Bess," Abe said, pouring some wine, "I assume you were conducting this trial before I arrived. I urge you to continue while I finish eating and wait for a migraine."

"Impasse," said Bess.

"What do you think should be done?" Abe asked his wife across the table. The wine wasn't bad. Or maybe he just needed it.

"Lisa goes back to California with her husband," said Bess. "Todd goes home or to court if he feels he must. Meanwhile, we keep the children."

"Anyone ask Melisa and Barry what they want?" Abe asked, considering the asparagus.

"No," said Bess.

"I'm willing to abide by their decision," said Todd.

"They're children," said Lisa. "It isn't their decision."

"Marvin?" Bess asked.

"I have an opinion," he said, "but there is no way I can give it without creating a greater problem. I'll just sit back and let those of the same blood as the children decide."

"Rhesus," Todd guessed.

"No," said Marvin, again adjusting his glasses. "My own idea, but it was a firm part of my father's basic philosophy. He had a very large extended family, and he survived by making as few familial decisions as possible."

"I say," said Bess, "that we sleep on this and tomorrow someone be designated to ask the children what they'd like after telling them that we are simply getting their input and that the adults will have to make the final decision. Now, who do you trust to discuss it with them?"

"You," said Abe.

"Fine," said Todd. "You talk to them, Bess."

"Okay," said Lisa.

"Lisa, you can sleep with Melisa again tonight or go to the hotel with your husband," said Bess.

Lisa looked at Marvin, who gave her a small smile. "I'll go with Marvin."

"And, Todd," Bess said, "you should go discuss it further with your wife."

"We have nothing more to discuss," he said in a way that made it clear that his wife was less than thrilled by her husband's decision to do battle for the children.

Lieberman had talked to Todd's wife several times about the situation. She was older than her husband, well known in her profession, and not at all anxious to take on someone else's children. Not that she wouldn't do it if it turned out to be the best thing and she would certainly do her best, but it wasn't something she was looking forward to. If she had a vote, Lieberman was sure, it would be for the children to stay with Bess and Abe.

"One more thing," said Lisa. "I don't think this is a safe environment for my children. Last night crazy Mexicans dragged a one-armed Vietnamese —"

"Korean," Lieberman corrected.

"Korean," said Lisa, "into this house, where he threatened to kill you and they volunteered to kill him. That is not a safe environment and I don't think a judge will disagree."

"Mr. Kim and I have had a heart-to-heart talk and he is on his way to San Francisco," Abe said as he ate his still-crisp salad. "The other gentlemen were business acquaintances. Now I'm tired. I've had a long day. I'm afraid I'm getting a migraine. I want a hot bath and I want a few hours of peace with my wife. Which means I am fond of you all, but it's time to say good night."

"Agreed," said Marvin.

"Agreed," Todd said reluctantly.

Lisa and Bess said nothing though Bess nodded almost imperceptibly to let her husband know that he had, in her opinion, said exactly the right thing.

Ten minutes later, an exhausted Lieberman and his wife were in the kitchen cleaning the glasses and his dinner plate. They managed to talk for fifteen whole minutes before the phone rang. Abe picked it up.

"Abe" came the gravelly voice of Desk Sergeant Nestor Briggs, who was closer to retirement than Lieberman. "Thought you'd like to know. Body found about ten minutes ago in an alley behind Lunt not far from Sheridan.

Looks like it's Clark Mills. Couple of bullets in the back of the head."

Abe stood silent.

"You there, Abe?"

"I'm here," he said. "What's the cross street? . . . I'm heading over there now. You call Bill?"

"Not yet."

"Do it."

There was a space almost in front of his house in Ravenswood, less than three blocks from the Ravenswood Hospital. He had been aware that there were lights on in the house even before he was looking at them. Hanrahan knew the house that well. He and Maureen had lived there for a quarter of a century, raised their two boys there. He had become an alcoholic both in and out of that house, and when his wife left, it was from the house in front of which he was now parked.

There was a FOR SALE sign in the small front yard. Hanrahan had put it there himself a few weeks ago. There were plenty of reasons not to keep the place, particularly the bad memories; some of the more recent ones, like the shooting of Frankie Kraylaw, were especially bad.

There had been a time Hanrahan would have assumed that the lights on the house meant that Maureen had returned. He had kept the house dust-free, sheets changed, kitchen floor polished, and dishes put away for years while he waited. He had gone to AA and managed with pain to get sober. And he had waited, waited for Maureen to return, until, in spite of the fact that they were Catholics, she had filed for divorce. Hanrahan had taken it hard, but he had neither let the house go to ruin nor fallen off the wagon.

The day before he had decided to go to AA, on the same night that he had been too drunk to keep alive a woman he was supposed to be watching, he had met Iris Chen in the Chinese restaurant right across from the apartment building he was supposed to keep an eye on. Iris's father owned the restaurant. Iris had looked at the big half-drunk Irish cop with concern. Later that concern turned to love. Iris had, much to his surprise, been there for him when everything had fallen apart. Iris had now agreed to marry him, and she had a key to the house. She had never used it before, but Hanrahan was sure she was inside, wondering why he hadn't come to see her or call since he had fouled up on the Gornitz murder and the kidnapping of the boy.

He walked up the front steps noticing that the *Tribune* wasn't on the doorstep. Iris must have brought it in. Just in case it wasn't Iris,

Hanrahan checked his weapon, put it in his right hand, and opened the door with his left. There were people out there who might want William "Hardrock" Hanrahan dead.

Every downstairs light in the house seemed to be on. Nothing seemed disturbed. He moved forward toward the kitchen and found himself looking at a crowded table, much as his partner had been doing at almost the same moment. Iris, beautiful Iris, sat next to her father, a tiny man who spoke little English. Iris's father, Huang Chen, was looking at the old man at the far end of the small table. Liao Woo could have been any age, but he was certainly old. He carried a silver-handled cane and wore thick glasses. Liao Woo was, officially, an importer of Oriental goods. He was, unofficially, the most powerful man in Chinatown. He quietly ruled the area around 22nd Street that contained a concentration of 100 percent Chinese except for tourists and Chicagoans who came for dinners and dim sum breakfasts. Liao Woo was also well acquainted with members of the aging Chicago mob.

Seated on either side of the chair left open for Hanrahan were two young Chinese men whom Hanrahan recognized as Liao Woo's bodyguards. Both, Hanrahan knew, were armed. Both, Hanrahan knew, had already done severe, possibly lethal bodily harm to those who threatened or displeased Liao Woo. Hanrahan had clashed with the well-dressed duo for the simple reason that Liao Woo had, for years, quietly harbored the certainty that he would wed Iris Chen. After several confrontations and a number of warnings, Woo and the Irish detective had reached an understanding and declared a truce, providing Hanrahan remained sober, attentive, and a good husband after the marriage took place.

Iris's smile was the same as always, but Hanrahan had learned to recognize when it was forced, a beautiful mask. Iris was, in fact, several years older than Bill though she could easily have passed for his daughter. He had no doubt that he loved her and wanted to marry her. He also had no doubt that this gathering was not going to be an hour of joyous talking about old times and preparations for the marriage reception.

"I see Iris made you some tea," Hanrahan said, putting his gun back in his holster.

"I hope we haven't offended you," said Liao Woo, "but we brought our own tea."

"I'm not offended," Hanrahan said sitting.

The five Chinese around the table were looking at him as if he were expected to speak.

"To what do I owe this honor, Mr. Woo?" Hanrahan said.

"Trouble follows you," said Woo. "People are hurt, die. We think, as I understand you do, that you are carrying a curse, and we do not wish Miss Chen to be a victim of this curse."

"Curse?" Hanrahan asked.

"I do not mean witch doctors and medicine men," Woo said slowly. "I believe you carry the curse in your heart, that you bring destruction wherever you go, that it is you who have cursed yourself. You seek danger and those around you suffer."

"And?" Hanrahan asked, recognizing the same basic argument he had heard from Sam Parker.

"I know what happened in Ohio," said Woo. "I have even been informed of your dangerous behavior earlier today in capturing a man with a shotgun. That cannot continue."

Hanrahan, wondering how Woo had found out but not surprised, rose and said, "I'm getting coffee. Anyone else?"

No one answered.

There was silence while the detective got some cold coffee from the pot, poured it into a cup, put it in the microwave, and stood listening to the hum of the machine, his back turned to his "guests." It didn't surprise Hanrahan that Woo would have an informant in the department, informants all over the place. Woo dealt in information.

The microwave *pinged*. Hanrahan removed the hot cup and went back to his seat. No one had moved. He looked at Iris, who seemed to try to convey something he wasn't sure he understood.

"I think this is up to me and Miss Chen," Hanrahan said.

Woo nodded, looked at the silver handle of his cane, and said softly, "Detective, I suppose to you we look like something out of an old movie, Chinese following traditions which make little sense to you and other Americans. The traditions are nearly dead both in mainland China and Taiwan. The traditions are maintained by those who left China when such traditions still existed and had meaning. They settled in communities all over the world and maintained those traditions which gave and give meaning to their existence. There are such Chinese communities in Vancouver, Seattle, San Francisco, and many other cities including Chicago. You are a Catholic. Would you like someone to tell you that your traditions, your church, are no longer meaningful?"

"No," said Hanrahan who, in fact, wasn't at all sure that all of what the Catholic church stood for was still meaningful, at least to him.

He drank his coffee and waited, silent while Woo looked at his withered hands and then at Iris.

"I propose, with the agreement of Mr. Chen, that the wedding be postponed for a period of one year during which we observe your behavior and see if death continues to leap upon you."

"Iris and I want to get married next month," said Hanrahan.

"Do you find my conditions unacceptable and unreasonable?"

Hanrahan started to say something and realized that, whatever the motives of the old Chinese at the table, considering his own behavior, there was certainly some sense in what the man said. In fact, it wasn't much different from what he had been thinking himself.

"Iris?" he said.

At first he couldn't understand her, she spoke so softly.

"I wish to marry you as soon as possible," she said. "It is difficult for me to go against my father who values the advice of Mr. Woo and who has done much for us. They have not said they wish us to not marry. They wish to be careful."

"During the year," said Woo, "you may certainly continue to see each other and I give you my word, as I have before, that I will not press my attentions on Miss Chen. You may ask her if I have done so since our agreement."

Iris looked down and shook her head no.

"Okay," said Hanrahan, wanting to go for some of the aspirin with codeine he kept upstairs in his medicine cabinet. "It makes sense."

"Good," said Woo, rising. "Then you agree?"

"If Iris agrees," Hanrahan said.

Iris's nod was almost imperceptible.

All the others around the table also rose, including Hanrahan.

"As a token of good faith," Woo said, looking at the detective, "I wish to give you some information. I do not know where the missing boy is who you are seeking. However, I suggest that you look in the boy's past for information which can help you. I have people inside of Mr. Stashall's organization who give me information in exchange for considerations. I do not believe that Stashall has the boy or took him. He may know where he is, but he did not do the deed himself. There is another male you seek."

The phone rang.

Hanrahan wanted to ask some questions, talk to Iris whose father took her arm. He wanted to let the phone ring, but he couldn't.

He had no answering machine. He had smashed it against the kitchen wall after a message from Maureen about the divorce. Then he had carefully replastered the hole he had made in the wall and covered it with perfectly matching paint. The story of my life, he thought. I break it and then I try to fix it.

The call might be from his son Michael who had recently stayed with his father during Michael's own battle with alcohol. It might be from Abe saying there was a lead on the Gornitz kid.

He answered the phone and heard a voice say, "Bill?"

"Yeah."

"Clark Mills was found dead about half an hour ago in an alley. Lieberman is on his way."

Nestor Briggs gave Hanrahan the location and hung up.

"I've got to go," said Hanrahan.

"You might wish to shave before you do," said Woo. "In your bathroom you will find a new, highly efficient electric razor. The one you have is ancient and useless. Please consider it an engagement gift. It would be good if you are to marry Miss Chen if you could be clean shaven and neatly dressed at all times. Respect, Detective Hanrahan."

"Respect is what makes calamity of so long

a life," said Hanrahan.

Woo paused. "Is that Shakespeare?"

"It is," said Hanrahan. "Can't say I remember much of what I had to learn in school, but that and a few other things stuck with me."

"You will have to, at your leisure, tell me other things which have stuck with you. I assume some of the religious rituals of your faith can be included."

"It can," said Hanrahan. "Meaning no disrespect, I can't keep the razor."

Woo smiled, pleased, and nodded at one of his young men, who bounded toward the stairs leading to the bedrooms. They all stood waiting the few seconds till the young man brought down a small box.

"You should make a good husband," said Woo. "It is a pity you are not Chinese."

"I think I agree with you on both counts," said Hanrahan.

As they left, Hanrahan touched Iris's arm and said aloud, "I'll call you tomorrow, okay?"

"Okay," she said, touching him back. "Do you want the key back?"

"No," said Hanrahan. "Never."

Her father escorted her out of the kitchen and Hanrahan followed as the five visitors left the house. He gave them time to move slowly with the old man. Hanrahan, standing in the doorway, listened to the sound of Woo's cane tapping against the concrete walk. A limousine was waiting double parked. It had not been there when Hanrahan came home. The windows were dark and he watched Woo, Iris, and Iris's father disappear into the backseat and the two young men disappear into the front. When the limo pulled away, Hanrahan felt his face of stubble, sighed, closed the door, and went upstairs to shave with a fresh blade.

Clark Mills lay in the middle of the alley. A woman in a nearby building had heard the shots and called the police. A few people were gathered in the alley watching though it was past midnight. The area had been taped off by the first two officers on the scene. When Lieberman had arrived he asked them what they had done. Fortunately, they had done almost nothing except determine that the big man lying on his face was dead with two holes in the back of his head. The evidence, what Abe, Bill, and Rutgers, from downtown Homicide and Forensics could find of it, would be reasonably intact.

"Rabbi," said Hanrahan arriving at the scene.

"Father Murph," said Lieberman. "Rutgers from Homicide'll be here in a few minutes."

Hanrahan nodded in understanding. Rutgers would give some orders to the medical examiner's people, say a few things to the evidence technicians, and disappear. The murder of a homeless man who had been harassing the neighborhood wasn't worth the effort he could be putting into domestic, drug, and gang murders. Rutgers probably caught an average of one murder every two days. This one, left to Homicide, would stay on the board for a few weeks unless the evidence search turned up a miracle. Then, either way, Clark Mills would be forgotten unless Hanrahan and Lieberman worked on it, which they were entitled to do since Mills was already their case on misdemeanor counts.

"Wish it could have been inside," said Lieberman. "Inside you get the prints, blood, all kinds of things. Out here, who knows what was trampled on and what, if anything, you can get prints from."

Lieberman wasn't telling his partner anything he didn't know. It was just something to say while they both looked.

Hanrahan watched where he was walking as he approached the body and knelt to examine it without touching. The first thing that struck him was that Mills still had the thick, solid neck of a pro lineman. It was in the man as it had been and still was in Hanrahan in spite of the years of alcohol and lack of exercise.

Hanrahan got up and returned to his partner who was looking at faces in the small crowd at the end of the alley behind the yellow tape. He didn't see anyone who might be a likely suspect, but you never know. Maybe that couple still in their robes in spite of the night chill had killed the man who had terrorized their neighborhood. Maybe a lot of things.

"One thing's sure, he died long after he was supposed to meet us in the park."

"Yeah," said Lieberman. "Shall we?"

"Let's," said Hanrahan.

For the next two hours, the two men searched the alley with their flashlights. Rutgers showed up, gave the body a quick look, and said a few words to the medical examiner's men and the two cops who had taken the call. He watched the police photographer take pictures, probably more than would be needed or carefully examined, but mistakes had been made in the past and would be again and again. He didn't say anything to Lieberman and his partner beyond an initial "I hate alleys. Seems like half the victims want to get killed in alleys."

He had nothing against them, but he had nothing to say to them. Actually, Rutgers was

239

happy to see them. The two detectives had taken a good number of homicides over the years and cleared them from the homicide board. They had helped make the statistics look reasonable, and he was lucky to get this call because he knew Lieberman and Hanrahan would follow up.

Rutgers had left after fifteen minutes of taking notes and asking the uniformed cops what they had learned. It turned out to be nothing except the time of the murder when the gunshots were heard. The woman who had made the call had not seen the shooting. No one had seen it unless it was someone who was not in the alley.

In a case like this, it wasn't likely that witnesses, even if they existed, would step forward to identify a person who had rid their neighborhood of a man who had caused them months of terror.

When the body was finally removed, what remained of the crowd disappeared. Eventually it was just Lieberman and Hanrahan looking through the alley, moving garbage cans and mounds of dirt, seeing two cats and a few rats. They had put on rubber gloves for the search though a rubber glove wouldn't stop the needle in a syringe from infecting them with HIV. They moved slowly, carefully, eventually making their way all the way down both sides of the alley.

They were into their second hour and Lieberman was on his knees shining his light into the grating of a sewer. Hanrahan had gone off on his own. There was nothing down the sewer that he could see, but that didn't mean much. He would ask Forensics to come back and check out the sewers. It would not make them happy. Depending on whom he talked to, it might even result in a serious argument, but the detectives on the case, Lieberman and Hanrahan, had the final say though Forensics could appeal to Kearney or Homicide. Both Kearney and Rutgers would back them up.

Lieberman got up with an ache in his knees and moved to some cracked concrete steps leading down to a small square of space and a basement door. In front of the basement door stood a dog that had, until this moment, been totally silent. Now the mess of a creature stood erect, showing his teeth and growling low at the person who was blocking his escape.

Lieberman sat on the top of six steps. His behind felt the cold concrete.

"You a witness?" Lieberman asked. "I'll take your statement."

The dog with no name cocked his head to one side. No human had ever spoken to him like this. He had heard anger, fear, but not this. He had no idea of what to make of it. He wanted to escape, but the man sat in his way.

"You are one of, if not *the,* mangiest mongrel I have ever seen. That's a fact, not an insult."

The dog stopped growling.

"No collar, no tags, and from the filthy mess you are, I'd guess you have no owner. I'm not going to arrest you. Don't worry. I can do without dog bites. I like the way you stand. I wish I had —"

Lieberman stopped and remembered that he did have half a bagel in his pocket wrapped in a small zip-lock plastic bag. It was supposed to be emergency food to keep him from being tempted by something he should not eat. He took out the package. The dog growled and took a step forward.

"Most dogs would have gone back a few feet. You've got spunk."

Lieberman slowly opened the bag and threw the bagel slice in front of the dog with no name. The dog backed away not knowing what this thing was. It was still in the air when he knew it was food.

"What I do not like about dogs," Lieberman said, "is that they want to be loved, petted, played with, walked. And when you go somewhere you've got to find someone to take care of them. I think you are definitely a different kind of dog."

The dog sniffed at the bagel, looked at Lieberman, and tore the food between his teeth. He began to gnaw, finding it difficult to tear off pieces small enough to chew.

"That," said Lieberman, "is a good bagel. My brother made it. It's not soft like they sell now. It's hard, lean like a bagel should be."

The dog wondered about the sounds without anger or fear that were coming from the man. The dog kept eating.

"Take care of yourself," Lieberman said, standing and wiping the rear of his pants. "I've got to get back to work."

Lieberman stepped away from the stairway and the dog came up slowly, watching him, wondering if the man had one of those things that spit death. He had some of the bagel between his teeth, but he could drop it and either run or attack if this was some trick of the man.

"Go home or wherever," Lieberman said with a sigh. "Maybe we'll have another nice heart-to-heart conversation some other time."

The dog started to run down the alley, night parking lights pointing him out as he ran. He was about fifty feet away when he stopped, turned, and looked at the man. Lieberman waved to him and the dog disappeared.

Hanrahan came back and said wearily, "Found the weapon."

Lieberman stood.

"Where?"

"Garbage can," said Hanrahan, "inside someone's plastic garbage liner. Probably stopped for a second or two, opened the liner, threw it in, tied it, and put the lid back on."

"Let's take a look at the can and get the gun in to the lab," Lieberman said looking around the alley once more though he didn't expect to see anything.

"Weapon looks old, Rabbi," said Hanrahan. "Real old."

"So do I," said Lieberman. "It wasn't too old to kill Clark Mills."

"I'll take this in and start doing some checking," said Hanrahan. "You got a few hours to go home and sleep."

Hanrahan had told his partner about the visit from Woo and the others. Hanrahan didn't want to go back to the empty house, not this morning. In fact, it was getting harder and harder to go back to the house. Working for a few more hours suited him.

"See you in a few hours," Lieberman said, gladly accepting his partner's offer.

"A few hours," Hanrahan said, looking at the weapon in the see-through bag.

CHAPTER 9

The sun was considering whether to come up or not when Lieberman got home. Parking was a little hard, but not hard enough to have to wrestle with the garage door. He found a spot about a block from the house, took it, and walked back. There was a smell of rain in the air and a strong breeze. Lieberman liked it this way.

He entered the dark house quietly. No one seemed to be up, probably wouldn't be for at least three hours when the children had to be awakened for school. Lieberman's plan was simple: Have some cereal, set the alarm, and go to sleep. He had a feeling that his insomnia demon was as tired as he was.

At first, things were just fine. He took off his shoes and left them in front of the hall closet. He didn't want to open the closet door because of the squeal the door would make. He walked to the kitchen, turned on the light, and closed the door.

Lieberman poured himself a bowl of something called Oat Clusters. Bess had told him to eat Cheerios. She had been reading and watching the news. They were good for his heart. Lieberman didn't like Cheerios. They had compromised with the other oat cereal. He got a spoon and the milk and sat down to eat more quickly than Bess would have approved of.

And then the kitchen door opened.

His daughter, Lisa, stood in the open doorway in a blue trench coat over her pajamas. Her hair was disheveled.

"I was waiting for you," she said, closing the door and sitting across from her father at the table while he continued to eat. "Marvin's at the hotel. I heard you come in. Actually, I heard the refrigerator close. Abe, I have to talk."

"Lisa," he said, tilting the bowl to get at the last of the milk. "I've been up all night and I've got about two or three hours to try to sleep. You can talk, but I can't guarantee I'll be able to listen. Or, if I do, I can't guarantee that I'll absorb it or that anything I say will make a hell of a lot of sense. I suggest we talk tonight when I get back home or maybe for a while when I get up, before I have to go back to work."

"Five minutes, Abe," Lisa said, leaning forward. "You might be in another big hurry when you get up and I'll be gone when you come home from work."

There was definitely a plea in his daughter's voice, a sound he was not accustomed to in Lisa who had, in the past, been critically silent, occasionally demanding, often angry. To hear something that might be more than a request from his daughter was more than the exhausted Lieberman could resist.

"I'm listening," he said.

"I'm going back with Marvin this afternoon," she said. "I love my children. I love my husband. I'm not a good mother. I talked to Todd. Actually, Bess talked to him. We agreed to leave things as they are, maybe review the situation with the kids in a year."

The word "love" was an alien one coming from the mouth of his reserved, dispassionate daughter. It would take Abe some time to absorb what all this meant.

"You're coming back for Barry's Bar Mitzvah?" he asked.

"Yes, both of us, if it's all right with you and Bess."

"Why wouldn't it . . . ah," Lieberman said, understanding.

Marvin Alexander might be a doctor. He might speak all kinds of languages including Hebrew. He might be well versed in Shakespeare and Greek tragedy, but Marvin

247

Alexander was black.

"Marvin and I don't want to embarrass Barry, Melisa, you, and Bess," she said. "Abe, I've changed since I married Marvin."

"You certainly have," Lieberman said, pushing his bowl away. "But you're not being particularly perceptive about your mother, your father, and your children. You can ask them in private, but I'd say the odds are one hundred percent that we all want Marvin there. Lisa, I like your husband. All my life other cops have said to me, cops who've had to work the streets for twenty years or more, cops who had seen ghetto drug murders and family butcherings, mostly in black neighborhoods, 'You talk the game, Abe, but would you want your daughter to marry one?' Well, you did marry one and your mother and I are delighted with him. How I would feel if you'd married a drug dealer is a different story, but that wouldn't have been because he was black. It would be because he dealt drugs."

"I know," Lisa said, brushing strands of hair from her face. Combing her hair out would be a nightmare.

"Good," Abe said, standing and walking to the sink to rinse the bowl and spoon before putting them in the dishwasher. "And you know your mother and I love you."

"I know," she repeated softly. "You think

248

I'm a bad person for not wanting to take Barry and Melisa to California?"

"No," Lieberman said, turning to face his still-seated daughter. "I can't say I understand it, but we've had one hell of a time understanding each other since you were old enough to prove you were nearly a genius and to make clear that I was going to be the cause of all your misfortune."

"I'll work on that," she said.

"Good," Lieberman said, moving to his daughter and leaning over to kiss the top of her head.

She didn't pull back.

"If you have to leave before I get back," Abe said, "call me and I'll get away long enough to say good-bye."

"I will," she said.

"And one more thing I'll throw in while you're feeling vulnerable. It's one of the things cops do when they want something. If you can't make an effort to call me Pop or Dad, at least make an effort to call your mother Mom more often. The only time you call me Dad is when you're exasperated with me, usually for reasons that remain forever a mystery to my aging and addled brain. You need a ride?"

"No, I've got the rental car. I parked right outside in front of the fire plug."

"You're probably safe," he said. "Good night. If I don't see you, have a good trip back and I'll call."

Lisa nodded and left the kitchen. A few seconds later he heard the front door open and close.

Lieberman moved quickly to the bedroom. The sun was definitely starting to come up. He put his weapon in the drawer, locked it, and got undressed. He'd shave when he got up. Lieberman shaved often. He didn't like seeing his father in the mirror. He had gotten along with his father. There had been problems, but the two had gotten along though his father had been sorely disappointed that neither of his two sons had gone to college.

He put his clothes on the chair, moving as quietly as he could, and then climbed into bed under the covers. Bess, accustomed to her husband's unpredictable sleep, which was a result both of his job and his insomnia, rolled on her side.

Lieberman checked the alarm. It was already set for 7:30 A.M. That would give him a few hours of sleep. He was sure he could sleep if he could keep his conversation with Lisa in a small sealed sack in his chest.

If things were as they usually were, Abe would not have bad dreams, not that he couldn't remember Clark Mills dead in the alley. No, he had learned to cope with such images, to turn them into causes. The people were dead. It was Abe's job to find out who had killed them and why. The only thing that still caused him nightmares were brutal murders of children. Fortunately, the last one like that he and Bill had caught was almost a year ago. Now . . . and Abe was asleep.

When Abe Lieberman walked into the T&L Delicatessen at nine-thirty, he was running far behind his plan for the day. First, Bess had turned off the alarm and let him sleep. He had had a solid four hours when his wife finally woke him.

"Kids?" he had asked, sitting up.

"Already took them to school. Lisa and Marvin came and helped them get ready. Something's happened to our daughter," she said, adjusting an earring.

"I noticed."

"I think it's good," she said. "How do I look?"

She was wearing a peach suit with a pearl necklace and pearl earrings. Her still-dark hair was cut short and off her neck the way he liked it.

"Great," he said, getting up. "Meeting?"

"Temple presidents of the North Shore," she said. "Brunch. Now that the temple is in

Skokie, we're North Shore. What can I tell you?"

"Calls?"

"None," she said. "Abe, I've got to run."

They came together, the same height with her heels. Maybe she was even a little taller. He kissed her and he said, "Quick coffee?"

"No time," she said. "Stop and see Maish before you go in. I'm very worried about him, and so is Yetta."

"I'll stop," he said.

He had shaved with the electric razor though it wasn't as close as a blade. No reason it should be. The electric was almost thirty years old. He tried not to look in the mirror when he shaved, but he couldn't resist. There was his father. The depressing thing was that even after he had finished shaving, his father was still in the mirror.

And so he walked into Maish's deli on Devon at the height of the convening of the *Alter Cockers.*

"Nice jacket," said Al Bloombach.

"Matches the pants," said Rosen.

Howie Chen added, "You look like a real goddammit, Abe."

"I appreciate the compliment, gentlemen, and I will try to continue to live up to my present state of sartorial splendor," Abe said, looking around.

252

Except for the Cockers, the place was empty. The breakfast crowd was gone. It was a nice day and people weren't ducking in to get out of the rain, cold, snow, or mad winds. Lieberman moved to his usual booth and Maish came out from behind the counter carrying a bowl, which he placed in front of his brother with a spoon.

"What's this?" Abe asked, looking at the thick tan soupy mixture.

"Oatmeal," said Maish. "Bess called. Said give Abe oatmeal."

"I had something with oats last night," Lieberman said, shaking his head and putting two spoons of sugar into the steaming oatmeal. The sugar did not alter texture or color. "I think I read somewhere you could go into convulsions from an overdose of oats."

"I'll call the paramedics," Maish said, starting to turn.

"Sit, Maish," Abe said. "You can watch to be sure I eat it all and don't pour it someplace unsanitary."

Maish shrugged and slid his 240 pounds into the seat across from his brother. Before his son David's death, he had weighed more than 300.

"Heard Lisa's back," said Bloombach.

"For a few days," Lieberman said, taking a spoon of oatmeal. He had eaten the stuff before and it wasn't so bad. It just wasn't all that good when one was yearning for a lox, onion, and cream cheese omelette. "She's going back today."

Terrell came from the kitchen with a cup and a pot of coffee. He put the cup in front of Abe and poured.

"Talk to the man," Terrell said, nodding at Maish. "He needs some new tires. He's skidding all over the place."

"I'll talk, Terrell. How's it going?"

"Fine," said Terrell. "My ex-wife sent me a card. My son Ben is graduating from high school this summer back in Texas. He's goin' to the University of Texas. First one on either side to go to college."

"It's good to have a son," said Maish. "But watch out for God, Terrell. I told you. He's evil."

"Congratulations, Terrell," Abe said, thinking that oatmeal wouldn't exactly become a staple in his diet but it wasn't as bad as he remembered.

Time moved so damn fast. He remembered Terrell as a kid. Now he was a father with a boy going to college.

Terrell walked back toward the kitchen.

"We're giving Terrell a bachelor party when his son graduates," called Bloombach.

"We considered a graduation party but

Weintraub, that dirty old man, said we'd have more fun at a bachelor party and Terrell qualifies."

Weintraub, eighty-one years old, shook his head knowingly. Weintraub husbanded his smiles, but when he gave one, it was a sincere reward. The other *Alter Cockers* courted his approval. There was, however, no chance that Weintraub would ever suggest a bachelor party.

"I'll be there," said Abe.

"What's that song?" asked Bloombach. "I'll be there in the morning if I live. I'll be there in the morning if I don't get killed."

"Change of subject," said Rosen, and the *Alter Cockers* lowered their collective voice to a level where it would remain for three whole minutes.

"So, Maish?" asked Abe.

"So?"

Today Maish looked more like a bloodhound than a bulldog. He always looked like some kind of sad-faced dog.

Until his son David, Abe's nephew, was murdered a year earlier, everyone called him Nothing-Bothers Maish. It had seemed to be true. It wasn't any longer.

"So, you remember Mickey Gornitz?"

"High school," Maish said without interest.

"His son's been kidnapped." Abe worked

on his oatmeal. "He was working for some bad people and he wants to be a witness against them. They took his kid. They want Mickey to kill himself before they let the kid go. Personally, I don't think they're going to let the kid go. I think we've got to find him."

"So?" asked Maish. "This you're telling me? You're supposed to be arguing with me, telling me to snap out of it, be good old Maish again, stop disrupting religious classes, find a hobby. Avrum, I tried. For a year I tried, but I'm never going to forget or forgive God for what happened to David."

"I'm not going to argue with you, Maish," Lieberman said. "Do what you want to do, what you have to do. Who cares if you start going crazy? Me, your wife, your other son, Bess, those Cockers by the window? Terrell? Do what you have to do, Maish. I could never talk you into anything you didn't want to do."

"Avrum," Maish whispered. "I know who I'm hurting, but I have to curse God. It's all that's keeping me sane."

"Maybe it's what's driving you crazy?" Lieberman finished his coffee. He wanted to check his watch, but he didn't.

"Maybe," Maish said with a shrug. "More oatmeal?"

"A little."

Maish got up, took the bowl, and came

back with a serving even bigger than the first.

"Minor point," said Maish. "But you know what else isn't fair? We're brothers. I hardly eat and I'm fat. You eat like a . . . Florida State lineman and you're a skinny little thing."

"Like Pa," said Lieberman. "You take after Ma's side. Would you be happier if I was fat?"

"No," said Maish. "I'm just making a small point about 'fair.' "

"Don't wait for me to say 'Who said life was fair?' I'm not saying it. I'm a cop. I don't walk into traps that obvious. I want you to see a friend of mine, a psychiatrist."

"Never," said Maish.

"Enjoying your misery too much?"

"You better go to work, Avrum," Maish said, getting up.

"This isn't an ordinary psychiatrist," said Abe. "He lost his wife and little daughter in a car accident. Only daughter. He'll understand. Can it hurt? I'll pay. I'll set it up. I'll even carry you to meet him. No, I'll get Bill to carry you."

"He couldn't do it," said Maish.

"Probably not," agreed Abe standing and facing his brother. "I just happen to have his card with me. Took me an extra ten minutes to find it this morning. Take it. What can it hurt? You can tell him about God. You can

257

get angry in front of him. It's what he's paid for."

"A man who lost his wife and only child?" Maish said, taking the card.

"For Yetta, for me, for whoever but mostly for you. You're my only brother, literally my big brother. See the man. Tell him you're my brother. He'll give you a rate."

"I'll consider." Maish looked at the card. "He's not Jewish."

"No," said Lieberman. "Dr. Mustapha Aziz is an Arab, a devout Muslim. You two should have a lot to talk about."

Abe touched his brother's shoulder and moved past him toward the door where the *Alter Cocker* chorus gave him one last warning,

"Watch out for pickle pockets," Bloombach called.

Weintraub did not smile. It was one of Bloombach's recurring jokes.

"We decided Terrell's bachelor party will be at your house, Lieberman," said Rosen.

"My pleasure," said Lieberman. "And you're all going to get invitations to my grandson's Bar Mitzvah. Come and bring a nice present. He's planning to say something insulting about you, but I think he can be bribed out of it."

"Blackmail," said Howie Chen.

" 'That,' as my granddaughter would say, 'is what Tiggers do best,' " Lieberman said, walking out into the morning and hurrying to his car.

The squad room of the Clark Street station was eerily quiet. Harley Buel and Rene Catolino were the only ones at their desks. Harley, who looked like a school principal complete with rimless glasses, was talking quietly to a thin Hispanic young man in a leather jacket. Harley played his role well. When you had a suspect or reluctant witness who looked like he or she would fall for an interrogation tone of disappointment, you got Harley on the job. People didn't want to disappoint their favorite teacher. Rene was the only woman on the squad. Dark, pretty, maybe a touch hard, she never turned away from a case and she could curse with the best in the squad, though Abe was sure the cursing was just self-defense.

No Hanrahan. Lieberman went to Kearney's office and knocked.

"Come in."

Kearney and Hanrahan sat at the small table. Kearney hardly ever went behind his desk anymore. He was either standing at the window or sitting at the small conference desk unless he was catching a few hours of restless sleep on the less-than-comfortable couch.

Hanrahan's eyes were a little baggy, but he was clean shaven, soaped, and neat. He was drinking coffee.

"Detective Hanrahan has been busy," said Kearney.

Hanrahan held a sheet of paper out to his partner. Lieberman took it. It was a message from Desk Sergeant Nestor Briggs dated the day before and with the time of the call in the right-hand corner, 5:50 P.M. The message was for Hardrock Hanrahan. It read:

COULDN'T COME TO THE PARK. I'M GONNA DO THIS ON MY OWN. NO FREE BUS TICKETS. NO COPS TAKING ME TO BE SURE I LEAVE. I'LL CALL YOU FROM GEORGIA SO YOU KNOW I'M NOT LYING.

The message was from Clark Mills.

"Son of a —" Lieberman started.

"The murder weapon is Chinese," said Hanrahan. "Lab tech knows all about them. Old Weapon. There's a name scratched on the handle. No prints. Name is in Korean. Weapon was standard issue to North Korean officers."

"Looks like a Korean War souvenir," said Kearney. "Whoever fired it was lucky it didn't explode in his hand."

Lieberman wanted a cup of coffee, a *good*

cup of coffee, not the stuff that was brewing in the squad room in the seldom-cleaned ancient coffeemaker. He wanted to sit, drink, close his eyes, and not be bothered by the world in general and his job and family in particular, and he had good reason.

"I may know a suspect," said Lieberman. "May be nothing, but it's probably worth checking."

"Well?" the captain asked.

"I'm probably wrong," said Lieberman. "I'll check it out. If it looks like something, I'll follow through."

"See the papers this morning?" Kearney asked.

Lieberman now felt like sitting down. Was he feeling his age or the weight caused by his suspicion? Lieberman, in fact, was not the oldest detective in the department. O'Neill on the West Side was almost sixty-five and came in early every day and was the last to leave at night. Some people said O'Neill worked harder every year just to prove he could handle the load. Lieberman thought it was easier. The department and job were his life. Then there was Albert "Big Bells" Bertinelli in the Organized Crime Division. Big Bells might be even older than O'Neill. Now that the old mobsters, whom he knew personally on a first-name basis, were dying off, Big Bells wasn't quite as essential, but as long as there were a few left and a second and third generation coming up, Bertinelli was too valuable to push into retirement. There were others. At the moment, Lieberman didn't feel like pulling them up for scrutiny. There would come a time soon when some sixty-year-old detective would be thinking or saying "Lieberman up on Clark is a hell of a lot older than I am."

Lieberman sat at the table knowing that Kearney was talking but not really hearing.

"I don't know how they got it," Kearney was saying when Lieberman forced himself to concentrate on the captain's words. "My guess is it's a leak in the department."

"Maybe a good reporter," said Hanrahan.

"Maybe," agreed Kearney. "But I like to think the worst so it doesn't come up behind you and kick you in the ass when you're not looking."

Hanrahan took the *Sun-Times* from Kearney and passed it to Lieberman. The paper was folded to page two. On the lower half of the page was a story and a photograph of a smiling young black man in a football uniform. The headline read: "Ex-Football Star Murdered. Clark Mills Was Living Homeless."

"Long headline," said Lieberman, handing the paper back to the captain.

"Hey, they had half a page to fill," said Kearney. "You've got a suspect?"

"Maybe," said Lieberman.

"Go for it, both of you. Now. Shit. Druggies, drunks, and homeless drifters get murdered every day and don't even make a paragraph in the papers."

"Clark Mills finally gets his moment of fame," murmured Lieberman.

Hanrahan looked at his partner. Hanrahan didn't want a half page in the *Sun-Times* if he died on duty. He didn't want a headline that said: "Detective Hardrock Hanrahan, Ex-Football Star, Found shot in Sewage Canal." They'd probably use some ancient file photograph of him in a Southern Illinois uniform a thousand years ago. Hanrahan had a good smile back then, like Clark Mills.

The bags under Lieberman's eyes were heavier than usual and there was no doubt that the man was showing signs that some heavy weights were coming down on his thin shoulders.

"Let's go." Hanrahan got up.

"Let's," Lieberman agreed joining him.

"Nothing new from Carbin on the Gornitz kid," said Kearney. "Carbin called early. May want you to go talk to Gornitz again. Keeps changing his mind about you, Abe. Now he thinks you said something that's got Gornitz thinking of staying alive."

"Maybe," said Lieberman following his partner to the door.

Kearney turned his head and looked at a plaque on the wall. Lieberman had the feeling that the younger man wasn't thinking of the glory days when the plaque had been awarded to him for being the outstanding detective on the force for that year. Lieberman felt Kearney was looking through that plaque into forever and the way things might have been. With all he was carrying, Lieberman would have been willing to talk to Kearney about his problems, but it wouldn't happen. Kearney wouldn't open up, probably wouldn't even admit it to himself. Maybe a time would come.

When they were back in the squad room, Rene Catolino was having a cup of coffee at her desk with Detective Lorber, the weight lifter, who had come in and was listening, smiling, and trying to hide his feelings of lust for his fellow officer.

"So," said Catolino, "this guy calls and says he'll tell me where the perp is hiding if I promise he'll remain monogamous. So, straightface, I said, 'Sir, that is completely up to you.' "

Lorber laughed, loud, much more than the tale was worth.

"I'd say the odds are even that Muscles will get through to our tough lady," Hanrahan said as they moved toward the squad room door.

"I've got more faith in her," said Lieberman. "I'll say he has one chance in a hundred."

"Of getting to her?" asked Hanrahan.

"Of getting *away* from her."

It wasn't until they were in the car, Lieberman driving, that Hanrahan said, "I got a tip yesterday, a little vague like the Chinese gentleman who gave it to me . . ."

"From racy to racist," said Lieberman.

"I'm beginning to think there are no limits to the tortures the Oriental mind can think up," said Hanrahan.

"Sounds like one of Cary Grant's lines in *Gunga Din*," said Lieberman. "God, I love that movie. So, your Chinese informant . . ."

They were heading toward Lake Michigan on Devon. Traffic was late-morning normal and slow so they could have made good time, but Lieberman was crawling, as if he were in no hurry to get where he had to go.

"I'll cut to the heart," said Hanrahan. "I'm gonna need a few hours on something soft where I can take a nap somewhere quiet real soon. I called a detective I know in Washington."

"Cunningham," Lieberman guessed.

"Cunningham it was," said Hanrahan, realizing that in his state of exhaustion, he was starting to talk like his father. "Well, I ask Cunningham, who I'm pleased to say was on the midnight–to–nine A.M. shift, if he'd check out a few things. He says 'Yes,' and calls me back in a couple of hours while I've got my head on my desk and my eyes closed imagining Kim coming back with that Korean gun and shooting Clark Mills."

"Didn't happen," said Lieberman.

"I know. I was dreaming. Cunningham tells me that Matt Gornitz Firth had no friends at all in the neighborhood where he lived with his mother. He had gone to private schools since his parents divorced when he was twelve. So, I call the private school Matthew is about to graduate from, but I wait till this morning. I talk to the headmaster. They call them 'headmasters' in those schools, Rabbi."

"I know," said Lieberman. "That's because they're in charge of your head."

"Reasonably funny," said Hanrahan, "but I find it hard to judge. I'm a wee bit on the weary side. Well, the headmaster knows every kid. Only one hundred fifty students in the school. We had a couple of thousand at Chicago Vocational when I went there. Principal

266

couldn't have known anybody, probably didn't want to."

"Proceed," said Lieberman. "You're wandering a little, Father Murphy."

Lieberman turned north on Sheridan moving slowly past the line-up of bookstores, fast-food delis, and pizza parlors, CD shops and other businesses that catered to the faculty and students at Loyola University, which stretched to the east right to the lake.

"Headmaster asks questions about Matt Firth, gets me to promise to call him as soon as we know anything. I promise and scrawl a note to myself to keep the promise. It seems Matt doesn't have many friends at his prep school though the headmaster assures me that everyone there who isn't an atheist is praying for him. So, I push him on the friend business and find out that not only does our kidnap victim have a friend, his roommate for four years, but the roommate did not return to school today when everyone was due back."

"Roommate have a name?"

"David Donald Wilhite," said Hanrahan as Lieberman made a left through traffic onto Lunt and slowed down even more as he searched for a parking space.

"Interesting," said Lieberman.

"I find it so," said Hanrahan, knowing he

wouldn't chase the voice of his father without at least two solid hours of sleep. "It gets even more interesting."

"How?" Abe prompted.

"Got a description of Wilhite. Tall for his age, maybe a little overweight. Smart. Old man's a stocks and bonds whiz-bang. I call the Wilhite house and talk to Mom. She sounds like prep school herself. She also sounds like she's not all that surprised to hear from a cop. She says David was staying with a friend and told her he might be a day or two late for school because he and his friend and the friend's mother were going on a short trip. However, Junior Wilhite has been known to listen to a different piper and lose his way a bit, according to Mom, who assured me her boy was as close to Mother Teresa as a human could get. I gave Mom a tale of terror befitting the Druids and got her to one-day a photograph of Junior Wilhite immediately. She added that she was sure Junior was fine, that he had called her last night. I told her for certain he was okay, and sure he was, I agreed with her."

"Matt Gornitz," Lieberman said, finding a space.

"That's the name our David Donald Wilhite gave his mom, Rabbi. The friend he's taking a trip with under the watchful eye of

Matthew's mother."

"Proud of yourself, Father Murph?"

"A little, maybe, but we've got a way to go. I checked back with Cunningham. He checked Juvenile in five states. Donald David Wilhite has been in trouble with the law since he was thirteen. Got out of everything with good lawyers, maybe his parents paying a bit of a bribe here and there."

"Trouble?" asked Lieberman.

"Joyriding in a stolen car, cocaine possession, assault."

"The assault is interesting."

"Remember, he's a big boy. Smart. I'm thinkin' maybe this situation is more perplexing than the Troubles."

"You're sounding like your father," said Lieberman.

"I know. I need some sleep. I told you. There's a kicker, Rabbi. When I figured we were done talking, Cunningham asks why I didn't get this information from the other policeman. I ask, 'What other policeman?' and he says, 'The one who called yesterday and asked the same questions.' I ask for the cop's name and Cunningham says he has it somewhere. Takes him a few seconds and he comes back with 'August Vogel.' Vogel left no number."

"State attorney?" asked Lieberman.

"Nobody by the name Vogel," said Hanrahan. "I checked."

"Interesting."

They were out of the car now and heading across the street for an apartment building. They were less than a block from where the body of Clark Mills had been found and maybe half a block or so from where Hanrahan had found the North Korean handgun.

Hanrahan didn't ask questions as they moved to the apartment building. The hallway they entered was brightly lit by a twenty-four-hour bulb and protected by a video camera. Lieberman found the bell and pressed it.

"Who is it?" came a wavering female voice.

"Abe Lieberman," he said.

"I'm not feeling well," said Rita Blitzstein. "I had to stay home from work."

Which was exactly what Lieberman had counted on. Had she gone to work, he had another stop to make that might have worked just as well.

"Just take a few minutes," Lieberman said.

The wait was long with a hum on the intercom to let the two men know the connection hadn't been cut.

"A few minutes," she said, and the door buzzed and clicked.

The detectives walked up the two flights of stairs and found the door. Even though she was now expecting two policemen, she had not opened the door and didn't do so till they knocked and again identified themselves. Only then did she open the locks and let them in.

She was a mess, hardly recognizable as the woman he had spoken to at the T&L. Her dark hair was uncombed. There was a definite smudge on her glasses. She wore a robe heavier than the weather and the heat of the apartment called for.

The detectives went in and looked around. The apartment was neat, expensively decorated in whites and blacks, very modern, not to either detective's taste.

"Sorry about your illness," Lieberman said, standing to face the woman. "What's wrong?"

"I'm just sick," she said. "Sometimes a person is just sick."

"Have you read the papers this morning, listened to the news, watched television?" asked Lieberman.

"No," she said.

"Mind if I ask 'Why?' "

"I'm sick."

"Rita, Clark Mills, the man who threatened you on the street day before yesterday, is dead."

Lieberman took the folded-up newspaper Kearney had given him and handed it to her.

271

"I was eating crackers," she said, not seeming to absorb the information, not looking at the newspaper in her hand. "Would you like some?"

"No, thanks," Abe and Bill said together.

Rita went to sit down on the chrome-and-white leather sofa. The detectives weren't invited to join her but they did, sitting on furniture that was as uncomfortable as it looked.

"Rita," Lieberman said gently, "do you know who killed Clark Mills?"

"No," she said emphatically, shaking her head.

"Want to know how he was killed?" he asked.

"No."

"Then maybe you'll be interested in knowing that he was leaving the city today, if he had lived," said Lieberman.

Rita looked up in disbelief from detective to detective. "That's not true."

"It's true." Hanrahan came in. "He called me last night, said he'd be gone today. I believe him."

"So do I," said Abe. "Can we get you something?"

"Crackers are dry. Maybe some water."

Hanrahan rose and moved toward the kitchen that could be seen beyond the open door of the dining area.

"In the refrigerator," she said. "Not the tap."

"Your father was in the Korean War," said Lieberman.

"Yes," Rita answered.

"He bring back any trophies? Guns, flags, you know."

"I don't remember."

"I'm going to make a statement," he said softly. "You don't have to respond. I believe you or your father killed Clark Mills last night in the alley across the street."

Hanrahan was discreetly taking his time in the kitchen. He had caught a sign from Lieberman, almost imperceptible, that he wanted to be alone with the woman.

"No," she said. "Was he really leaving?"

"He was."

"Oh my God," she said, looking at the newspaper in her hand and scanning the article on Mills the paper was folded to reveal. "He had a family. He was famous."

"He was a man," said Lieberman. "He could have been better, but he could have been worse."

She looked away and said, "Ten years ago I was raped. I didn't report it. I was . . . I needed a lot of help and some hospital time. My parents were at my side, paid for everything. Eventually I came out and climbed back."

"And I understand that you've done very well," said Lieberman.

"I thought so until the other night," she said. "Now I'm afraid to go out, afraid to go to work. He's dead, but there are others. There'll always be others."

Hanrahan returned with a glass of water and handed it to the woman, who took it with a cracked-lip, vacant smile.

"Rita, I'm afraid we're going to ask you to come with us to answer a few questions," Lieberman said gently.

"I know the law," she said. "I don't have to go. I don't have to talk to you."

"We can get a warrant for you as a possible witness to murder," said Lieberman.

Hanrahan continued to stand though he took several steps back to give the woman room. She downed the water in one long gulp and closed her eyes.

"I didn't kill him," she said.

"And you don't and didn't have a gun in this apartment?" Lieberman asked, knowing he was walking thin, but she was still only a possible witness. If he was going to charge her, he would need more evidence, and then he would come back with a warrant and deliver the Miranda.

"No," she said, putting down the empty glass and looking at it.

"You know, don't you?" asked Lieberman. He had not said what it was he thought she knew. It could have been a thousand and one things, but there was no doubt for either one of them.

"Nothing more to say," she said. "Sorry he's dead. No, he did this to me. He set me back a decade. I'm not sorry. He was just going somewhere else to terrorize other people and eventually hurt some woman like me. I'm not sorry he's dead."

"Maybe you want to think about it," said Lieberman. "Maybe you'll be interested in talking to his mother. We're going to invite her to come and take the body back to Georgia after the autopsy."

"No," said Rita. "Why should I want to talk to his mother? Everybody has a mother."

"Suit yourself," Lieberman said, rising. "Thanks for talking to us. If you don't mind, Detective Hanrahan has a few more questions about what happened that night and some of the other people in the neighborhood who might have been confronted by Clark Mills."

"I don't know anyone in the neighborhood," Rita said. "And this isn't a neighborhood. It's houses and apartments where people generally leave each other alone."

"Indulge me," Lieberman said. "Your father and I have known each other a long time."

The woman did not see the look between the two men, but Hanrahan gave that almost imperceptible nod that showed he understood.

As soon as he was in the hall, Lieberman moved ahead quickly, down the stairs and across the street. Hanrahan's job was to keep Rita Blitzstein talking and away from the phone. The second he was in the car Abe radioed for a phone number and then dialed it. There was no answer. He hit the button after six rings and called the station to ask that a couple of uniforms go to Robert Blitzstein's office in his children's furniture shop in Wilmette. They were to bring him in immediately for questioning in the Clark Mills murder. They were to keep him from making any calls, and no one was to talk to them.

Hanrahan came out fifteen minutes later, enough time for the uniforms, if they hurried, to get to Blitzstein. Abe hoped they had hurried. Hanrahan got in the car with a tired grunt.

"You kept her long enough," Lieberman said.

"Wasn't easy, but from deep inside my old man, the Irish charm burst like . . . gotta stop talking like this."

They drove back to the station quickly.

"David Donald Wilhite," said Lieberman.

"David Donald Wilhite," Hanrahan repeated. "Could be nothing. Could be Stashall worked something out with him. Could be he did it on his own. Could be lots of things, but we look for Wilhite. I got more than a feeling the kid's in Chicago, and one way or the other way my boy, our David, has some answers."

"It's a lead," said Lieberman.

"Maybe a good one," said Hanrahan. "Want to handle Mr. Blitzstein by yourself? I need a few hours on the sofa at home."

"Make it the rest of the day if you like," said Lieberman. "I'll get someone in the squad to take the interrogation room window."

"A tempting offer."

"I'm not always this generous." Lieberman pulled into the small parking lot behind the station. "Maybe I've been taken by the muse."

"Escape," said Hanrahan. "Take the advice of your priest. Muses lead you astray. I know."

Hanrahan and Lieberman got out of the car and Hanrahan headed for his own. Lieberman went through the back door of the station, passed a few uniforms, went up the stairs and into the squad room, which was relatively busy. The people he would have liked to back him were tied up or out of the office. He could ask Kearney or a uniform, but it would go down better with a detective who could put in for decent overtime if he had to testify.

The only one who was there without a witness or suspect next to his desk in the middle of the room was Tony Munoz. Tony was big. Tony was tough. Tony was nearly fearless, which was a bad idea in a cop. Tony also lost control, let his sense of justice kick in and come out with a rage directed at a suspect or reluctant witness. He had been disciplined three times, suspended once, but Tony was the youngest member of the squad. There was a chance he would change. Everyone knew Tony would take a bullet for you and that if he thought there was any chance of tracking down a felony, he would stay with it without asking for overtime and working double shifts.

"Tony," Lieberman said, approaching the young man's desk. "You got a minute to give me a hand?"

"You got it," Munoz said, putting aside the report he was working on and rising.

"I need you behind the mirror to witness an interrogation."

That, Tony knew, might mean testifying in court down the road, but he didn't hesitate and didn't ask where Hanrahan was.

"Let's go," he said.

And they went, Tony to the room behind

the interrogation room window and Lieberman to the interrogation room. Blitzstein was already there sitting behind the table, his back to the wall facing whoever sat across from him and the mirror. He kept glancing over Lieberman's shoulder as they talked.

"How are you, Bob?" Lieberman said before Blitzstein could ask for a lawyer.

"I'm fine," said the thin, gaunt man whose face and movements Lieberman knew well from dozens of temple committee meetings.

Lieberman and Bess had bought Lisa's baby bedroom furniture from Blitzstein when Blitzstein was a very young man working for his father. Later Lisa and Todd had bought furniture for Lieberman's grandchildren. Bob Blitzstein had given them a very generous discount.

"I just came back from talking to Rita," Lieberman said, sitting across from the man. "She told me."

"No." Blitzstein shook his head.

"Yes," said Lieberman. "Your daughter is distraught, torn between loyalty, anger, and an upbringing by you and your wife that taught her to do the right thing."

Blitzstein looked as if he wanted to say something. His thin white fingers were folded on the table in front of him. The tabletop was a mess. It had been thrown around by cops and criminals. It looked as if it had been through some major violence. Suspects and witnesses did not like the table. Before Blitzstein could get out a word, Lieberman stopped him by saying "I'm going to read you your rights. When I'm done and you sign the form saying you understand, I'll listen to you. I want to listen to you, Bob. I want to help."

"This is —" Blitzstein shouted, rising from the chair.

Lieberman found the performance sad. He had seen much better righteous indignation from street kids and drug dealers who had done each other in with large guns at close range. Lieberman read the rights at an even pace, pausing to ask Blitzstein, who had resumed his seat, if he understood. He nodded his head yes the first time and Lieberman asked him to say yes or no. When he was done, Lieberman passed the sheet to Blitzstein along with a click pen. Blitzstein looked at it and signed.

While Blitzstein was writing, Lieberman said gently, "Did he come after you in the alley, Bob?"

Blitzstein looked up and pushed the paper back. His eyes were moist and his hand shaking. "Can I ask for a lawyer now?"

"You can," said Lieberman. "May I say something before you decide?"

"Speak." Blitzstein rubbed his thin neck with his left hand, a nervous habit Lieberman had noted at many a meeting.

"Clark Mills was leaving Chicago today," said Lieberman. "He called my partner, told us where he was going. He wasn't going to be a threat to anyone anymore."

"That doesn't change anything," Blitzstein said, forgetting about asking for a lawyer. "My only child was set back ten years and I don't know if she can ever recover. You have an only child Abe, a girl. What would you do?"

"What did you do, Bob?" Lieberman asked.

"You know."

"I think things'll go easier if you talk to me. You had provocation. You were distraught, maybe temporarily out of your mind. The gun is yours, Bob. I recognize it. You showed it to me once."

Nothing of the sort had ever happened. Lieberman held his breath.

"I showed it to a lot of people," said Blitzstein. "I was proud of what I did in Korea. That's the forgotten war. All that's left of it is *M*A*S*H* reruns. I saw . . . what does it matter."

"You killed Clark Mills," Lieberman said. He didn't ask.

"I don't care if he was a football star, if he had a family, if he was leaving town. He destroyed my baby. The goddamn city is full of people like that, and the police don't do anything about it."

"You admit that you shot Clark Mills in that alley?" Lieberman asked.

"Yes," said Blitzstein. "Forty years ago when I was a kid, I shot North Koreans and went back behind the lines for a hot meal, a few hours' sleep, and a beer or two. I'm too old for what I did last night. I'm still shaking, Abe. God help me, I killed a man. I told myself I was killing an animal, but it was a man."

Blitzstein's head hung down. He bit his tongue to keep from crying.

"I think you better call a lawyer now, Bob. Don't say anything more."

"Yes. I'll call my sister. She'll get a lawyer. I'll lose the business, go to jail, be in all the newspapers. Abe, I love kids. You know that."

"I know it," Lieberman said, acting as if he understood the relevance of the remark, which, at some level, he did.

"I did the right thing," Blitzstein said, lifting his head. "I'd —"

"Stop talking, Bob," Lieberman said. "You want a phone?"

"A phone?"

282

"To call your sister, whoever you want."

Blitzstein nodded yes and Lieberman leaned over the table to touch his shoulder. Lieberman did understand what the quivering man in front of him had done and why. Lieberman had done worse, choosing to act as God, determine life and death for people who he thought deserved immediate extinction instead of a trial and a prison term that would get them back out on the street. Lieberman had exacted old-fashioned revenge more than once. Lieberman understood.

Lieberman waved a finger at the mirror to signal Munoz that the interview was over. Then he led the disoriented Blitzstein out and to his desk. He backed away to give Blitzstein some privacy in the noisy, now-crowded squad room.

"Lieberman," Munoz said with a grin, "that was the fastest turnover I've ever seen."

"You're still young." Lieberman watched Blitzstein pause, probably forgetting his sister's phone number, and then start to dial. "The man wanted to talk. He wants the world to forgive him. He wants me to forgive him. He wants the members of our temple to forgive him. He thinks I'm his friend."

"Are you?" asked Munoz.

"In a way," said Lieberman.

"Righteous," said Munoz. "Like me. Turn

him over if he did the felony, even if he's your best friend."

Lieberman said nothing. Not only had he exacted his own sentences on more than one occasion, he had arranged for the unrighteous and the unholy to walk free when it promised a more long-range payoff down the calender.

"You lock him up while I fill out the papers?" Lieberman asked, not wanting to face Blitzstein, not now.

"Sure."

Lieberman walked to Hanrahan's desk. There was an envelope on it, a special delivery one-day. The return address was to Elizabeth Wilhite in Rockville, Maryland. Lieberman opened the package and found himself looking at the face of a young man. The young man was pudgy with straight blond hair. David Donald Wilhite was wearing a suit. David Donald Wilhite was wearing a smile. Lieberman didn't care for the suit or tie with little clocks on it. He didn't care for the smile either.

He sat at his partner's desk and single-finger-typed a simple note as Blitzstein finished his call and was led away from the desk. He needed Munoz's hand on his arm to keep from stumbling. Lieberman would visit him later. Now he composed a note asking if a David Donald Wilhite were registered at the hotel or motel. He asked if whoever received the fax of the notice and the photograph would check with the staff to see if anyone recognized him. The young man, he explained, was wanted for questioning in a possible felony. A computer downtown would check the name with the computers of every hotel and motel in and around the city. Circulating the faxed photograph would take longer. The big hotels could get the photograph on their computer screens, but that covered only a small number of possible places Wilhite might be staying.

When he was finished, Lieberman wove his way out of the squad room and walked down to communications and dispatch where the fax machine was. He sent the copy of the photo downtown. If they weren't backed up at the moment, it would go out in minutes. The cost would be more than a few hundred dollars, maybe much more. Abe would worry about that later. Now he had a kidnapper to catch and at least one life to be saved.

He vaguely heard the dispatcher on the radio behind him and the hum of the computer in the corner. Maybe he should have been pleased with how quickly they had put this homicide into the black. Rutgers would be happy. It would look good to the brass and the media, but Abe wasn't pleased. He desperately wanted a cup of coffee and a big, fat lox and cream cheese sandwich on a garlic bagel with a thick slice of sweet onion. He decided not to have the sandwich before the faxing was even halfway through. He would settle for the coffee and a bagel with sugar-free jam from the Bagel Barn.

He stood at the machine trying to remember the name of Bob Blitzstein's dead wife. Not only could he not remember her name, he couldn't remember her face.

CHAPTER 10

"Mikhail Piniescu, the driveway repair saint, is back in business," Hanrahan said when he checked into the station a little after noon. "Just checked with the state attorney's office."

"Can't keep a bad man down," Lieberman said, offering his partner a Life Saver.

Hanrahan took it.

They were at Hanrahan's desk with Lieberman sucking a mint and standing with arms folded trying to come back from a distant thought.

"Seems Mike had enough sense and money to hire Herberts," said Hanrahan. "Kid he was up against in the state attorney's office was ready to deal after five minutes with Herberts. Misdemeanor fraud. Five-hundred-dollar fine. Probation. Judge said, 'Fine.' Mike walked and we've already got a call in from downtown that an old lady on the South Side talked to good old Mike and he convinced her that her roof was dangerous and needed immediate replacement, four thousand bucks. Lady says she'll think about it and ask her grandson. Mike says she has to take the special offer now or . . . The lady is about to celebrate her eighty-fourth birthday, is almost blind, Black, a devout Baptist living on Social Security and a very small pension, but she insists that she has to talk to her grandson. Our friend to the old homeowners of our metropolis says he simply can't let the offer stay open. It's a one-day special. Lady says, 'Then no thank you.' Mike gets unpleasant, puts his hands on the lady. She has lived a life and a half of purse snatchers, muggers, and worse. Mike has met his match. She starts screaming and scratching at his face. Mike shoves her, breaks her leg, and runs to his van and drives into the sunset, no posse on his tail."

"I've got it," Lieberman said over the hubbub in the squad room where a beautiful, tall blonde with the figure of a model was being interviewed by Lorber. "How's the old lady?"

"Looks like a long recovery, but she should be okay," said Hanrahan. "Problem is she couldn't see well enough to be sure it was anything but a white man. M.O. is different enough . . ."

"Roofs instead of driveways," said Lieberman.

". . . different enough and he has Herberts in the wings waiting to come out and do his act."

The blonde with Lorber looked around as she talked. The witnesses and perps, male and female, were trying not to watch her. The unfamiliar and uninitiated were making the usual comments to detectives who didn't bother to tell them that the beautiful blonde was Ivan Sorno, a transvestite prostitute who was HIV positive. Ivana, as he called himself, simply couldn't stop. Most of the detectives felt sorry for Ivan, but they felt sorrier for his victims.

Lieberman told Hanrahan about the fax and photo of David Donald Wilhite he had sent out. They checked. No identification had been made.

"Some good news, Abe," said Hanrahan. "My son Michael called this morning before I hit the bed. He and Holly are doing fine. Mike is sober. They want me to come visit them, with Iris."

"Great."

"With you?"

"Maish is almost suicidal. Lisa doesn't know what she wants. The Bar Mitzvah is coming in a month, and we're dipping deep in the bank to make it happen. I dream about pastrami and chopped liver sandwiches, and I need a vacation."

"Sounds good," said Hanrahan.

"Couldn't be better. You wanna see Gornitz with me?"

"No, you do better without me. I'll keep looking for the elusive young David Donald Wilhite. Should we go have a talk with Driveway Mike?"

"Give him a day to worry. Late lunch at the T&L?"

"Two?" asked Hanrahan.

The blond transvestite had suddenly risen and bolted for the squad room door, a move destined for failure, particularly in a tight dress and silver high heels, but he ran with a yelp. Everyone watched as the momentarily stunned Lorber finally jumped out of his chair and started after the transvestite just as Ivan, looking quite feminine, had reached the door.

"Watch where you grab her," called a suspect.

Everyone who wasn't crying or worrying about their own troubles laughed. Even a few cops.

Lorber was out the door. The sound of feminine screaming came through the squad room door as it snapped shut.

"I've got a stop to make after Gornitz," Lieberman said. "I'll let you know what's going on at Maish's."

Lieberman moved out of the squad room and Hanrahan sat thinking whether he should have said anything about the call from Iris. She had called this morning after he got up. No, the truth was that her call had awakened him. He probably would have slept a few more hours, maybe the whole day. But Iris had called. She had thought over what her father and Woo had said, had decided that they might be right but that she was prepared to marry Bill whenever he wished. The former Catholic priest and present Unitarian minister who had agreed to marry them was ready when they were. Bill had told Iris that he wasn't sure that her father and Woo were wrong. Iris had not commented. They both said they loved each other, and Bill said he would call her later.

"William," said Iris.

"Yes."

"Will things really be better in a year? The longer we wait, the more time Mr. Woo will have to pressure my father and the more time my father has to make me feel guilty. I would prefer not to wait a year."

"Holy mother," he said. "You're not that different from Irish Catholics."

"I can ask them to meet at the restaurant tonight," she said. "Tell them that you have something more to say."

"You're not worried about . . . the way I've been behaving?"

"Very worried," she said. "There will be something else to worry about in a year. That is life."

"I think I'd better go see Woo," he had said. "I don't think it's polite to ask someone to come to your turf to say you're thinking of breaking a deal."

"That would be a good idea, William."

He loved when she called him William. He had hung up. Now he wondered why he had not told Lieberman. Inspiration struck him. What about bringing Lieberman with him to see Woo? Abe would probably be a match for Woo. Besides, it would be an interesting encounter. He would think about it and ask his partner later.

Now he would wonder who had called Detective Cunningham about David Donald Wilhite before Hanrahan.

There had been no one in the small waiting room when Maish arrived. If the office of Mustapha Aziz had been any farther than Skokie, Maish would probably not have gone. He expected little from this. In a way, he was humoring his brother. Maybe, in a very small way, he was curious. The office was on Skokie Boulevard not far from the Old Orchard

Shopping Center. It was a modest yellow brick building called Mason-Wright Office Courtyard. The building was two stories high and there were no vacancies.

Maish had located the office and entered the unlocked door. Aziz was on the first floor.

There were photographs on the yellow walls of the waiting room. All of the photographs were of a distinctly foreign city or town — a marketplace, Arabs stopping on the street to look with suspicion at the camera, mountains rising in the distance behind a minaret. Maish was decidedly uncomfortable. He considered simply leaving, but the inner office door opened and a man stepped out. The man was no more than forty, dark, modestly built, and wearing what appeared to be a sincere smile. His suit was dark and his tie was neatly knotted.

"I, obviously, am Mustapha Aziz," the man said, holding out his hand.

"And I can be no one but Morris Lieberman. I'll call you Dr. Aziz. You call me Maish. We'll both be as comfortable as we can be."

"Won't you come in, Maish," Aziz said.

Maish followed the man into the inner office. He glanced around, thankful that there was no couch. If he had been asked to lie on a couch, Maish would have left. There was a desk, paneled walls, degrees and certificates on the walls, and a bookcase. There were also four matching green chairs with arms, in a circle in front of the desk.

"Pick one," said Aziz.

"I could use two," Maish said, selecting a chair and easing into it.

"Perhaps if you return, I will find one for you."

"*If*," Maish said warily.

Aziz hitched up his trousers and sat facing Maish. Maish didn't like people hitching up their trousers.

"I have insurance," Maish said.

"Good," said Aziz. "I'll get the information when we conclude our session."

"This isn't a session," said Maish. "I told my brother I'd talk to you."

"When we conclude our talk then," Aziz replied.

Then came silence.

"I consider your brother a friend," said Aziz. "He was very helpful to me when my wife and daughter died."

Maish shifted his considerable weight uneasily and watched the smiling man. "I'm a Jew," he said.

"That fact has not escaped my notice," said Aziz. "I am, obviously, an Arab. What is less obvious is that I am also a Moslem and what is even less obvious is that before I became a citizen of the United States I was an Israeli."

"A Palestinian," said Maish.

"No, an Israeli," said Aziz. "There are many of us."

"Your wife and —" Maish began and then stopped.

"Drunken driver downtown," said Aziz. "We were coming home from a Saturday afternoon concert at Orchestra Hall. My daughter died instantly. My wife was unconscious till she died the next day. I was unhurt."

"This is none of my business," said Maish.

"I know about your son and unborn grandchild," said Aziz. "Your brother informed me."

More silence.

"What happened to him?" Maish asked. "The driver who killed your family."

"Her," Aziz corrected. "The drunken driver was a woman. She survived. Her license was taken away and because she was old, she was given a very light sentence, a lecture, and a warning. She lives still and I understand she has twice more been arrested for drunken driving without a license. She gets no younger and the judges get no more harsh."

"You wanted her dead, didn't you?" asked Maish.

Aziz shrugged. "It crossed my mind unbidden," he said. "I found myself daydreaming about violent and just destructions of the woman who was white and without real remorse. I tried to return to work but found my mind wandering and even found myself disliking my patients for coming to me with their small problems while I tried to deal with what had happened. I asked God. He did not answer."

"Yes," said Maish.

"Now," said Aziz, "I have revealed myself. Tell me about your son if you would."

"Your mind won't wander?" asked Maish.

"I will never forget what has happened," said Aziz. "But I find that I can function and that there are those I can sometimes delude myself that I am helping. From time to time, I am even convinced that I am helping them and, by some illogical and logical extension, helping myself to survive."

"Yes," Maish said with a sigh. "Well, it was a cold night, a very cold night . . ."

Gornitz had insisted that his old friend Abe Lieberman could see him whenever Lieberman wanted to do so. Carbin had balked. Gornitz had insisted. And now Lieberman was at the hotel sitting on the lumpy sofa with a cup of coffee in his hand. He was facing

Gornitz, who looked more haggard each day.

The state attorney's men were both outside the door, and the woman from the day before and a different man were sitting at a table in the corner pretending to carry on a conversation.

"They tell me they're closing in on where Stashall may have my son," Gornitz said, leaning toward Abe and whispering. "Are they?"

Lieberman shook his head no.

"I knew it," Gornitz said nervously, tapping his thighs with the palms of both hands. "Abe, I've got no choice here. I've got to take the chance. I've got to take myself out. Even if I refuse to testify now, Stashall'll have to get me on the streets and I won't have any protection. If he's gonna kill Matt, he'll do it either way. I know that."

Lieberman drank more of the bitter brew of some cut-rate instant brand from the nearest supermarket and then whispered to Gornitz while the woman from the state attorney's office stood up. Lieberman talked fast as the woman approached.

"Mr. Carbin said there were to be no secrets," she said almost apologetically.

"We were talking about sexual dysfunction," said Lieberman. "It's up close and personal at our age."

"No secrets, Detective," she said.

Lieberman shrugged and looked at Gornitz.

"Do what you have to do," said Mickey. "I'm talking big here. I'm talking, for God's sake, about killing myself. I don't even know if I'd be able to do it. I'm not a brave man, Abe. Numbers I know. Killing myself I don't know. But for my son . . ."

"You want to talk some basketball?" Lieberman asked.

"Why not?" Mickey said with a shrug. "Watched the Bulls yesterday. Beat the Sonics. Brand kept hitting from the inside. He had — I don't know — forty points."

"Mickey Gornitz can't remember an exact number?" Lieberman said with a smile, putting the rest of his coffee down.

"Mickey Gornitz is in a state of nearly constant panic. I don't think I'm up to talk. Sorry, Abe. Maybe later. Maybe tomorrow."

Lieberman got up and so did Gornitz. The two men shook hands.

"Hold on, Mickey," said Lieberman.

"I wish I believed in God enough to pray."

"Listen, I go to the temple with my wife almost every Friday night and all the holidays. I pray. I don't know if anyone's listening. I don't know if I want to pray to a God who'd solve my problems and screw up someone else's life in the process, but I'll tell you something, Mickey. I pray and it makes me feel better. I don't ask for much and never for myself. If there's a trick, that might be it. I'm hitting about fifty-fifty with that plan. It doesn't hurt."

"It's Friday," Mickey said. "You gonna pray for me?"

"During a silent reading," said Lieberman. "I'll put in a good word for you."

"It's fifty-fifty," Gornitz said, trying a smile. "What have I got to lose?"

Lieberman was barely in the hall when the woman from inside the room followed him out.

"What did you whisper to him?" she asked politely.

"Sexual dysfunction," Lieberman said.

"Yours or his?" she asked.

"The answer to that I'll take to the grave," Lieberman said with a smile. "Now, we'd better stop the questions because I might make a flattering sexist remark which would be apropos at this point and which you might be forced to report to Mr. Carbin."

The woman shook her head and tried to hide a grin. "Go on."

"I'm gone," Lieberman replied.

He went to a Vietnamese restaurant across from the hotel, ordered a Vietnamese iced coffee to wash away the taste of instant coffee, and called the station. Nestor Briggs told him there was one call. God was already listening. It was from the person Abe was planning to call when he finished his coffee.

Lieberman was the only customer in the restaurant darkened by closed blinds. He watched the lone little waiter bring the coffee to the table. Then Abe carried the chilled glass to the phone near the door and made his call.

The answer came on the first ring.

"Ola," said a young man.

"*Lieberman aqui, El Viejo, quiero a hablar con Emiliano.*"

"Okay," said the voice at the other end.

There was a pause. He sipped the coffee. The sweet jolt was perfect.

"*¿Viejo?*" came El Perro.

"I'm returning your call," Lieberman said.

"*Viene a mi resturante, por favor. Es muy important.*"

"*¿Cuando?*" asked Lieberman.

"Hey," said El Perro. "I said it's important. You want to meet some place else, *bueno*. I trus' you, *Viejo*."

"The restaurant'll be fine," said Lieberman. "I'll be there inside an hour."

"*Bueno,*" El Perro said happily. "*Hasta luego.*"

Lieberman hung up and went to sit down and finish his coffee. It was very cold, very sweet, and very good. He savored it, drinking slowly imagining Mickey Gornitz erode away under the acrid terror of bitter instant coffee. When he was finished, Lieberman would have to go see Eugene Carbin.

Lieberman drank slowly.

Jimmy Stashall sat behind his desk, hands folded. He didn't raise his head high but looked up at the big man across the desk. This, Heine Manush knew, was a very bad sign. He had seen it several times before and usually watched this look and manner lead to an explosion. Jimmy Stashall's explosions were legendary. He took tablets to keep his blood pressure down and downed Xanax tablets with every meal to control his anxiety. Stashall knew that both his father and grandfather had died of strokes. His grandfather had been with Jimmy's father at a clothing store. Stashall's grandfather had gone wild with anger when he had insisted that a sweater was green and the clerk had calmly insisted that the sweater was teal. Then came the stroke. Jimmy's father had learned nothing from the graphic lesson he had witnessed. He too had died of a stroke after screaming at Jimmy's mother over the consistency of

Thanksgiving cranberry sauce. First they had thanked God. Then Jimmy's father had started with the cranberry sauce.

Jimmy Stashall had far more cause for a broken blood vessel in his head than cranberry sauce and sweaters. Jimmy's very freedom was at stake, and he was commanding a small gang of total incompetents. The last person who worked for him that had any brains was Mickey Gornitz, who Jimmy now wanted dead.

"You've got the Wilhite kid's picture. You've got his name. You've got his credit card numbers. You've got his out-of-state plate number," said Jimmy. "And we know he's in town. And you can't find him."

"Maybe," said the big man. "If we ask some of the other guys. Sal, Solly One, the Greek, Schwartz, you know?"

"I don't want to do that," Jimmy said calmly. "I don't want them in if I can help it. That phone's gonna ring in a few seconds. I'm gonna be very careful because I and anyone with any brains is gonna know that the line is tapped by the FBI, state attorney, city cops, and maybe even the producers of fuckin' *Law and Order*. And you're gonna keep —"

The phone rang. Jimmy watched the small monitor below the receiver where the number being called from appeared. Not only did he not recognize it, he could tell by a glance at his pad that it was a different number from the one from which he had been called three times before. He picked up the phone.

"Phone booth," said the voice at the other end. "Downstairs."

The caller hung up.

Starshall listened to the droning sound for a few seconds and then gently, very gently, put the phone down.

"That," he said, "was the Wilhite kid. Find him. And remember, you dumb . . . remember, he doesn't know we know who he is. Just find him and tell me where he is. Don't touch him. Don't talk to him. Don't whack him. Call our contact downtown. He must know something."

Jimmy was up now. He had a phone booth to get to fast and he didn't like it. He didn't like being pushed by a punk.

"We'll find him," said Heine.

"Your assurance fills me with confidence," Jimmy said adjusting the sleeves of his jacket. "Find him."

Stashall rushed past his secretary and the man sitting in a chair against the wall reading a magazine. Heine would soon be passing curses onto the man reading peacefully. That was fine with Stashall. He was suffering. Everybody should suffer all up and down the food chain.

The phone booth was half a block away. The sky was overcast and the day cool. He refused to run. They might be watching him, calling him from nearby. A woman was using the phone. Jimmy listened, hoping she was about to end her conversation.

"You think I don't know that?" she said angrily. She was about forty, maybe older, because she had the haggard look of a loser and user. Her arms were probably dead sore and her nose and throat raw. Maybe she had been pretty once. Maybe.

"I'm not comin' in," the woman said, pushing uncombed black hair from her pale face. "We can talk now . . . go ahead. You talk. I listen, but this is Pauley's phone and he's gonna come by in a while and want to use it . . . any minute . . . You talk . . . No, you. I'll listen and then maybe I'll talk about coming back to the house . . . Because I don't want to face you and the others . . . There. I said it. Happy? . . . No . . ."

Jimmy checked his watch. It had been almost three minutes since the Wilhite kid's call to his office. A cop would be watching him from somewhere, and maybe one of them would try to come close enough to hear what he was saying.

"Lady," Jimmy said politely, tapping the woman on the shoulder.

She waved him away, pressing her lips together and trying to ignore him.

"Lady," he repeated. "Tell whoever that is that you'll call back later."

The woman turned her back on Jimmy.

Enough. Cops and punks push him around and now a wasted bitch druggie. Enough. He would dearly love to be carrying heat or even a knife though he hadn't used any blade on a human in almost twenty years. Jimmy reached over and pushed down on the phone cradle to cut the connection. The pale woman looked at Jimmy and swung the phone toward his face. He had been dealing with this kind of thing for most of his life. He caught her arm with his and punched her with the other. His blow hit the woman low in the stomach. She dropped the phone. She folded forward clutching her gut and moaned. Jimmy hung up the phone, which almost immediately began to ring.

"I'm gonna tear your heart out," the woman screamed.

Jimmy fumbled for his wad of bills, pealed off one of them, and handed it to her as she tried to rise. It was probably a fifty, maybe a hundred. He didn't look. He wanted to answer the goddamn phone.

She took the offered bill, looked at it and at him with a murderous hate. Then she tried to spit at him but she was dry. She pushed the bill into the pocket of her jacket, turned her back, and limped down the sidewalk holding her stomach and moaning, but much more softly than a few seconds ago.

Jimmy picked up the phone.

"Someone using the phone?" asked the voice.

"I got rid of them," Stashall said, finding it nearly impossible to control his anger.

"I'm calling Gornitz in fifteen minutes," the voice said. "I'm going to tell him his time is up, that his son is about to be killed. I'll make a suggestion about what he has to do, and when it's done, you pay the money we agreed on, the way we agreed on."

"I keep my word, and like I said last time, if you're a cop, I know this is all a setup and I'm joking."

"It's not a setup," said the voice.

As a matter of fact, Jimmy's word on the street was as good as the bitter coffee that Lieberman had tried to drink in Gornitz's room. He had double-crossed, lied, cheated, stabbed, and shot his way about halfway up the mob ladder. Now, at a time when it looked like things were looking even higher up, the Gornitz thing had blown. Everyone knew about it or soon would. If Jimmy had connections in the police department, so did everyone else he knew. If it looked like Jimmy was going down, someone might decide he might talk to make a deal. Somebody, and he knew who, might put out a contract on Jimmy. It was likely. So, Jimmy would lie and probably kill or have killed anyone, including his own family, to save his behind.

"Listen," said Stashall. "No more calls. I —"

Stashall felt rough, cold fingers on his neck. A thumb was digging deeply into his throat. He choked.

"What's going on?" the caller asked, but Jimmy couldn't speak.

He felt himself being turned around to face a burly, dark man with a bushy well-trimmed mustache. The man wore a raincoat.

"This is my phone," said the man. "Lorraine, when anyone wants her, which nobody does much, works for me. You hurt her."

"Look," Jimmy tried to say, knowing that if he survived this, he would have the man choking him, Pauley, killed in an alley. He might even take a chance and do it himself.

"You're getting off easy," Pauley said softly, showing remarkably white, and possibly false, teeth. "I'm just gonna cut your old face a little."

"What's going on?" cried the voice on the phone.

A knife appeared. Jimmy shot a knee toward big Pauley's groin. Pauley turned to his right and the knee hit him in the thigh. Jimmy went for the man's eyes, but Pauley turned away and held the knife down, probably, Jimmy guessed, now planning murder, murder for using a goddamn public phone. Jimmy kept struggling, the pain in his neck pumping, throbbing. Jimmy closed his eyes and gritted his teeth, waiting for the blade.

And then the hand on his neck loosened and big Pauley let out a gagging sound. Pauley stepped back, his arm behind him, the knife clattering to the sidewalk. Someone was behind him. One arm around Pauley's neck, the other lifting his arm in a hammerlock. Pauley grimaced.

"I'm a cop," said Hanrahan. "I'm a big cop. I'm a tired cop. I'm a cop with a lot of problems we can share over a cup of coffee some time. But right now I'm feeling a bit hopeful. So, I want to see you running down the street, not walking, running. If you do anything less, I haul you in and have you searched and . . . you know the fire drill. Nod."

Pauley, his face turning red, nodded. Hanrahan let him go and Pauley reached

308

down for his knife. Hanrahan grabbed the reaching hand and squeezed.

"Leave it and run," he said. "Now."

Pauley did as he was told. For a drug dealer and an addict, he was in pretty good shape. A few people stood across the street watching, not understanding. No one enlightened them.

Hanrahan took the phone and put it to his ear.

The caller had hung up. So did Hanrahan.

Stashall was rubbing his bruised neck with both hands.

"That's a dead man running down the street," Stashall croaked.

"That he is," said Hanrahan, "but he doesn't need your help to come to the realization. Your caller'll call back. Maybe right away. Find out what you can. I've been watching. I've heard enough."

"I was talking to my wife," Stashall whispered in pain. "I —"

"Call her back," said Hanrahan. "I'll just ask her."

"No, I was on my way to my car," he said his pain obvious to the policeman and the audience across the street. "I just remembered I promised to call her in case she wanted me to pick anything up."

"Your car is in the other direction," said Hanrahan.

"This is the nearest —"

He was cut off by the ringing of the phone. Stashall started to reach for it.

"Do the right thing, Jimmy."

"Hello?" the voice said cautiously.

"I'm here," croaked Stashall.

"Who're you?"

"Stashall. Some drug dealer choked me. Trying to rob me. I got rid of him."

Hanrahan, who was listening, nodded that Jimmy was doing just fine.

"You sure?"

"I'm sure. Some drunk dealer talkin' to another one," said Stashall. "How the hell do I know with these crazy people?"

"Good-bye," said the voice, and the phone went dead.

Hanrahan and Stashall faced each other and the detective said, "David Donald Wilhite. You know that name?"

Stashall, the pain staying at a high level, tried to meet the detective's eyes.

"Don't know that name," he said, closing his eyes in agony.

"I think he just called you," said Hanrahan. "I think you're lookin' for him. Well, Mr. Jimmy Stashall, so am I, and I mean to find him and I mean to be very upset with anyone who stands in the way or has the bad luck to get to the young man first. I know you're

310

hurtin'. So just nod to show we understand each other."

Stashall nodded.

The nod was a lie. Both men knew it, but the policeman thought it might make the mobster a little cautious.

Hanrahan turned and walked away. Stashall considered saying, "Thanks," but it wasn't worth the effort.

CHAPTER 11

"So, *Viejo,* again you tickle my *tochus* and I tickle yours," said Emiliano "El Perro" Del Sol, rubbing the white scar that ran down his face and smiling at three members of his gang to see if they got the joke. They didn't.

Abe Lieberman was sitting in the darkened restaurant owned by El Perro. It was a small but very good Mexican restaurant on North Avenue. Emiliano had the good sense to convince a retired and illegal Mexican cook who spoke no English to return to the kitchen. Since Emiliano paid in cash and paid reasonably, the man had been eager to return to work though he was over seventy years old. Emiliano had also persuaded the previous owners, who had done their own cooking, to sell to El Perro at a reasonable price. The old couple had rationalized that they were planning to retire soon anyway, move in with their son and his family, and contribute to the rent. They had also rationalized that it was better to be alive with a pocketful of cash and well than dead or maimed.

The CD player in the corner on a wooden table blared out salsa, Ruben Blades and Julio Iglesias nonstop, during the conversation between the policeman and the gang leader. The salsa, according to Lieberman's taste, was okay. Blades was terrific and Julio, El Perro's idol, could be done without.

There was an almost finished plate of food in front of Lieberman. It had been prepared the moment he had entered the restaurant. It was some kind of spicy omelette with onions, peppers, and a covering of red sauce. Since he could not offend his host, Lieberman ate. It was great. It might well kill him, but at the moment, it was great.

As it turned out, the mad gang leader and the detective had mutual favors to ask.

"Viejo," El Perro had said over someone belting out a salsa song that sounded like *"Cuando Yo Sueno."* "There's a stupid dumb jerk your guys are holding over on the West Side. Name's Willie Coles. Black loco from the Lawndale Razors. Most times I don't give a shit about them guys, you know? But their top man, he calls me. He says, 'Emiliano, you get my guy out and I owe you. They say you got connections.' I been waitin' for that piss to owe me. I got somethin' I want from him. An' I wanna show him I got the

313

connection. You, *Viejo*."

"What's this citizen being held for?" asked Lieberman finishing the last of the omelette and taking a sip of Diet Coke.

"Beatin' somebody up. *¿Quien sabe?* He didn' kill nobody. But Willie Coles, he got a big record."

"You got a phone?"

"Telephone, *ahora*," El Perro said to Piedras, who lumbered over to retrieve a white portable phone from the darkness near the CD player.

Lieberman dialed the number. He knew it and almost every station in the city not because of his phenomenal memory but because he had called them all thousands of times.

When a weary desk sergeant — they're all weary — answered the phone, Lieberman identified himself and asked who was handling Willie Coles.

"You're still alive, Abe?" the desk sergeant joked.

"I'll still be getting the bad guys when you're in a bar in Boca Raton drinking Bud, wearing ugly shirts you don't tuck in, and telling lies about what a hero you are."

"You may be right at that," said the sergeant. "Andy Moore's on the Coles arrest. You're lucky. Andy's in. Hold on."

There was a click and a buzz and a very

314

deep voice: "Detective Moore."

Andy Moore was somewhere in his forties, late forties. He was tall, lean, black, and wore horn-rimmed glasses. He looked like a college professor and talked like one. Andy Moore had gone to college, had a degree in criminal justice. Andy Moore was also the most feared police officer on the West Side. Even the toughest gang members didn't want to be left alone in an interrogation room with Moore, who had perfected the art of painful beating from years of practice and a black belt in some kind of martial art with a Japanese name. Andy Moore was a greater deterrent to crime in the Lawndale district than the death penalty.

"Andy, it's Abe Lieberman."

"Abe, broken any of my laws lately?"

"They're my laws, Andy."

"Our laws, then."

"Every day." Lieberman looked at El Perro, who continued to stroke his scar and listen to Julio wail plaintively behind him.

"What you need, Abe?" asked Moore.

"Willie Coles."

"He's a sweetheart," said Moore. "Beat up a girl and her mother who wouldn't let him get ahead of them in line at a hot dog stand. Willie's got a list of priors as long as my *schmuck*."

315

"I'm impressed," said Abe. "If it were as long as mine, on the other hand, you'd have to let him go with an apology and a cash bonus."

"I've got to run, Abe. Not that I don't like talking about the relative length of our bodily appendages. What can I do for you?"

"Can you let Willie Coles walk?"

"It can be arranged," said Moore. "He'll probably beat the charge anyway. The girl and her mother will probably get a visit or a phone call from one of the Lawndale Razors as soon as they get out of the hospital, maybe before. I won't ask you why you want our creature from the Black Lagoon walking down Cermak Road, but I'll do it after I have a sincere private talk with him about why he should become a better person. After that you owe me one, Abe."

"I owe you, Andy. Thanks."

Lieberman hung up and looked at El Perro, who stopped touching his scar and looked at the detective.

"He'll be out today," said Lieberman. "A few bruises, maybe a sore stomach, but he'll be out."

"Bueno," cried El Perro, taking the phone back and dialing a number written with Magic Marker on the back of a menu. Someone must have picked up almost immediately.

"I wanna talk to J.T. Tell him it's El Perro . . . J.T.? He'll be out today. Now you do what you said you'd do. Good. Maybe we do business again."

El Perro hung up grinning. His was a grin to frighten even a hungry alligator.

"I'm not going to ask you what you want J.T. to do."

"You don' wanna know," said El Perro. "I think I'll have a Coke. You wan' another one?"

"No, thanks. I want to tell you what you can do for me. There's a man named Mike or Mikhail Pinescu, lives up on the North Side, on Nordica. I'll give you the address. Mike has a van, a white van with 'Mike's Driveways' written on the side. It might say 'Mike's Roofs.' Something like that. I heard that my friend Mike's vehicle was going to be totally destroyed by vandals tonight, very late. It'll be done very quickly and someone, maybe three or four someones, will knock on Mike's door and politely tell him that his truck has been destroyed and that he is out of business. They're going to tell him that he is out of business forever or he'll wind up like his truck."

"Sounds like fun, *Viejo*," said El Perro.

"I thought you might like it."

"Why you wan' this done?"

317

"He's a bad man," said Lieberman. "My job is to put bad men out of business. Once in a while the system doesn't help me do that."

"So we need each other again," Emiliano said happily.

"Let's say that our relationship has continued to be mutually beneficial." Lieberman accepted the Coke that another member of the Tentaculos had brought to him. "By the way, our Korean friend has left town. Won't be back."

"Woulda been more easy to shoot him in the head," said El Perro. "I tell you he's comin' back."

"What can I say?" asked Lieberman. "I'm a sweetheart."

"You always been this funny, *Viejo?*"

"It's a gift," Lieberman said, drinking his Coke and enjoying the plaintive singing of some woman in Spanish. Her heart was broken. There was nothing left for her in the world. There was nothing to live for. She was through with men forever.

"You know the odds against the Cubs winning the World Series next year?" asked El Perro.

"No."

"Fifteen to one," El Perro said, leaning over to whisper louder than he had been talking. "You're a fan, you bet on things like that, you know? I'm gonna put down a few hundred bucks before the odds drop."

"They may go up," said Lieberman.

"Then I'll bet more," said El Perro.

Lieberman rose and took a small brown paper bag out of his pocket. He handed it to Emiliano.

"What's this?"

"A present," said Lieberman. "I picked it up on my way here."

The gang leader reached inside and pulled a compact disc from the bag. He held it up and read, "Klaz . . . Kless. *Viejo, no puedo de leerlo.*"

"Klezmer," said Lieberman.

"What's that?"

"Jew music," said Lieberman. "Next time I come, put it on, another favor."

El Perro examined the photograph on the front of the CD, a young woman and three young men all with beards, all smiling.

"I'll listen," Emiliano said.

Three minutes later, almost unable to hear, his stomach punishing him with jalapeño sauce, Lieberman was back on North Avenue. The sky was overcast and thunder rumbled. Three young Latinos walked toward the little old man as he headed for his car. Lieberman sighed and before they were ten feet away, pulled his gun from underneath his jacket, and pointed it at them. The trio stopped.

"I'm a cop. I've got a headache. I've got a stomachache and I've got a hell of a lot to do. Go away. Mug someone else. *¿Comprende?*"

"*Sí,*" said the smallest of the three.

They were all wearing light jackets and black jeans.

"*Andale entonces,*" said Lieberman. "I haven't shot anyone in weeks. Shooting people is like *la leche de mi madre por mi.* Just ask El Perro. Go."

The three looked at each other, turned around, and walked away. Lieberman would have liked them to walk faster. He was in a foul mood. He even considered firing his gun in the air, but they might be armed and decide that they had to fight it out or die, and more than one stray bullet had hit an innocent or guilty bystander over the last few decades. He got in his car and drove. He didn't turn on the radio.

The meeting was not going well. The group was small — Irving Hammel, the lawyer whom Abe called Rommel, Rabbi Wass, and Ida Katzman who was nearing ninety and remained the primary contributor to everything Temple Mir Shavot did. Ida was wealthy. Ida's husband had left her a string of successful jewelry stores throughout the city. Ida had sold the stores to a chain. Ida was good for about three or four million, maybe more. Bess didn't know. She was sure Irving Hammel, who wasn't even forty yet, knew exactly what Ida Katzman was worth.

The meeting was in Rabbi Wass's office. The rabbi sat behind his desk, slightly pale, dressed in a conservative blue suit and a raven-black *kepuh* on his head, trying to look very rabbinical and wise and failing miserably, Bess Lieberman thought. Ida Katzman was definitely showing signs of problems with her aging. Her hearing had always been good. It was going rapidly. She was beginning to have trouble sorting out arguments and positions. It was a shame that tore at Bess's heart. Ida had been a rock. She and her husband had once had a son. He died in Vietnam. Now, Irving Hammel was certain, when she died she would leave all or most of her money and assets to the temple. In his heart, Rabbi Wass agreed.

It was Bess's plan to honor Ida while she could still possibly enjoy the honor. Hammel and the rabbi were enthusiastic. Ida didn't care for the idea. Bess promised that it could be small and tasteful or big, whatever Ida wanted.

"Money can be spent better on the temple,

the religious school," said Ida. "I don't need a party. I don't want a party."

"Well," Bess tried, "how about we have a very small ceremony to officially recognize your contributions and to dedicate a plaque in the temple lobby honoring you and your husband for your years of support?"

The very office in which they sat had a plaque on the wall indicating that the room had been bought and paid for in honor of Ida's son.

"How small?" asked Ida, her hands resting on the cane in her lap.

"As small as you like," said Bess. "Maybe just the temple officers."

"The president, vice president, president of the men's club, president of the women's club, chair of the fund-raising committee, all of you and who knows who else," Ida Katzman said. "You want a plaque. *Gey gezundt.* A plaque. Maybe dinner with you and Lieberman."

"Ida," Irving Hammel said gently. He wanted a big bash, a fund-raiser. He wanted to run it. He wanted to invite prominent Jews, potential clients, to the gala at a big hotel. "I hope you don't mind me calling you Ida. We've known each other and worked together for more than five years now."

"You can call me Mrs. Katzman," the old

woman said. "When you're maybe ten years older, if I'm still alive, which would be a miracle and a joke played by God, you can call me Ida. You're a good boy, Hammel, but you are a devious good boy and I think you should have more fun. Fats Waller was dead when he was your age. He had fun. That's all I have to say."

The old woman stood with the help of her cane and looked at the rabbi and then at Bess. Everyone had joined Ida in standing.

"Whatever you want to do, Ida, we'll do," said Bess.

"I want to die in my sleep and find out there's a heaven," Ida Katzman said. "I hope that I'm there because I belong there and not because the Lord keeps a book of those who donated enough to a synagogue building fund to make a hundred heaven points. Mr. Small is waiting outside to drive me home. I'm tired. Good-bye."

Bess accompanied the old woman to her car where Mr. Small, her driver and guardian, opened the door for her.

"Driving Miss Daisy," Ida said, getting in with the help of Mr. Small, who defied the remark by the fact that he was white and as dedicated to the old woman as he had been to her husband. Mr. Small had been the manager of one of the jewelry stores. He had suffered a pair of small strokes and the Katzmans had taken him into their house and helped him as much as he helped them.

The car drove off and Bess straightened her dress, took a deep breath, stood upright, and went back to face the always wavering rabbi and the always determined Rommel who was, she was sure, ready with some plan to save the idea of a big fund-raiser and law practice builder in honor of Ida Katzman.

Bess was now equally determined that such an event would not be if Ida didn't want it. There would be no surprise parties, no visit from the women's auxiliary board, not even a visit from old Rabbi Wass who was retired but could always be persuaded to come back from Florida to save the Jewish people.

Bess was the president of the temple. She would bully the rabbi and persuade the board while Irving Hammel did the same.

It never stops, Bess thought, going back into the rabbi's office. She glanced at her watch. She had to pick up the children at school at three.

The call came at four. The caller had said he wanted to talk to Gornitz very soon. Carbin gave him a number and told him to call at four. Gornitz would answer. The caller had hung up.

Now it was four and the phone in the hotel room was ringing.

Mickey Gornitz picked up the phone and said, "Hello."

"You're still alive," the male voice said. "We're disappointed. Very disappointed. We keep our word, Mickey. Matthew dies in fifteen minutes and his body will be someplace where it won't look pretty and it might not be found for weeks, maybe longer."

"Give me a little more time," Mickey pleaded.

"No more time," said the caller. "Talk to your son for the last time."

"Dad" came Matthew's voice. "He's going to kill me."

The boy began to sob and the phone was taken from him by the caller.

"You didn't say 'good-bye,'" the caller said.

There was a sudden, loud howl from Mickey and the sound of the phone dropping. Then the caller heard a male voice say "Stop him. Stop —"

The sound of breaking glass and a howl of fear fading away.

"Oh, Christ" came a man's voice.

The caller was about to hang up. Gornitz had gone through the window. The caller hoped the window was high enough.

"This is Eugene Carbin in the state attorney's office, you son of a bitch" came the deep, steady voice of a man obviously making an attempt to remain calm. Behind him were voices arguing and what sounded like someone crying. "Let the boy go now. If anything happens to him, when we catch you, and we *will* catch you, there won't be any goddamn plea bargains."

The man who had called himself Eugene Carbin hung up the phone. Hard.

"Iris and I are getting married a week from Sunday," said Bill Hanrahan, sitting in the chair next to Abe Lieberman's desk. "Unitarian. Ex-priest Vince DiPino. His church is out in Des Plaines."

"Iris's father?" asked Abe drinking one of the two coffees he had picked up at Dunkin' Donuts. Bill had the other.

"He'll come around," Hanrahan said with what sounded like less than total conviction.

The squad room was relatively quiet. Two uniforms were standing near the water fountain arguing about something. Detectives were doing paperwork, paperwork, paperwork. Typewriters were clattering. They had been told for years that they were all getting computers . . . sometime. Only Lorber really wanted one. The others were used to the typewriters. Cops don't change easily.

"Woo?"

"He'll come around too, and if he doesn't, the hell with him. Iris and I want to get married. We don't want to wait."

"Your life, Father Murphy. Congratulations."

"Rabbi, let me ask you something."

"Ask," said Lieberman.

"You think I'm suicidal?"

Lieberman had some more coffee, thought for a few seconds. "Yes, I do. I also think you want to stay alive. You don't know why you do things? Welcome to the congregation. People get hurt, killed because you think you screwed up. You've made it to the board of directors of the Society of Screwed-Up Police Officers. You've got a conscience you don't think you can live with. Congratulations on that too. You're the president of the human race, Father Murphy."

"Not that easy, Abe."

"I should have taped this conversation. When did I say it was easy? When did I say you'd find answers? One day I'm in a good mood and I let three kids who want to mug me get away. Another day I feel like Darth Vader — my grandson's favorite character of all time — and I pull in a woman for standing in the middle of the street and impeding traffic."

Hanrahan finished his coffee and dropped the paper cup in the trash can near his feet. The can was almost overflowing.

"My old friend Woo isn't going to like this," he said.

"As we've already observed. Then maybe we should go see Mr. Woo and soothe his moral indignation." Abe nursed his coffee.

"Won't do any good, Rabbi," said Hanrahan.

"Won't know if we don't try," said Lieberman. "We're off in a few minutes. Let's pick up some hot and sour soup in Chinatown and engage in some friendly discussion with Mr. Woo."

"If I'm living and Iris doesn't change her mind, I'd like you to be best man and Bess to stand up with us. You know, bridesmaid, something like that."

"Okay with Iris?"

"More than okay."

"Then you've got yourself —"

The phone on the desk rang. Lieberman reached over and picked it up.

"Lieberman," he said. And then he listened for a long time before he spoke again. "What do I think? It's your call. No surprise. In a few years when I'm ready for retirement, I'll run into those two and they'll shoot a big hole in me or I'll shoot a big hole in them . . . know you don't have to get my permission. You're just feeling like a compromising . . . forget it. Have a nice day."

Lieberman hung up the phone and looked at his partner.

"One day," he said, "one day and Salt and Pepper's public defender plea-bargains them down to attempted robbery. The prisons are full. They'd both appear in court with cast, bandages, their mothers, their ministers — who they haven't seen before in —"

"Saviello's a Catholic," said Hanrahan.

"His lawyer would find a priest. They'll both be out in less than two years, probably one year. They're going to kill some poor Pakistani some time, probably not together. Maybe if the State of Illinois is lucky, they'll kill each other. Hell, William, you should have shot the bastard. *I* should have shot the bastard."

"I've done enough of that for a while, Rabbi."

Lieberman got up, dropped his cup in the garbage where it teetered precariously and decided to remain magically balanced within the ring of garbage.

"Let's go see Mr. Woo," he said.

It was after five.

"You are a remarkably well informed Jewish detective," Woo said a little more than an hour after Abe and Bill had left the Clark Street station. The hot and sour soup was in two white pint cartons in the backseat of their car. They would drink it like coffee when they finished talking to the ancient man.

They were in a room behind the Chinese import shop that Liao Woo owned and that was a front for activities both legal and questionable. Lieberman had the bad taste to have brought up some of the questionable activities to their host in the office tastefully decorated with teak furniture, a large Oriental rug, and Chinese paintings on the wall. Woo was wearing dark slacks and a black silk Chinese shirt that buttoned to his neck.

"I'm a remarkably well informed detective," said Lieberman.

The two detectives had sat in large finely polished wooden chairs with sturdy carved arms. Woo sat in a plainer version of the two chairs facing the men.

"It comes from living a long time and paying attention to the past," said Lieberman. "I think we share that."

Woo nodded and looked at Hanrahan.

"I am disappointed in you, William Hanrahan," he said. "We have always conducted our conversations in a civilized manner and between the two of us."

"Things have changed," said Hanrahan. "Iris and I don't want to wait. It's got nothing to do with you. We can step back and respect each other and you can give Iris a nice wedding present, or my partner and I . . ."

Woo smiled.

"Officers," he said, "I cannot be intimidated. I'll not bore you with my boyhood and youth in China, but for every horror you have witnessed, I have witnessed a hundred. For every threat that you issue, I have survived a dozen. I have come near starvation and have engaged in acts which were beneath me, but one survives. Do not threaten me with misery. Do not bother to hint at it. You have no experience of real misery. I need not remind you that I am old, that my knees and back are beyond the help of physicians or acupuncture. William Hanrahan, you agreed to my proposal in your own home. You agreed to wait. You will live by that agreement. That is not a threat. It is what shall be whatever I must do to make it so."

"When was it, Woo? Back in the early eighties, a cocaine shipment," said Lieberman. "Narcotics tore this place apart, found one of those big vases sitting right out in your shop filled with packages of cocaine."

Woo rose and looked at Lieberman. There was no emotion in Woo's face.

"That was an error," said Woo. "My attorneys rectified the error."

"You've done a lot of rectifying," said Lieberman. "You were a poor street kid in a little town in China where, I understand, people survived by eating each other. You made it to Shanghai and found out how to stay alive in the dark alleys, and now you're playing Fu Man Chu right up to the top of your silk shirt, which, I must say, is quite classy."

"I do not know what you seek in this attempt at provocation," said Woo leaning on his cane. "I believe it is a characteristic of your race. It has seemed so in my experience. Jews have a tendency toward abrupt transitions. I assure you, neither flattery nor threats will sway me from my duty, and it should not sway Detective Hanrahan from his promise."

"Mr. Woo," said Lieberman. "They don't want to wait."

"Then he should not have promised," said Woo. "I have a modest but sufficient income and am able to help friends in my community and to chastise those who would take advantage of me or my friends in this community. It is not my access to money which has brought me respect. It is that I keep my word. Always. I would prefer to die than break my word."

"You've got a point," Lieberman said.

"If you like," Woo said, "I will have coffee

or tea brought in to you and you may take as much time as you wish. Meanwhile, I have other business."

"More important than this?" asked Lieberman.

"No," said Woo. "Simply more likely to have an affirmative conclusion."

"We'll leave," Hanrahan said, rising.

"I think I might like some coffee," said Lieberman. "Provided it's good coffee."

"Espresso." Woo went through a door behind the desk and closed it. "Egyptian. Very strong."

And the old man was gone.

"Abe," Hanrahan said with some exasperation when the door had closed. "You were supposed to help me."

"I like the old guy," Lieberman said, sitting comfortably and admiring the chair. "I didn't know I'd like him, and he has a point, Father Murphy."

"I know." Hanrahan got up and moved to the desk. He turned to face his partner and leaned back against the solid support.

"Woo has a reputation for being reasonable," said Lieberman. "Had it from the first time I first heard of him back in the late sixties. I've seen him around, but this was the first time I've really talked to him."

"He's not reasonable when it comes to

Iris," Hanrahan said. "He'd have me killed on the street tomorrow if I weren't a cop and he thought it would win him Iris. He's old enough to be her father."

"If he started young," said Lieberman.

At that moment the coffee was brought in by one of Woo's two young men. He wore a perfectly pressed dark suit and conservative tie. He placed the tray between the two policemen on a solid, dark small table. There were little cookies on a plate on the tray.

"Thanks," said Lieberman.

The young man stared. The man was considerably younger than his employer and far less able to hide his feelings, not that he wanted to. He definitely did not like the gray-haired policeman. The young man left without a word. The two detectives drank strong coffee and ate cookies.

"He loves her, Abe. I think that old man really damn loves her. Can you imagine the two of them together? I'd —"

"And I used to be in love with Cyd Charisse."

"But you got over it, Rabbi."

"Who says? Let's go home, Father Murph. I've got a daughter to say good-bye to and a science project I promised to work on with Melisa."

"You came here to help me and you wind

up almost agreeing with Woo."

"I like him," said Lieberman. "I also know he can have bad things done. Now, after he has six or seven men cut you into forty or fifty pieces, I promise I'll come here and shoot him right in the face, but that won't do you and Iris any good. Besides, Murph, I think he's right."

"Maybe, Rabbi," Hanrahan said with a deep sigh. "I'll think about it."

"If you don't, you just prove to him that he was right about your being reckless, suicidal, and unwilling to learn the game of gin rummy. Back away from it, partner. I got a feeling the Unitarian Universalist minister may well have an opening after you live up to your agreement."

"Damn it, Abe." Hanrahan clenched his fist.

"Damn it, indeed," said Lieberman. "One more cookie. Let's go. Our soup is getting cold."

They left their empty cups and went back through the door leading to the shop. It seemed to be empty. They were out on the street when Woo stepped back into the shop with both of the young men who protected him.

"I like the Jewish policeman," said Woo.

Both of the young men wanted to ask what

they should do about the two detectives, about Iris, about her father, but they had learned long ago to initiate nothing unless it was absolutely necessary. This was not such a case. They would do what they were told.

CHAPTER 12

That night two police officers in uniform in an official vehicle drove to O'Hare Airport, met a man with a bulging blue carry-on. The man was named Carlo. He was short, bald, fat in a tight-fitting suit. Carlo handed the carry-on to one of the officers and, without a word, wheezed toward the crowded moving walkway to retrieve his luggage. The two policemen, one very young, the other no more than forty, took the bag to their illegally parked car, placed it in the backseat, and drove to a far-north suburb to personally deliver the bag containing over a million dollars skimmed from Vegas gambling houses. The two policemen had no idea what, if anything, their reward for the delivery would be. They both hoped and assumed it would be generous. The younger man had a very pregnant wife and very heavy debts.

That night a drunken man named Suede Nichols put on his gloves and got in the car parked in front of the bar on Ashland Avenue. Suede tried to drive carefully and thought he was succeeding. He definitely did not want to be stopped. Suede Nichols did not own the car. He was a burglar who had stolen the neat little Mazda for the night. His tools and the goods he had collected from the house in Winnetka were in the backseat. Suede did not have a driver's license. In addition to two short sentences for breaking and entering, he had three times been nailed on DUI charges.

Traffic wasn't heavy that late at night, especially not on Ashland. Suede sang, a wordless song with no melody that simply came to him. He would drive home with his goods, hide them, and dump the car about four or five blocks away. The take had been good, very good. Suede would make a nice profit from Wasko the fence. They had a good relationship. Wasko would cheat him only a little bit. Suede told himself as he sang "Bum biddle bee, now, now" that he would send some of the money to his daughter in Bakersfield. He would give her a call and say she was getting a present. He imagined her asking him to come for a visit, see his grandchildren, but he knew she wouldn't. Oh hell, Suede liked living alone, at night, when honest people were sleeping.

When he made the left turn on Leland, he saw the woman crossing the street at the corner. She seemed to be crying. She was crossing slowly. Suede's plan was to let her get across and go behind her. He stepped on the brake to slow down, but hit the gas instead. When the car struck the woman, she went flying straight up about five feet in the air and landed on his hood as he tried to find the brake. She looked directly at him, blood oozing from her nose and mouth, a look of surprise on her face. She was young, younger than his daughter. Suede hit the gas again, this time on purpose, and the young woman, who looked dark and foreign, slid from the hood into the street. Suede's car bounced off a pickup truck and then he straightened it out. He didn't want to look in the rearview mirror, but he couldn't stop himself. She was lying in the street not moving. She kept getting smaller and smaller.

He pulled himself together, drove home, got the tools and goods from the backseat, and took them into the apartment. He went out quickly and drove four blocks to Leavitt, where he parked next to the Ravenswood El tracks. When he got out, he tore off his gloves, threw them into some bushes, and pushed the door closed. His left handprint on the window was clear enough for any moderately intelligent person to notice. Suede had no little finger on his left hand, never mind the fingerprints.

On that night, a nineteen-year-old black drug dealer named Butchie Courts stood on his usual corner with a couple of friends waiting for customers. It was getting cold. Butchie and his friends weren't worried about the police. There were dealers all around, and it wasn't worth picking them up for the little they had in their pockets. The dealers with brains had a spot where they stashed and went to, from time to time. People came and went, bought and pleaded. One of Butchie's friends, who was fourteen but big for his age, kept his hand on the nine millimeter in his pocket. It was a heavy two pounds and the love of his short life. The three of them talked shit, mostly about people they were going to get even with and girls they were going to get or had already gotten. Tisa Lings, hands in pockets, crossed the street and headed for Butchie Courts. The three saw her coming and Butchie grinned. Tisa was young. Tisa was light-skinned and pretty and she had a body. You could tell that even with the jacket she was wearing. She didn't need money to collect a bag, a good bag.

"Tisa," Butchie said. "I'll tell you what I

can do for you and you tell me what you can do for —"

Butchie never finished. The kitchen knife had come out from behind Tisa's back and she plunged it deeply into Butchie's neck. The fourteen-year-old with the gun and his friend turned and ran down the street. Butchie staggered to the brick wall of the housing project in front of which he had been dealing for four years. Tisa watched him try to get the knife out of his neck, but his hands wouldn't listen to his need. His lips moved forming a word "Why?"

"I'm going to college" was Tisa's answer.

She turned and walked away. Butchie finally got his hands on the knife, thus covering Tisa's fingerprints. Then he slid down the wall and died, a very puzzled look on his face.

On that night, two homeless men in their fifties but looking at least eighty had an argument where they lived over a warm-air exhaust behind a Thai restaurant on Clark Street. Both men, strange as it seemed, even to them, were named Tom Evans. One was black. One white. Other homeless people they knew and the people at the Salvation Army had taken to calling both of them Long Tom. Now the two of them were arguing loudly over who deserved the nickname.

"I'm taller," said white Tom.

"I'm thinner," said black Tom.

They were in each other's face now. They kept repeating "I'm taller." "I'm thinner." Their noses almost touched. Since they both had the same terrible breath, they didn't notice the smell. White Tom had spent much of his life in state mental hospitals. Black Tom had owned a successful used car lot on the South Side. A black gang, which he felt should support black businesses, had started extorting money from him. Soon there were no profits. Soon there was no business. Black Tom had gone into a terrible depression and wandered, winding up in this alley.

White Tom threw the first punch. It caught Black Tom on the forehead, breaking two knuckles on White Tom's right hand. It also gave Black Tom a terrible headache. He threw his punch and caught White Tom in the stomach when he wasn't ready. White Tom bent over. Even in the dim light Black Tom could see that his friend and enemy was spitting blood. He could hear him moan.

"Oh, shit," said Black Tom. "Sit down. I'll get some help. Don't die. You're Long Tom. You got respect. Don't die."

When Black Tom ran down the alley, White Tom repeated, "I'm Long Tom, dammit," and smiled.

His stomach cancer was far advanced, and the punch had done him no good. He sat down still smiling.

That night the dog with no name stood in the shadows and watched the two men who smelled of human excrement shout and fight. When one of the men fell down, the dog smelled the blood. It was not the good blood smell but the smell of something bad.

The dog watched the other man run down the alley, and then the dog ran past the fallen man whose eyes were closed. He ran silently. Something inside told him to go to the place where the man had talked to him like a person and had given him food.

That man was a puzzle, something curious. Maybe he would talk again, give him food. But those weren't the only reasons the dog was running silently through alleys for miles.

The man had smelled of, sounded of, something the dog had never known, something that made him feel calm, even safe. The dog wanted to feel that again.

On that night Dr. Mustapha Aziz sat in the one-bedroom condo he had bought a month after his wife and daughter had been killed. The house and all its possessions had been sold at a significant loss.

The condo was in an old building in Evanston right past the turn on Sheridan Road beyond the cemetery. It was rumored that Marlon Brando and Wally Cox had once shared the large third-floor apartment two buildings down. That apartment, like Dr. Aziz's, faced Lake Michigan. Even in the darkness, with his lights out Aziz could see occasional whitecaps along the waves that hit the rocks. He could also hear the lazy powerful *whoosh* of the waves as they rolled and crashed.

There were nights when he would sit till two or three in the morning listening, watching. There were nights when he would fall asleep in his chair. The chair was deep and comfortable. Most of the furniture had been picked up by a cousin in the Oriental rug business who had connections with furniture dealers in the Arab Moslem community.

Aziz's pleasures were few. He had given away his collection of classical CDs and records. His family had died coming home from a concert. Any classical music was a reminder. Now he watched old movies on television, read articles and books on psychiatric treatment, had an occasional evening and meal with relatives and friends, and listened to the lake.

Since the accident, Aziz had begun to get

more and more referrals of patients suffering from extreme grief. The assumption was that these patients would be more willing to talk to someone who had also suffered and that he would be more capable of dealing with their problems because of what they had suffered.

In a sense, they had been right. Aziz had more referrals than he could handle. The rich, the old, the young, the nearly poor came to him with a pain he recognized even when it was masked with anger or defiance. Many of them dared him to help. Others came in the hope of getting something that he knew he might not be able to deliver.

As his specialty as a grief therapist grew, Aziz feared it would lead him into an even deeper depression, but he gradually realized that the opposite had happened. He wanted to help. He had returned to his religion in a cautious manner and begun to have some life, had even thought, with the urging of his family, that he might some day consider marrying again. He was a young man.

With his return to religion had come an interest in his culture and the food of his culture. He had begun to collect art work — vases, paintings, furniture — made by Israeli Moslem artists. Gradually, he knew, these acquisitions would replace all the furnishings with which his cousin had decorated his apartment. The culture in which he had grown and to which he had paid scant attention in his hope of escaping from it now interested him as few things did.

Although he was not a happy man, Dr. Mustapha Aziz had taught himself how to be a man reasonably at peace with himself. It was the goal he set for his patients.

A particularly large wave crashed against the shore below him.

Aziz smiled and closed his eyes.

The heavy, homely sad face of Lieberman's brother came to him as he quickly moved into sleep. There, Mustapha Aziz was sure, was someone whom he might be able to help.

On that night, 106 babies were born in Chicago hospitals and who knows how many in bedrooms, washrooms, and alleys. Five adults and teens died as a result of homicide. Births still outnumbered the deaths. Television and fear made a bad problem seem worse. Less than 1 percent of the deaths in Chicago each year were results of homicides. It wasn't even close statistically to other causes, and that night was no different.

Agnes Sheffer was a fifty-two-year-old African American nurse at Michael Reese Hospital. That night she helped deliver a baby, and the mother, who was rich and white, said she

346

wanted to name the baby Agnes. Agnes had saved her tears till she was alone in the women's room. Agnes had been through this before.

In the morning, free from drugs and after a talk with her husband, the woman whose baby she had helped to deliver would apologize to Agnes and say that she had been carried away by the nurse's kindness and the baby had to be named after a grandmother or someone. Agnes understood. Over the years, though, there had been three girls named Agnes born and named. Now Agnes cleaned up, checked the clock, got into her street clothes, and went to the OB desk to be sure her replacement had come. She had. It was a little after five and still dark when Agnes left the hospital and crossed the parking lot. She could have asked for an escort. She should have asked for an escort. But she didn't and nothing happened to her. She would work for a dozen more years and then retire to Mobile where she had family.

That night Lieberman walked through the door of his house prepared to eat quickly and work with his granddaughter on her science project. The child had chosen causes of death in the United States, a subject about which Bess had worried and which Lieberman found not in the least bit morbid.

"People die," said Lieberman.

"God knows," Bess had said.

"And so do I," Lieberman had said as they sat in the kitchen one night almost two weeks earlier having tea and some hard, toasted bagels. "We'll take her to the library, get some poster board. She's got crayons. The other kids in her class will love it. They must be sick of seeing sprouting potatoes and two plastic bottles taped together with water inside them. Morbidity is not morbid. It's life."

"She's eight," said Bess.

"If she wants this to be the time she knows, let it be," said Lieberman.

Now, Lieberman walked through the door prepared to say good-bye to his daughter if she were still there, have a quick dinner, and work with Melisa, but it was not to be.

The dining room table was alive with people, and the smell of kosher food was beautifully overwhelming.

"You're late, Abe, but we waited," Bess said, sitting at the far end of the table.

He had forgotten. It was Friday, *Shabbat*.

There were the kids, Maish and Yetta, Lisa and her husband, Marvin.

"Maish brought the food," Yetta said.

Maish always brought food when he came to the Sabbath dinner. It was always prepared with special care by Terrell.

The men and Barry were all wearing *kepuhs*. There was one at Lieberman's plate. Lieberman recognized it. It was one of the purple satin ones given out at some wedding at the temple last year. For the moment, Lieberman couldn't remember who it was who got married. He would check inside the little cap where the names and date were written.

"I'll wash my hands," he said, and Bess knew that meant he would put his gun in the drawer and take off his holster. "Maish, did you? . . ."

"I did," Maish said looking normally glum.

"Later we'll talk," Lieberman said, heading for his and Bess's bedroom.

In three minutes, he was back at his place across from his wife. He put on the purple *kepuh* and Bess started immediately with the blessing over the candles. The women covered their eyes, held out their hands, and prayed. The loudest was Melisa. Then came the blessing over the wine. Lieberman didn't bother to ask his brother if he wanted to say the blessing. In the past, before David died, Maish had always shrugged and said, "Why not?" and said the blessing. He hadn't said the blessing since. So Lieberman said it, holding up the *kiddish* cup, pouring the wine, a bottle of the good kosher California red, not the sweet, sweet kosher of his childhood. The cup was passed, everyone drank. Maish hesitated and drank and the cup came back to Lieberman empty.

Melisa said the *hammotzeh*, the blessing over the *challah*, and proceeded with great gusto to tear the bread into pieces, sprinkling a little salt on each piece and passing the pieces around.

Only then did Abe pass the wine bottle while Yetta and Bess brought in the food from the kitchen. Matzoh ball soup, chicken in the pot, noodle kugel.

"Marvin and Lisa have an eleven o'clock flight," said Bess. "I said we would drive them."

"Can we go?" asked Barry, looking not at his mother but his grandfather.

"Tomorrow's Saturday," said Lieberman. "You can sleep in the car on the way back if your grandmother says okay."

"Okay," Bess said, passing the food.

Lieberman noticed that Marvin Alexander's dark hand touched Lisa's from time to time and Lieberman's daughter smiled when it did. From time to time she touched his shoulder. Alexander was the best-dressed man at the table. This was a holy weekly dinner and he planned to respect it. Not for the first time, Lieberman wondered what this doctor who spoke Hebrew and knew the classics saw in his moody but brilliant daughter. It was a puzzle Abe would never solve.

In contrast to Dr. Marvin Alexander, Maish was an indifferent *shlump*. He wore a wrinkled white shirt and no tie and a jacket that was beginning to show signs not only of decay but impending doom.

"Basketball practice starts next week at the JCC," said Barry. "Just found out today. Grandpa, I told them you'd coach again."

"Maish, you gonna help again this year?" Abe asked.

Maish shrugged noncommittally. Abe was sure his brother would help. He might be able to scorn God for a while, but the lure of that basketball, which he handled like a magic floating ball when he was younger, would be too much to resist. Maish knew the rankings of all the college teams. Maish knew the stats and standings of every NBA team and even the women's league. He had worried about Michael Jordan's threats to retire and hoped Kobe Bryant wouldn't burn out young. He searched nearly in vain for a Jewish player.

Sad to say, Barry had not inherited his grandfather's or his granduncle's ability on the court, but he had inherited their heart and no sense of fear. He was of average height, but he was one of the top rebounders in his age bracket.

"Bar Mitzvah," Bess reminded all present.

"I've got it down," said Barry. "English, Hebrew, the *Torah* reading, my speech. Rabbi Wass says I've got it down."

"We'll be back for the Bar Mitzvah," said Marvin.

"You gonna convert, Marvin?" Barry asked, cutting into an extremely tender piece of chicken.

"I don't think so, Barry," he said. "Methodist, Methodist is my belief. I'm a Methodist till I die. Till old grim death comes knocking at my door, I'll be eating Methodist pie."

"If you eat too much pie, it clogs your arteries and you die of heart disease," said Melisa. "That's a heart problem. More people die of heart problems in the United States than anything else, twenty-two percent."

"That's interesting," said Marvin, who, Lieberman was sure, as a pathologist, could tell the child more about failed and diseased hearts than she could ever learn from the library.

The dinner went well, right down to the rice pudding dessert, which was low cal and low fat. Lieberman's stomach had not fully recovered from his lunch with El Perro, but it had come back enough to enjoy the meal that had been placed in front of him tonight.

"We have to go," Bess said, checking her watch.

"Maish and I will clean up," Yetta volunteered.

Maish said nothing.

"A word with Maish while Marvin and Lisa get their bags," said Abe.

Bess and Yetta began to clear immediately. All the men and Barry removed their *kepuhs* and placed them on top of each other on the table. Maish and Abe moved into the living room.

"I saw him, Aziz," said Maish.

"And?"

"I'm cured," Maish said flatly.

"You're a very funny man."

"It's a gift."

The two brothers, a study in contrasts, stood whispering near the front door. The fat bulldog and the lean bloodhound.

"Maish."

"He's all right," he said reluctantly. "He likes you."

"That's nice," said Abe. "Well?"

"I thought I had been punished by God for no reason," said Maish. "He has had it even worse. His wife, child . . . and he endures. My problem isn't that I lost my belief in God. It's that I believe and I don't like him. If I could just lose my faith . . . but I can't. I've tried. It's driving me nuts, Avrum."

"That's why you're seeing a shrink," whispered Abe.

"That's why I'm seeing a shrink," Maish agreed. "I got another appointment Wednesday."

"So it helped?"

"Long run, who knows?" said the man who had once been known as Nothing-Bothers Maish. "We'll see."

"Maish," called Yetta. "You gonna help, you gonna talk?"

"I'm gonna help," Maish called, and then to Abe in a whisper, "We'll see."

Maish wandered back to the dining room as Lisa and Marvin came down the stairs with their luggage. There wasn't much.

"We've got a few minutes to help," said Bess.

"Leave, go go, *gey avek, avek gagaingan*," said Yetta, the thinnest person in the room who was carrying a pile of plates like a waitress. "Maish and I are professionals, remember. Lisa, good-bye. Dr. Alexander, a pleasure to see you again. We'll see you for the Bar Mitzvah."

Yetta disappeared into the kitchen.

Maish shook Marvin Alexander's hand and said good-bye to Lisa, taking her hand. Lisa had never liked hugs and kisses, tears and secrets, but she suffered her favorite uncle to take her hand and she didn't pull it away.

The kids were ready and Melisa was carrying her teddy bear.

Five minutes later they were stuffed into Bess's car. She drove. Abe sat stoically next to her. In the backseat, Lisa sat by the window, Barry sat in the middle, Marvin by the other window with Melisa in his lap. The two suitcases were in the trunk.

The drive was only half an hour. The timing was nearly perfect. There was another half hour till the flight to Los Angeles, and they had boarding passes.

Lieberman had placed an official police business sign on Bess's sun visor two years ago. She had argued that it was an abuse of his position. He had argued that he occasionally used her car for official business. Bess had reluctantly agreed. At first she had resisted using it when she couldn't find a parking space, but gradually, and only for an emergency, she had pulled down the visor and parked illegally. Now they pulled up directly in front of the arrival gate near baggage claim and dropped the visor.

They went up the escalator and directly to the gate. Abe carried Marvin's trifold carry-on and Marvin carried the sleeping Melisa.

They did not move quickly. Barry carried his mother's cloth suitcase and Lisa carried a tote bag. They had hurried to the gate. Bess had led the way.

By the time they got to the check-in desk, an attendant was already calling for boarding.

Marvin reached under the sleeping child to shake Abe's hand. Then he handed Melisa to Lieberman. Her dark, wavy hair brushed his face and smelled of something sweet.

"Be patient with Lisa if you can," said Lieberman. "God knows, I've tried."

"I will, Abraham," Marvin said, gently moving strands of Melisa's hair from her grandfather's face.

Lisa actually hugged her son and mother and came over to kiss the sleeping child who clutched her bear. Melisa believed in the tooth fairy. Melisa believed her teddy bear had a touch of life. Melisa believed her mother would come back to Chicago and everyone would live happily ever after. Melisa was asleep.

"For you," Lisa said, putting an envelope in her father's pocket.

She was very serious, probably a good sign.

The couple waved, promised to call the next day, and waved again as they boarded. Lisa and Marvin got looks of curiosity and guarded or masked disapproval, but it was a new generation and many people simply noted the mixed-race couple and went about their own business. Lieberman, however, was an observer. It was his job to observe. Life had been hard for his daughter. She had made it hard and was making it harder.

Lieberman shifted the child. He was short, thin, and surprisingly strong, but he had a long way back to the car with the full fifty pounds of his granddaughter.

Bess and Barry led the way, talking, with Lieberman slightly behind.

When they got to the car, Barry opened the back door and Lieberman put his grand-daughter inside, snapping the sleeping girl into her seat belt as she made a little grunt, clutched her bear, and slept. Barry climbed over her, buckled in, and closed his eyes.

The police car in front of them had not been there when they parked. As Bess pushed up the visor bearing the OFFICIAL POLICE BUSINESS sign, two uniformed officers, one carrying a big bag, moved to the police car and climbed in. Lieberman thought he recognized the older of the two, but he couldn't remember his name, at least not at the moment.

He wondered briefly what they were doing, but there were always calls to the airport. The bulging bag was a curiosity, but not enough to give Lieberman more than a few seconds of thought. He filed the event deep in his memory.

Half an hour later the children were home in bed and Bess said, "Look at the job Yetta and Maish did. Perfect. I'm worried about your brother, Abe."

"I'm working on it," he said. "I got him to see a shrink today."

"Thank God."

They moved to the bedroom, turned on the lights, and began to undress. Then Lieberman remembered the envelope his daughter had handed him.

"Ida Katzman doesn't want a tribute," Bess said.

"It's her decision," Abe said, standing in his shorts and socks, the chain with the key to the drawer where he kept his gun and holster around his neck.

"She deserves it and the temple needs the money for the religious school," she said, carefully stepping out of her dress.

Abe watched. It always delighted him that his wife had the svelte figure of a model, though her breasts, which pleased him mightily, were too large for a model.

"You wanna?" he asked.

"It's late, Abe, and as irresistible as you look standing there in shorts and socks, I think I'll suggest that we get up early and see what develops. Let's just hold each other. I could use it."

"You've got it," he said, opening the envelope.

"Abe," Bess said, moving toward the small bathroom off the bedroom. "I think you could talk Ida into it. I think you could do it if you took over as chairman of the dinner."

Lieberman paused before he removed the note in the envelope. Bess was going to get him again. Heading the building committee fund drive had been a nightmare. Organizing a huge dinner would be as bad, maybe worse. He knew Irving Hammel wanted the job, but it was up to Bess to appoint whomever she wanted, and if she didn't pick someone Ida would find acceptable, there would be no testimonial. Lieberman envisioned arguments, arrangements, committee meetings, caterers, finding a hotel, collecting checks. He hated it, but he knew that it was no use resisting. He would lose. Better to accept gracefully and get as much help as he could, provided he could talk Ida into allowing the temple to do it.

"To save us both a lot of time, trouble, and anguish," Abe said, unfolding the note from his daughter. "And to make my wife grateful, I'll talk to Ida."

Bess returned to the bedroom with a smile, wearing a black lacy thing.

He read the note. It was to both of them and very short. He handed it to Bess, took off his socks, and stood with them in his hand as she read:

MOM AND DAD, THANKS FOR YOUR PATIENCE, THANKS FOR EVERYTHING. LOVE, YOUR DAUGHTER LISA.

" 'Mom and Dad,' " Bess said. "Not Bess and Abe."

"We're making progress," said Lieberman, moving to the bathroom to put his dirty socks and shirt in the laundry hamper and hang up his pants and jacket so he could put them in the closet.

"Thanks," she writes. "Twice."

"I think Marvin Alexander is the best thing that ever happened to her," said Lieberman.

" 'Your daughter,' she writes," said Bess. "Not just Lisa."

Abe was back in the bedroom, skinny, nude except for the chain and key around his neck. The gray hairs on his chest were curly and abundant. His mustache was trimmed, his teeth cleaned, and his face freshly and electrically shaved.

"Maybe I'm not that tired," Bess said, looking at him with a smile.

"Ah, that, my dear, is the promise of a consummation devoutly to be wished," he said.

He knew he would be up in a few hours with the curse of insomnia and thoughts about Ida Katzman and what had happened to Mickey Gornitz. He would hope. He would pray that Mickey's son, Matthew, turned up and soon.

Bess had put down the note and crawled into bed under the covers. Lieberman turned off all but one small light and joined her. The one light had been an impulse gift. It was brass, the figure of a nearly nude nymph holding a curved bar that led to a light and chain under a pink flower-shaped glass shade. It was ugly. It was beautiful. It probably belonged in a nineteenth-century bordello. Lieberman had fallen in love with it at first sight, and Bess had accepted the gift with curiosity and respect for the impulse.

Abe reached for his wife and she reached back under the cool blanket.

Bill Hanrahan had avoided going home. He was almost at the point where the memories were too much for him. The house had once been rich with memories, good and bad, but the memories of his life. Now all he wanted to do was sell it and find someplace fresh and clean for himself and Iris. Iris. He would have to talk to her, tell her they had made a mistake, that they would have to honor his agreement with her father and Woo. Woo and Lieberman were right. Bill had been suicidal, hadn't yet dealt with his guilt and fears.

He had spent the evening with Father Parker. Whiz had done little of the talking in the coffeehouse on Argyle in Little Viet Nam. Parker had worn a black knit turtleneck shirt and his black zipper jacket. Hanrahan was still in his work clothes — jacket, slacks, button-down shirt. He had taken off his tie.

"So," Hanrahan had said when the place was almost empty and should have been closed and would have been had the owner not been a member of Father Parker's congregation and felt that he and his family owed the priest much for having taken them into his care when they had arrived in Chicago ten years ago after a decade of internment in Borneo. The family that owned the coffeehouse would have stayed up all night for Father Parker, and they nearly did.

"Can I get a little religious on you for a minute or two, Bill?" Parker had asked, eyeing his cup of tea, which had just been refilled by the proprietor.

"It can't hurt," said Hanrahan.

"Our Lord kept his word and won the devotion and belief of millions of people for two thousand years. If you like, I'll talk to Woo."

"He's not a Catholic," said Bill.

"The possibility still exists for us to carry on a conversation," the priest said.

"Not necessary," Hanrahan said. "I'll keep my word. Hard part's gonna be telling Iris."

"Want my help?"

"Maybe," said Bill.

"Let me know. Hardrock Hanrahan, I'm going to take a chance and say something you may have trouble dealing with. You're afraid to go home, aren't you?"

"Since Michael left I . . . yes, I guess, but I can live with the fear."

"You mean you think you deserve it?"

"Could be," Hanrahan agreed, finishing his coffee. He had switched to decaf almost an hour earlier.

"You can stay with me tonight," Parker said. "Lot's of room, but —"

"Sometime I'll have to go home. Might as well be tonight. Let's go."

"You're all right?" asked the priest.

"All right for now," said Hanrahan. "Father, I had a dream last night. Gornitz's ex-wife and Frankie Kraylaw were at the foot of my bed. I thought I was awake, could have sworn it. She had no face, just one filmy eye. He was a walking pain of bleeding shotgun wounds. They just stood facing me, saying nothing. The door opened behind them and more people started to come in. I didn't want to see them. A cop can't live with such nightmares, Sam. I woke up. I don't want that dream again."

"Who would?" asked the priest. "So your nightmares are part of the reason you want the marriage to take place soon and why you want out of the house."

"Part of the reason. Most of it," agreed Hanrahan.

"And guilt."

"For sure."

"Move out of the house tonight," said Parker. "Find an apartment while you try to sell it. Stay at the rectory tonight or go to a hotel. There's no shame in it, Bill."

"But will the ghosts follow me?" Hanrahan asked.

"Possibly," said Parker, "but I think they're haunting the house where you keep your memories."

"You really believe that?"

"I think I do," Parker said with a smile. "It's late, William, and I've got a lot to do in the morning, which is right now. Let's go. The people keeping this place open for us need some sleep too."

Hanrahan nodded and rose. The man who had served them came out instantly and started to clean up.

"Sure you finished, Father?" asked the man.

"I'm sure. Thanks, Nguyen."

"You are always welcome," said the man who stood thin, short, and erect before them.

Parker didn't go through the formality of trying to pay. He knew the man wouldn't take his money and was more than pleased to serve the priest.

Hanrahan drove home.

On the way, driving down Ashland Avenue, a Mazda wove north almost leaving its lane. The driver came close enough to Hanrahan that the detective could see his face in the headlights. The man looked familiar. Bill Hanrahan could have driven up and down the streets trying to find him, but it was likely to be hopeless. Besides, he knew that he would just be stalling, convincing himself that he was doing his job when he was really trying to avoid going home.

Hanrahan drove to his house determined to live with his ghosts, at least for one more night. What he truly dreaded was facing Iris.

Going home turned out to be not nearly as bad as he thought it would be. He found a parking space with relative ease, half a block from the house. He parked and walked back. He had left some of the lights on. He did that more and more recently. He didn't want to come home to a dark house. He had no illusions that the lights would deter a professional burglar. The lights were for him.

Hanrahan went straight to the bedroom, leaving all the lights on.

He brushed his teeth, touched his bristly face, and decided to shave and shower in the morning. He put on a pair of pajamas Maureen had bought him for Christmas maybe eight or nine years earlier and got into bed, leaving one of the reading lamps on low.

In moments he felt himself sinking into sleep and remembering the name of the man he had seen in the headlights of his car. The man's name was Suede something and he was a burglar. Hanrahan should have followed him. Too late now.

He fell asleep, and he did not dream.

CHAPTER 13

Lieberman was not the first to wake up, which was unusual. As resident insomniac, he generally got the coffee going, put out the juice, chocolate milk, and cereal, frozen pancakes, or frozen waffles. He would bring in the *Tribune* after he had dressed and then awaken Bess and the kids with plenty of time for them to dress, eat, brush their teeth and hair, and be ready for the day. It might take two trips to get Barry and Melisa up, but he would simply inform Bess who would smell the coffee and rouse herself.

This morning was different. Barry came in to wake up his grandfather, who didn't simply feel groggy, he felt nearly catatonic.

"It's seven, Grandpa," said Barry.

"Night or day?" Lieberman asked, opening his eyes.

"Day. Your hair is sticking up like a devil."

"I feel like the devil," Lieberman said. "I'll be right out."

It was Saturday. Religious school at nine

367

for the kids, which gave them an extra hour of sleep or an extra hour to get ready. Lieberman was on the day shift for two more weekends. He had the coming Wednesday and Thursday off, if there were no emergencies related to cases he was working.

The kids and Bess were finishing breakfast when Abe came into the kitchen clean shaven, well groomed, and smelling of a mild after-shave. He had trimmed his mustache, gotten dressed, putting on his holster and gun and selecting one of his better sports jackets, a conservative blue one Bess had bought him about a year ago.

"Is my mother in California now?" asked Melisa.

"She is," Bess said, pouring her husband some coffee.

Before him sat a bowl of cereal. Next to the bowl was a small blue pitcher of milk. The kids were eating the same thing, Cheerios. Abe now hated Cheerios. He had been a Wheaties man from the days of Jack Armstrong, All-American Boy. Abe was generous in his adding sugar. Bess, who was watching, said nothing.

"Tonight we do the poster," Lieberman said, digging in with his spoon.

It wasn't bad. It wasn't good, but the box had a big heart on it that implied his heart, which was never a problem, would be as red and bright as a valentine.

"I'm overnighting at Laura's house," said Melisa. "It's her eighth birthday."

"Tomorrow then," Lieberman tried.

"I won't be back till after eleven."

"And I won't be home till six," said Lieberman. "We'll work in a creative frenzy."

"Creative Frenzy. Is that the one that looks like a Honda Civic?" asked Barry. "There's not much room in the back to work on a poster, and you'll get paint all over the uphol-stery."

"That's my kind of joke," said Lieberman. "Bess, tell your grandchild he's to find his own style."

"It's in the family," said Bess. "Abe, re-member Ida Katzman."

"Like I remember the Alamo, the *Maine*, and Pearl Harbor. I'll see her. I'll talk to her. How about I'm honorary chair of the dinner? I'll talk to Rommel about being the executive chair. He'll like that, probably assign some-one in his office to do the dirty work."

"If that's the best," Bess said.

"Barry —" Lieberman began.

"Grandpa," Barry said excitedly. "There's some things I don't have exactly clear about when you met Frankie Baumholtz. You asked him, what?"

"I asked him to stop trying to keep me from bringing up the subject of his Bar Mitzvah," said Lieberman. "Unfortunately for you, dear grandson who will carry on the name of Lieberman along with your cousin Arthur, I have grown a little bump in my brain that goes off when perpetrators and witnesses try to change the subject. It always means they have something they don't want to talk about. From now on, I think I'll call attempts to change the subject Frankie Baumholtzes. When I get tired of that, I'll call them Hal Jeffcoats. But I must admit you sensed the direction of my next line of inquiry brilliantly."

"Thanks," said Barry, working on his chocolate milk.

"Your speech," Abe said.

"Here? Now?" Barry looked at his sister and grandmother for support, which was not forthcoming.

"If not here, where? If not now, when?" asked Lieberman.

"I have to?"

"No," said Abe. "I'm still waking up. Later. Before or after dinner."

"I'm spending the night at my dad's," said Barry.

"Tomorrow, then," Lieberman said with a sigh. "At night you will recite your Bar Mitzvah speech while Melisa and I work on her death poster. It will be a night to be re-membered."

"Finished?" asked Bess.

The question was directed at all three of them regarding breakfast, not the conversa-tion. All answered affirmatively and all, in-cluding Abe, cleared their places, rinsed their dishes in the sink, and put them in the dish-washer.

While the kids went for their books, Lieberman got the phone from the wall and asked Bess for Ida Katzman's number. He di-aled. The phone rang twice and Mr. Smith picked it up.

"Mr. Smith, Lieberman."

"Good morning, Mr. Lieberman," Smith said.

"How are you?"

"Very well," said Smith. "Would you like to speak to Mrs. Katzman?"

"If available," Abe said as Bess hovered in the room doing small tasks and listening.

There was a pause and Ida Katzman came on with "Abraham?"

"Abraham," Lieberman said, loudly. "Can we get together tonight? Maybe you and me and Bess? For a few minutes?"

"Dinner," said Ida. "Here."

"You know what I want to talk about?"

"I'm old, but I am not unobservant," she

said. "Seven o'clock. You still have the grand-children?"

"Yes," he said.

"You can bring them, but there's not much to do in an old woman's apartment but watch television."

"They're going away for the night," Lieberman said, tucking the phone under his chin and holding up seven fingers for Bess who nodded "yes."

"See you at seven," said Lieberman. "We'll bring a dessert."

"You'll bring nothing," said Ida. "Mr. Smith will arrange for the dinner. As I remember, you eat everything."

"Right," said Lieberman. "How are you?"

"I survive, Abraham. I survive."

With that she hung up and so did he.

"I'll take the kids," Bess said, coming to kiss her husband.

"You smell like gardenias," he said. "My favorite."

"And you smell like after-shave. Here's a bagel in a Baggie if you get hungry."

He took the bagel and stuffed it in his pocket. He would probably eat it before he reached the station.

When the kids hurried into the room arguing about whether *Predator* was a good or bad movie, Lieberman kissed them atop the head and started out the door.

"Grandpa," Melisa said, seriously, "you haven't shot anyone in a long time."

"No one in my immediate vicinity needed shooting," Lieberman said, standing in the open door.

"Hard to believe," said Barry. "People are shooting, shooting, shooting each other every night."

"And we try to find them, bring them in, get witnesses and evidence, and, if we're lucky, get them to admit what they did. We seldom have to shoot them."

"But aren't there times when they're so bad, you want to do something bad back to them?" Melisa asked.

"You are, like your mother, a morbidly minded child," Bess said.

"Sometimes," said Lieberman. "See you later."

"Have you done bad things?" Barry asked.

Lieberman paused at the front door and considered lying. "I have," he said.

"A lot?" asked Melisa.

"Depends on what one calls 'bad,' " said Lieberman. "We can continue this tomorrow if you're still interested."

He escaped before his grandchildren could pursue this line of inquiry. Maybe by tomorrow they would have forgotten their question and his answer.

He went out the door. It was colder than he thought. He went back in and put on his three-quarter-length brown coat and called toward the kitchen, "Cold out there."

"We know," said Bess.

The bagel sat heavily in his pocket but Lieberman didn't reach for it as he drove, the memory of Cheerios still strong within him.

The Clark Street station parking lot was full with marked and unmarked cars. It was the weekend. It was always busy on Friday and Saturday nights, and Sunday nights weren't much better. Some of the revelers were now being interviewed about the fights they had gotten into, the automobiles and store windows they had destroyed, the houses they had burgled while the families slept, the early-morning acts of stupidity and violence, and, finally, the domestic battles. Lieberman hated taking those, and normally he didn't have to if no one had been seriously, even mortally hurt.

Once he had covered a call to an apartment where a Hispanic man opened the door when he knocked. The man was about forty, heavy, with a knife sticking out of his throat. Lieberman called for an ambulance while the man croaked his tale in Spanish. He had been drunk the night before. His wife had gotten a knife from the kitchen. He didn't remember her using it. He did remember hitting her. She had left screaming and he had gone to bed. He had slept all night with the knife in his throat and had noticed it there only when he went to the toilet when he got up. The man lived. He didn't press charges. He had beaten his wife too often to make the charges stick very firmly.

Lieberman hated domestic calls.

Hanrahan was nowhere in sight as Lieberman went to his desk and looked at his messages. One was from Kearney, who told him to come to his office the minute he came in. Lieberman didn't even take the time to remove his coat.

"So" came a loud male voice from one of the detectives' desks, a voice that had probably been the result of a botched tonsillectomy, "I say, nice as like now, please don't sit on my fucking car. I swear to God, and I'm a Catholic, I didn't hit him with the tool box till he didn't move. I gave him a good minute."

The man with the croaking voice was Fats Gerald, stolen auto parts dealer. He liked hitting people and God, if he was up there, had a file drawer full of the times Fats had lied in the name of his deity.

Lieberman knocked at the door. Kearney

told him to come in. The captain looked clean, well groomed, and reasonably rested. He had a haircut.

"I'm meeting with brass in an hour," Kearney explained.

"Saturday?"

"Homicide rate is up in the district," explained Kearney. "Television station is going to pick up on it. Others will too, plus the papers, radio, alarmists, and every man or woman in the force who wants my job."

"You need something to throw 'em?" Lieberman asked.

"It would help," said Kearney. "If they push too hard, Abe, they know I'm likely to blow up. Then I'd be in real trouble instead of just trouble. What have we got?"

"Clark Mills murder suspect," said Lieberman.

"I've got that. We've got a hit-and-run killing of a pregnant young woman down in Ravenswood. We got word from downtown to take it. It's not ours, but something's going down. We've got Butchie the dealer dead, murdered. Lorber's on it. What I need is a lid on the Gornitz kidnapping. Look . . ."

Kearney held out the newspaper he took from his desk and handed it to Lieberman.

Front page, bottom, *Sun-Times*. "Mob Informer Gornitz Takes His Own Life." Then a bold subhead, "Police Watch While Witness Plunges Through Hotel Window."

There was a photograph of the hotel and one of those dotted black lines with an arrow on the bottom. The arrow led from a broken window to the sidewalk.

Lieberman handed the paper back. He didn't bother to ask if Kearney had any idea of how the story leaked. The department, the state attorney's office, was full of leaks and, who knows, someone might have thought it was a good idea to let it out to the public, maybe give incentive to the people holding Matthew Gornitz to let him go.

"He'll turn up now," Lieberman said with a confidence he did not feel.

"Dead or alive?"

"Alive," said Lieberman.

"If anything breaks, I'll be downtown in the assistant chief's office with who knows who. Call me if you get anything. I think I'm in for a very long day."

Kearney headed for the door with Lieberman right behind him.

"One more thing," Kearney said as they stepped into the squad room with Kearney holding his thin briefcase. "You and your partner handled the Piniescu case."

"Right," Lieberman said with a decidedly uneasy feeling.

"Someone burned his truck last night, knocked at his door, and when he answered, they beat the hell out of him in front of his wife. He's in Edgewater hospital. You might want to go talk to him. Any ideas?"

"A disgruntled customer?"

"Abe, Piniescu's customers are all ancient."

They were weaving through the squad room. A toothless woman touched Kearney's sleeve as he moved past her.

"Lieutenant, Lieutenant, remember me? Remember me? Alberta Dwights. My boy got shot dead a year ago maybe. Now my other boy's here and they say he shot somebody. He's thirteen."

"Why don't you get your son to make a statement and tell the truth," Kearney said, touching the woman's arm.

She was at Harley Buel's desk. Buel sat behind it looking like a sympathetic professor with his balding head, erect posture, and glasses.

"Detective Buel will help you, Mrs. Dwights," Kearney said, then continued toward and out the door with Lieberman at his side.

They were on their way down the steps when they met Bill Hanrahan coming up.

"Captain," he said. "Got a call at the desk.

Gornitz kid walked up to a police vehicle downtown and identified himself."

Kearney stopped and something like a smile touched his handsome dark face, a smile that had broadened years earlier to charm brass and the ladies. He had never recaptured that smile and charm after the death of his partner.

"Good," Kearney said. "What shape is he in?"

"Call says he's okay. Some bruises, a cut or two and maybe a broken finger," said Hanrahan.

"Do it," Kearney said, hurrying past the two detectives and down the stairs.

"They're taking him to Grant Hospital for treatment," said Hanrahan.

"Friendly Mike the driveway paver lost his vehicle to vandalism last night and the vandals almost did the same thing to our Mike," said Lieberman. "He's in the hospital. Edgewater."

The partners stood looking at each other for about ten seconds and Hanrahan recognized his partner's look. Basically the look said "You don't want to know, Father Murphy."

"You take Mike, Abe," said Hanrahan. "How about I go to the hospital, ask Matthew about his ordeal, and bring him in if he's up to it?"

"Meet back here after lunch," said Abe.

"One?"

"Fine. You sleep all right?"

"Lonely there, Abe," Hanrahan said softly. "Even with the company of ghosts. But yeah, I slept. You?"

"Fine."

"You talk to Iris?"

"This morning," said Hanrahan. "Told her we should keep our word to her father and Woo. She not only seemed to understand, she sounded relieved."

They had to move out of the way for two uniformed officers, one man, one woman, who hurried up the stairs. There was nothing more to be said. Lieberman was sure that his partner suspected at least the possibility of Abe's knowing something about the mysterious vandalism and beating of Mike Piniescu. He may even suspect that the vandals would be identified as Hispanic. Since he approved, however, Hanrahan asked no questions.

Twenty minutes later Lieberman was at the bedside of Mikhail Piniescu. There were three other beds in the room. Piniescu had a bandage around his head. His right arm was broken, as was his nose, and he groaned pitifully. Lieberman closed the thin curtains around the bed to give them a little privacy.

Piniescu looked at Lieberman and said, "You."

"Me," Lieberman agreed. "Not your lucky day, Mike."

"They destroyed my only transportation." He wept. "They almost destroyed me."

"They say anything?"

"One of them while they were beating me in front of my wife said, 'You're out of business.' "

"Not bad advice," said Lieberman.

Piniescu looked at the policeman standing at the side of his bed and tried to read the meaning of what had been said.

"You get a good look at them?" Lieberman asked.

"Mexican bandits. One, the leader, had a scar on his face. He smiled all the time. He was having fun. He made me look at the burning van. People were in the street now, watching. I could identify that one. And a few more. So could my wife."

"I'll see what I can do," said Lieberman. "What were they wearing?"

"Who remembers?" Piniescu groaned. "What did I do, God, to deserve this?"

"Don't you know, Mike?"

"I'm a businessman," Mike cried in obvious pain. "This is America. This is my business."

"I think you're out of business, Mike. If

these people are crazy enough to come to your house while a crowd is gathering and beat you to a pulp, I wonder what they would do if you didn't heed their advice."

"Find them," said Piniescu, his fists tightening.

"You sure you want them found?"

"You're a policeman. It's your job. This is America."

"You've given me that valuable information twice. When you can move, we'll show you some pictures. Maybe you'll be able to identify your assailants. Maybe they'll have interesting criminal records that will help in your admirable determination to seek revenge and justice."

Mike looked puzzled.

"I —" he began.

"Take care of yourself, Mike," said Lieberman. "I'll get back to you."

Lieberman headed back to the station where Hanrahan was waiting at his desk.

"What'd he give you?" asked Lieberman.

"Got him in the captain's office. He's downing a Wendy's double cheese. He's talking fast and hard."

"Wanna make the call to Carbin?"

"My pleasure," said Hanrahan. "Piniescu?"

"Wants us to find the villains so the law can take its course."

"You gonna find them?"

"Who knows, Father Murphy? This is a big city. Even with a decent description it won't be easy. And I think our Mike might have second thoughts about identifying his attackers if they have a violent past that suggests they might be upset if he identified them."

While Hanrahan made his call to the assistant state attorney, Lieberman went to his desk and dialed a number. Someone answered and Lieberman asked for the person he was trying to reach.

"*Viejo,* what do you know? What do you say? I'm still in bed. Up late *la noche pasada.*"

"So I hear," said Lieberman. "You and your friends displayed more enthusiasm for your task than I asked."

"*Viejo,* we got carried away with our duty to the public," said El Perro.

"Our victim wants the perpetrators caught. He says he can identify them."

"No shit," exclaimed El Perro. "I thought he'd pack up and find some other part of the country. This is a big country."

"He may," said Lieberman. "Didn't you tell me you were planning to visit your relatives in Guatemala?"

"I got no relatives, *Viejo,*" he said, "an' I'm too busy here, you know?"

"Suit yourself," said Lieberman.

"I have faith in you, *Viejo*," said El Perro. "You know I got two girls here. One of them is very young. The other is her mother, who ain' all that old either. You ever have two women, *Viejo?*"

"I can't say that I've experienced that pleasure," said Lieberman watching Hanrahan get up from his desk and head toward his partner's.

"I can set it up," said El Perro. *"Dija la palabra y —"*

"Thanks, but I don't think so."

"I was kiddin' anyway," said El Perro. "Truth is I got the grandmother here too and she ain' so fuckin' old."

"I find that hard to believe," said Lieberman.

"You wanna talk to them?"

"No, but thanks for the offer. *Hasta luego.*"

"Hasta luego," said El Perro.

Lieberman hung up. He had been careful in his conversation as had Emiliano, just in case the call was being taped. It wasn't likely, but you never knew. If he were asked about the call, Lieberman would have a perfectly acceptable tale to spin.

Lieberman looked up at his partner.

"On the way," said Hanrahan.

"Let's work." Lieberman got up.

There weren't many detectives and citizens

in the squad room now, but there were a few. Business would pick up on the night shift. Hanrahan and Lieberman were not scheduled for the night shift for a month or so though they often worked overtime at night. Neither dreaded the night duty. On a good night, little or nothing happened, and besides, Lieberman slept better during the day. On a bad weekday night, both men wondered why they had become cops.

"Lieberman, Hanrahan," Tony Munoz called from his desk where he was taking a statement from a reasonably attractive woman old enough to be his mother. A single glance at his smile left no doubt that he was hitting on the woman.

"Blitzstein agreed to walk-through on the site," he said. "Got a call from the state attorney's office. I think they're making a deal with him. Who knows? They'll be here in an hour."

"Thanks," said Hanrahan. "If we're in the captain's office, ask them . . . no, tell them to wait."

"They made a deal," Lieberman said.

"TV, papers'll be all over it," Hanrahan said as they walked across the room. "White Jew kills poor homeless black man, a once sort of famous black man. Was it ever thus, Rabbi?"

"Ever," said Lieberman.

The boy sat at Kearney's table. There was an open box that had once contained a double burger and there was a bag of fries that was almost gone. The boy, his glasses in the pocket of his white T-shirt, looked up solemnly.

"This is my partner, Detective Lieberman," Hanrahan said, taking a seat across from the boy while Lieberman sat next to him. "Can you go over everything that happened? Your own words. Then we'll ask questions. 'Fraid you might have to go through this three or four times. You know, people forget details."

"They killed my father," said Matthew, eyes moist, a deep scratch on his cheek. "And my mother. I'm going to kill them. Torture them."

"Let's find them first," said Lieberman. "Mind if we tape?"

The thin young man nodded in agreement.

"In Ohio," he began when Hanrahan had produced a small cassette recorder and turned it on, "at the motel. They came through the window, two of them, fast, with guns. We were asleep. The breaking glass woke me up. I heard a loud noise, the shot, and they dragged me through the broken window, two of them. They were big, strong. Not too old. Italian or Greek maybe. I could identify them if I saw them. I'll never forget the bastards —"

Matthew paused, choked with emotion.

"Take your time," said Lieberman.

"I'm okay," the young man said. "They put me in the backseat of the car, covered my eyes. I asked them what they were doing. They told me to shut up. When I asked again, one of them hit me hard. They kept me in a basement. I was scared. They said they were going to kill me if my father didn't do what they wanted. They wanted . . . they wanted him . . ."

Again the young man couldn't speak. He put his head down and closed his eyes.

"To kill himself," Lieberman supplied.

Matthew pulled himself together, his narrow shoulders quivering for an instant. He rubbed his eyes with the sleeve of his soiled shirt and went on. "They said they were going to send my fingers to my father till he did what they wanted. They asked me if I had ever seen anyone with no fingers. They showed me pictures. God, I was so scared."

"So," said Hanrahan, "they never took the blindfold off?"

"No, except to look at the pictures. They even led me to the toilet and fed me with the blindfold on. I did get a look when they showed me the pictures but I was too scared to pay attention. Later I did get a peek under the wrapping once. I could see I was in a small room with concrete walls and some wooden steps leading up. There was a dirty little window. I didn't get a look at anyone's face that time, but several of them had really bad grammar. One, the one who was on the phone to my father, spoke much better. They pushed me around a lot. I think they wanted to be sure I was frightened when I talked to my father. I was. Very frightened."

"Seems reasonable," said Lieberman. "Go on."

"Not much more," Matthew said. "This morning they led me out. It was cold. They drove me where I guess was downtown. They didn't talk. Someone reached over me to push the door open and then shove me out. I tripped over a curb, stood up, and heard the car pulling away. I tore off the blindfold."

"You see the car pulling away?" asked Hanrahan.

"I think so. It was big and black. The sun was almost blinding me after those days in the dark, but it was big and black."

"What did you do with the blindfold?"

"Do? There was a garbage can. I threw it away and began looking for a policeman. My legs were a little weak. They still are."

"Where exactly were you?" Lieberman asked gently.

"In front of the Picasso," the boy said. "May I have some water?"

Hanrahan turned off the tape recorder. Lieberman went to the door to open it and call, "Tony, can we have a cup of water in here?"

Lieberman returned to the table and folded his hands in front of him. Hanrahan turned the tape recorder back on.

"Did you talk to your father very much over the past few years?" Abe asked.

"On the phone, maybe once a month," he said. "We talked about my coming to visit him when I went to college. You know, spend spring break, maybe Christmas."

"He write to you?"

"Yes," said Matthew. "Maybe three or four times a year. We were getting closer. I wanted to see him. Now —"

Munoz came with the water in a paper cup. He looked at the boy and then at Hanrahan, who gave no clue to how things were going or what they were learning if anything. Lieberman said something to Munoz, who nodded and departed. Matthew drank the entire cup.

"We'll go over all this again later, Matt," said Lieberman. "Just a few more questions."

"Sure."

"You sure the car pulling away was black, not white?" asked Hanrahan.

"White? No, it was black."

"You know someone named David Donald Wilhite?" Lieberman said immediately, but gently.

"David — he's my roommate at school. But —"

"Good friend?"

"Friend," Matthew said, looking puzzled.

"He has a white car, hasn't he?" asked Hanrahan.

"Yes," said Matt slowly.

"He's missing," said Lieberman. "Think that might have something to do with what happened to you? You think he could have been working with the people who kidnapped you, killed your mother?"

"David? No. Never."

There was a knock at the door and Hanrahan stopped the tape recorder again. Munoz came in before anyone could tell him to enter. He had a sheet of paper in his hand. He gave it to Lieberman and went out again.

Lieberman read the sheet and handed it to Hanrahan.

"This note is a piece of serendipity," said Lieberman. "David Donald Wilhite has been picked up on the turnpike in Michigan heading east. He was just outside of Detroit."

"Picked up?" Matthew asked, looking at both detectives.

"We sent out a bulletin with a description of his car and his plate number," said Hanrahan. "They're bringing him back here now. Should be here this afternoon some time."

"Why?"

"Suspicion of murder," said Lieberman.

"David? He didn't kill my mother. That's crazy. I told you it was two men who —"

"My partner thinks he killed your mother. I think you did. What color was the car they took you away from that motel in?" asked Lieberman.

"I don't remember. It was blue, black. I don't know. I didn't kill my mother. Are you crazy?"

"Not white?" asked Lieberman. "The car wasn't white?"

"No," said Matthew.

"It was white," said Hanrahan. "I watched it drive away."

"You were there?" asked Matthew.

"Room across from yours," said Hanrahan.

"No," the boy said, looking from detective to detective.

"Yes," said Hanrahan.

"We can wait till we talk to your friend David," said Lieberman. "We've got time."

"Garbage pickup downtown is midnight," said Hanrahan having no idea when the garbage pickup was. "We're sending a couple of men down to the Picasso to look through the trash cans for your blindfold. Dirty job, but it looks like it has to be done."

"Why?" asked Matthew.

"Because we don't think you're telling the truth," Lieberman said sympathetically. "You're smart, but we don't think you're smart enough to actually put a blindfold in the garbage. You expected us to believe you."

"So wait a minute. You really think I had something to do with killing my own mother and father?" Matthew asked, standing up.

"Please sit," said Lieberman.

The young man stood for a few seconds more and then sat.

"We know you didn't kill your father," said Hanrahan. "We know your friend David didn't kill him. We know Jimmy Stashall didn't kill him. Want to know why?"

"I . . . yes."

"Because your father's not dead," said Lieberman. "We staged the whole thing over the phone."

"No, he's dead," Matthew said with a smile of suspicion. "You think I had something to do with killing my parents. This is crazy. I want to see a lawyer."

"You've got it," said Hanrahan. "We'll stop the tape now and read you your rights. You don't have to say anything more till you get a lawyer."

Lieberman rattled off the Miranda in a monotone and closed with asking Matthew if he wanted a court-appointed lawyer.

"This is crazy," he repeated.

"We'll talk to your friend David," said Hanrahan.

"Want to see your father?" asked Lieberman.

"He's dead," the boy shouted.

Lieberman shook his head no.

"I think he's right outside the door by now," Lieberman said, standing. "We'll play the tape for him and see if he confirms the story of reconciliation between father and son, the phone calls, the letters. We don't know how tough your pal David is, but we'll see if he can be persuaded to tell his part."

"We think you planned the whole thing, got your buddy to help you with the promise of money you would be getting from your mother's life insurance and other holdings and the insurance policy and assets of your father."

"You killed your mother for money," Lieberman said, shaking his head.

"No," Matthew said emphatically.

"Then hate," said Hanrahan.

This time the young man did not respond.

"I'll check on your father," Lieberman said, moving to the door, opening it, and motioning to someone. He held the door open wide and Assistant State Attorney Eugene Carbin entered with Mickey Gornitz right behind.

"No!" Matthew shouted, backing against the wall. "You're dead."

"Matt," Mickey said softly, stepping toward his son.

"This isn't fair," Matthew cried. "You're supposed to be dead."

"I'm okay," said Mickey. "And you're not hurt. That's all that counts."

"You're supposed to be dead," Matthew screamed.

"You read his rights?" asked Carbin.

"All on the tape," said Lieberman. "He wants a lawyer."

"Needs one," said Carbin. "I understand they picked up the other kid."

Lieberman nodded.

"Matt," Mickey said. "It'll be okay."

"I don't want it to be okay," the boy shouted. "I want you dead. You're supposed to be dead."

"I love you, son," said Mickey.

"I hate you, Dad," the boy said, his back to the wall. "I hated her and I hate you. You weren't parents. She was a demanding, critical monster, a Medusa in tight dresses, a manipulating bitch. And you, you're a cringing piece of shit who never made any real effort to see me, talk to me, find out about how I was or wasn't. You love me? You're a fucking hypocrite."

With that, Matthew broke from the wall and threw himself against the window. The window didn't give. Hanrahan ran to the boy and threw his arms around him, lifting Matthew from the floor and turning him back into the room to face Lieberman and Carbin. Matthew went limp in defeat.

"Even if you went through it," Hanrahan said, "it's only one flight down. Most you'd probably do unless you took a dive is break a leg. Only know of one who had the nerve to take a head-first dive out of a low window."

"Matt," said Mickey. "Matt. Did you kill your mother?"

"He doesn't have to answer that," said Carbin. "He has a right to an attorney."

Matthew looked at his father with ugly hatred and nodded.

Hanrahan sat the boy back at the captain's small conference table and put the cuffs on him as gently as he could.

"Matt," Mickey tried.

"Go away," the boy shouted. "Go away. I

have nothing more to say to you ever except I hope Stashall finds you and kills you, tears your head off."

Mickey was going to speak again but Carbin, to whom Lieberman had handed the cassette of the interview with Matthew, took Gornitz by the arm and led him out of the office.

"We'll get you a lawyer," Lieberman said.

Matthew's head and shoulders were down in defeat. A lawyer might restore some confidence to him. Hell, a good lawyer might even get the boy off depending on what David Donald Wilhite had to say under pressure.

"I'll take him, Abe," Hanrahan said, helping Matthew to his feet. "You call Kearney."

Matthew didn't resist as Hanrahan led him out of the office.

Lieberman walked to the phone and dialed the central police headquarters downtown. He asked for the assistant chief's office and got a secretary, female.

"My name's Lieberman. Is Captain Kearney still in a meeting?"

"Yes," she said abruptly.

"He wants to talk to me," Lieberman said.

"I've been ordered not to interrupt."

"The assistant chief will want this information immediately," said Lieberman. "Believe me. Tell them I said it was urgent. I'll take the blame if there is any. I'm getting old. I'm getting tired. I can handle the irritation of the mayor if I have to."

"You're Abraham Lieberman out of Clark Street?" she asked.

"My reputation precedes me," he said.

"And it's not all bad," she said. "I'll get Captain Kearney on the line."

Lieberman didn't feel like sitting. He didn't feel like thinking about the boy who had shot his mother in the face and had been nearly maniacal because he had failed to drive his father to suicide. He didn't feel like it, knew he would think about Matthew.

"Kearney" came the voice.

"We've got the Gornitz kid back and we know who shot his mother," said Lieberman. "He did."

"Nailed tight?" asked Kearney.

"Looks that way," Lieberman said. "How's it going? Or can't you talk."

"Better than I thought. This will help. I'll see you back at the station."

Kearney hung up. So did Lieberman.

He went out into the squad room, which was almost deserted. The rush would come later. Three people were standing at his desk. He knew them all, no-nonsense Faye Lasher from the state attorney's office, Bob Blitzstein looking decidedly unrested, and Irving

Hammel, Lieberman's nemesis at the temple.

"To what do I owe this pleasure?" Lieberman asked.

"I'm representing Bob," said Hammel. "He called me."

"And?" asked Lieberman.

"Mr. Blitzstein has agreed to cooperate," Faye Lasher said.

"My client has been completely misunderstood," said Hammel. "My client is ready to make a clarifying statement."

"I'm looking forward to hearing his new tale," Lieberman said, looking at Blitzstein, who wouldn't meet his eyes.

"Mr. Blitzstein has agreed to go to the crime scene and show us what happened," said Faye Lasher. "As arresting officers, I'd like you and Detective Hanrahan to come with us."

"Detective Hanrahan is booking a suspect, and I don't think —"

The squad room door opened and Hanrahan came in walking toward the quartet at his partner's desk.

"Juvenile is coming for him," Hanrahan said. "Rene is booking him in. What's the party?"

"William, how would you like to spend an hour or so in an alley listening to a tale that promises to be worthy of Baron Munchausen?"

"Abe," Hammel said, "I resent that."

"I apologize," Lieberman said, bowing his head in false contrition.

"Sounds like fun," said Hanrahan.

"Then let's get it over with," Faye Lasher joined in, heading toward the squad room door, which opened ahead of her to a uniformed officer who was ushering in a thin man who looked like an emery board.

"What's that guy's name, Rabbi?" Bill asked Lieberman.

"Thin guy?"

"That's the one."

"Suede something."

"Wonder what he's in for. I saw him last night, driving drunk in a Mazda around Leland and Ashland. Maybe I should have stopped him, but I was long off duty and had a lot on my mind."

"When we come back, we'll see," said Lieberman. "Now we run after the Amazon woman."

Faye Lasher was almost as tall as Hanrahan, lean and fast. The four men had trouble keeping up with her. She didn't ask anyone when they were in the parking lot. She simply headed for a dark Buick LeSabre and motioned for everyone to get in.

CHAPTER 14

Ten minutes later the five of them were in the alley behind Lunt. It was definitely cold, definitely gray, and definitely a place where none of them wanted to be.

"I was going to visit my daughter," Bob Blitzstein said in a monotone. "He was in front of the apartment house, in the courtyard, looking at her window. I told him to get the hell away. He laughed at me."

"You had a gun in your pocket," said Lieberman.

"I was bringing it to Rita for her protection," said Blitzstein.

Irving Hammel nodded in agreement. Faye Lasher looked bored.

"He grabbed my arm, pushed me down the street," Blitzstein went on as they walked from the spot in the courtyard he was talking about. "We went this way. I told him to leave me alone."

"You can use his name," said Lieberman. "Clark Mills."

"We went this way. I thought someone would see us, call for help. I started to shout. He — Mills told me to shut up. He was big. I was afraid."

"But angry," said Hanrahan.

"At that point, just afraid," Blitzstein said, adjusting his glasses and looking at his attorney, who nodded to let him know he was saying the right thing.

"We came in the alley here," Blitzstein went on. "He pushed me this way. I knew he was going to beat me up, maybe kill me. I'm not a young man. I was afraid. He pushed me against that wall there."

Blitzstein pointed at a wall.

"Between two cars," he said. "He started looking around after he told me to stand still and shut up. Then he picked up this piece of wood. It was dark, broken at one end, sort of a broken board."

"We didn't find anything like that," said Hanrahan. "But we'll look again."

"It was probably picked up by the garbage men," said Hammel.

"Then?" Lieberman asked.

"I remembered the gun in my pocket."

"The one you were bringing your daughter?" asked Hanrahan.

"Yes. I took it out and when his, Mills's, back was turned to me, he said, 'I'm going to smash your head to a pulp.' I was terrified. I peed in my pants. I held up the gun. It was shaking in my hands. I shot. Once, twice, I don't remember. He went down. I was in total panic. I ran down the alley and threw the gun away. I should have stayed, but I was afraid, for myself, for my daughter."

"Good story," said Lieberman. "Panic notwithstanding, you managed to wipe your prints off the gun."

"I don't remember," Blitzstein said, looking at his lawyer.

"It's the truth," said Hammel. "For now, that is all my client has to say. He has cooperated fully."

"Let's go." Faye Lasher sounded as if she wanted the whole farce over with. She would look for holes in the story, but if Blitzstein stuck with it and could keep looking as if he were telling the truth, he would probably walk.

"I'll see you at services," said Lieberman. "Irving, Bob, what's the commandment that fits here?"

"Thou shalt not bear false witness," said Hanrahan.

Faye Lasher smiled, not much of a smile, but a smile. Lasher, Hammel, and Blitzstein left. Hanrahan and Lieberman stood in the alley in which they had spent the better part of the night.

"It's a living, Abe."

"It's a job."

Lieberman held up his hand and said, "You hear that?"

"I hear a lot of things, Rabbi. Traffic on Sheridan. The wind."

"No, I —"

Lieberman started back down the alley with his partner beside him. He stopped at concrete stairs leading down to a door. Standing next to the door looking up at them was the dog with no name.

"That is one ugly dog," said Hanrahan.

"I think he could clean up pretty good," said Lieberman, taking the Baggie with the bagel out of his pocket and holding it out as he knelt at the top of the steps.

"He's got half an ear missing. If he were cleaned up, I think we'd see some scars, and there's something wrong with his eye, the left one."

"He has character," said Lieberman.

The dog came slowly, cautiously up the steps watching the two men. He had never by his own choosing come this close to humans before.

"I like him," Lieberman said as the dog took the bagel gently in his teeth and retreated down the steps to eat it and watch the two men.

"So?" asked Hanrahan. "It's cold. Let's go."

"He look like anyone we know?" asked Lieberman.

"No," said Hanrahan. "Abe, can we do something besides watching a stray dog eat a bagel?"

"He reminds me of me, Father Murph," said Lieberman.

Hanrahan looked at the dog again and said, "I see the resemblance. Now that you point it out."

"If he's willing to come with us, I'm taking him to Augustino, the vet, for cleaning and shots or whatever," Lieberman said, standing up.

"You know what that costs?" Hanrahan said.

"Money is no object," said Lieberman, "not when one finds a soul mate."

"It's just a dog, Abe."

"We shall see. We shall see."

An omelette sat before Abraham Lieberman, an omelette with onions and just a touch of lox and cream cheese, real cream cheese, not the low-fat kind with the wrong texture and no taste. And the omelette was perfect, not brown. Terrell had created a work of art. Lieberman poured ketchup on the side and looked at the twin of his omelette on the plate in front of Hanrahan.

"So Iris took it all right?" Lieberman asked, digging in.

"I told you. She took it fine," said Hanrahan. "She takes everything fine."

"You are a fortunate man." Lieberman closed his eyes in ecstasy.

"Abe," Herschel Rosen called from the *Alter Cocker* table. "Howie's got a fortune cookie for you. You want I should read it?"

The *Alter Cocker* table was full: Rosen, Bloombach, Chen, Hurvitz the psychologist, and the quiet Sy Weintraub who had probably walked his five or ten miles hours ago.

"Read," said Abe, not bothering to look at the old men at the table.

"Says," said Rosen, " 'Beware of cholesterol or you'll die young.' "

"Too late for me to die young," said Lieberman.

"Too early for you to die old," Hurvitz said, looking over his glasses.

"I am touched by your concern," Lieberman said between bites.

"So what's with Blitzstein?" asked Bloombach.

"Irving Hammel's his lawyer," said Abe.

"Hammel?" asked Rosen. "He does criminal?"

"For friends," said Bloombach. "Friends with a chain of children's furniture stores. He handled Al Herskowitz's brother's case. The one where he backed his car into the guy who was pushing a cart at the supermarket. Got him off. Herskowitz's brother has *gelt* from his wife's insurance money. I don't trust Hammel. What is it you call him, Abe?"

"Rommel," said Howie Chen.

"Good name," said Bloombach. "Blitzkriegs and all that stuff. I was in North Africa in the war, the real war."

"We know," said Howie Chen.

"I can fill in details," said Bloombach.

"We wait in anticipation," said Rosen, who called to Lieberman. "Abe, we decided you got enough *tsuoris*. We talked it over. Retire early. Join the table. You're a born *kibitzer*."

"I'm touched," Lieberman said, finishing his omelette.

Hanrahan was still working on his between sips of coffee.

"What about the Irish?" said Rosen.

"Ask him," said Abe.

"Irish, you want to be an *Alter Cocker*? We can talk it over. We never had *goyim* at the table — except for the illustrious and honorary Jew, Howie Chen. Consider the honor. An Irish Catholic, a first. But you'd have to retire."

"He's too young," said Weintraub.

"He's lookin' older every day," said Rosen.

"Gentlemen, I appreciate the offer," said Hanrahan, "and I may consider it at some point in the future."

"No, you won't," said Hurvitz.

"I said 'may,' " Hanrahan countered. "But for now, I choose to sow my cultivated oats and say prayers for the endangered souls of all of you."

"Woe unto you, Irish," said Rosen. "We don't offer twice. Honors are difficult to come by in this life."

"I appreciate that," said Hanrahan. "I'm deeply touched."

"For now," said Bloombach, "we'll accept your decision to postpone making a decision."

"Without a vote?" said Rosen.

"Without a vote," said Bloombach.

At that moment, Maish came through the front door carrying two big brown paper shopping bags.

"The return of the Portugal," said Rosen.

"Ulysses back from his travels bearing treasure," said Chen.

Maish ignored them and moved to his brother's table. He put the shopping bags down. There was a series of clinking sounds from the bags.

"Just came from Aziz the shrink," said Maish. "He's a crazy person, Avrum."

"Why?"

"He told me to buy cheap pottery, go in the alley, and throw it against the wall. He said it would help if I yelled or screamed when I did it. If I run out of pottery, I'm supposed to throw eggs."

"Sounds like a good idea to me," said Hanrahan.

"You've done it?" Maish asked, looking at the policeman.

"Many times," Hanrahan said. "Inside my house. Ten minutes of 'who the hell cares' and forty-five minutes of cleaning up. Always helps. Well, almost."

"*Meshuganah auf tait.*" Maish shook his head.

"He says —" Abe began.

"That I'm crazy in the head," said Hanrahan. "Try it Maish, now."

"Now?" asked Maish.

"Now," said Hanrahan. "All by yourself. Smash the holy shit out of that stuff."

"How're the omelettes?" Maish asked.

"Delicious," Lieberman replied.

"Perfect," said Hanrahan.

"Maish," Bloombach called. "What's in the bags?"

"My salvation, according to a crazy shrink

408

and an Irish cop," he answered.

"Good," said Rosen.

Terrell stood behind the counter pouring coffee for a cab driver who was reading the paper and paying no attention to the banter behind him.

"Terrell," said Maish, "I'll be in the alley."

"Throw one small cup for me," said Hanrahan.

"And a big pitcher for mankind," added Lieberman.

When Lieberman and Hanrahan appeared at the door with the dog, Bess knew she was in for trouble. Before they even entered the house, she said, "What's that?"

"A dog," said her husband.

"It's not a dog," said Bess. "It's a . . . a . . . I don't know. You can't bring it in until you get it cleaned up."

"It *is* cleaned up," said Abe. "And he has all his shots."

The dog looked up at Bess. She was unmoved.

"I've got to go pick up the kids," she said. "I don't want it here when I get back, Abe."

"What makes you think I want to keep him?" asked Lieberman.

"Abe?"

"Let's make a deal," he said, still standing

in the doorway with his silent partner. "I take on the Katzman dinner and charm her completely. We keep the dog on a trial basis."

"You already agreed to do the Katzman dinner tonight," she said. "Abe, I'm sorry. If we took all the strays you've brought home over the years — human and animal — the house would be under investigation from the Board of Health and I'd be a nervous wreck. Abe, you know I'm right. It's not just because he's such an ugly creature."

"You're right," Abe said in defeat. "But maybe we can work something out."

"Abe. I love you. I always will. No dog and don't stall till the children come home and take your side. Go get a goldfish. I'll even talk about a cat, but no dog."

"I'll take him," said Hanrahan. "If he'll go with me."

Bess found her car keys in her purse and moved past the two men, closing the door behind her.

"Bless you, William," she said, kissing his cheek. "Avrum, you can visit the creature whenever you like."

Bess was down the stairs and getting into her car when the two detectives looked at each other.

"You sure, Father Murph?"

"I could use the company, Rabbi."

"Then he's yours," said Lieberman.

"No, he's nobody's, Abe. He can live with me if it suits him."

Lieberman's partner turned and walked back down the stairs. The dog with no name followed him.

The employees of Thorndike Press hope you have enjoyed this Large Print book. All our Large Print titles are designed for easy reading, and all our books are made to last. Other Thorndike Press Large Print books are available at your library, through selected bookstores, or directly from the publishers.

For more information about titles, please call:

(800) 223-1244
(800) 223-6121

To share your comments, please write:

Publisher
Thorndike Press
P.O. Box 159
Thorndike, Maine 04986